"You're pregnant?"

"I don't owe you any explanations." Bethany said, trying to push past Dylan. She might as well have tried to move a boulder.

"If you think I'm going to let you walk out of here by yourself, you're out of your mind. You told me yourself you'd do what it took to protect your child. No way am I going to risk you driving off into those mountains and never coming back."

"I appreciate your concern, Dylan, but I'm not some fragile flower, and I don't need you playing bodyguard or bounty hunter or whatever it is you think you're doing." Even if for a few dangerous moments she wanted to feel his arms close around her more than she'd ever wanted anything.

His expression darkened. "I'd call it father."

Everything inside her went very still.
"W-what?"

"This child you're carrying, Bethany. This child is mine."

D1413329

Dear Reader,

A new year has begun, so why not celebrate with six exciting new titles from Silhouette Intimate Moments? *What a Man's Gotta Do* is the newest from Karen Templeton, reuniting the one-time good girl, now a single mom, with the former bad boy who always made her heart pound, even though he never once sent a smile her way. Until now.

Kylie Brant introduces THE TREMAINE TRADITION with *Alias Smith and Jones,* an exciting novel about two people hiding everything about themselves—except the way they feel about each other. There's still TROUBLE IN EDEN in Virginia Kantra's *All a Man Can Ask,* in which an undercover assignment leads (predictably) to danger and (*un*predictably) to love. By now you know that the WINGMEN WARRIORS flash means you're about to experience top-notch military romance, courtesy of Catherine Mann. *Under Siege,* a marriage-of-inconvenience tale, won't disappoint. Who wouldn't like *A Kiss in the Dark* from a handsome hero? So run—don't walk—to pick up the book of the same name by rising star Jenna Mills. Finally, enjoy the winter chill—and the cozy cuddling that drives it away—in *Northern Exposure,* by Debra Lee Brown, who sends her heroine to Alaska to find love.

And, of course, we'll be back next month with six more of the best and most exciting romances around, so be sure not to miss a single one.

Enjoy!

Leslie J. Wainger
Executive Senior Editor

Please address questions and book requests to:
Silhouette Reader Service
U.S.: 3010 Walden Ave., P.O. Box 1325, Buffalo, NY 14269
Canadian: P.O. Box 609, Fort Erie, Ont. L2A 5X3

A Kiss in the Dark

JENNA MILLS

Silhouette®

INTIMATE MOMENTS™

Published by Silhouette Books

America's Publisher of Contemporary Romance

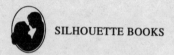

SILHOUETTE BOOKS

ISBN 0-373-27269-3

A KISS IN THE DARK

Books by Jenna Mills

Silhouette Intimate Moments

Smoke and Mirrors #1146
When Night Falls #1170
The Cop Next Door #1181
A Kiss in the Dark #1199

JENNA MILLS

grew up in south Louisiana, amid romantic plantation ruins, haunting swamps and timeless legends. It's not surprising, then, that she wrote her first romance at the ripe old age of six! Three years later, this librarian's daughter turned to romantic suspense with *Jacquie and the Swamp,* a harrowing tale of a young woman on the run in the swamp and the dashing hero who helps her find her way home. Since then her stories have grown in complexity, but her affinity for adventurous women and dangerous men has remained constant. She loves writing about strong characters torn between duty and desire, conscious choice and destiny.

When not writing award-winning stories brimming with deep emotion, steamy passion and page-turning suspense, Jenna spends her time with her husband, two cats, two dogs and a menagerie of plants in their Dallas, Texas, home. Jenna loves to hear from her readers. She can be reached via e-mail at writejennamills@aol.com, or via snail mail at P.O. Box 768, Coppell, Texas 75019.

A book about a woman who longs for the joys of motherhood deserves to be dedicated to the wonderful women who've loved, nurtured and supported me— my mother, Sharilynn Aucoin, my dear grandmothers, Rosemary Aucoin and the late Marie Allison, and my special mother-in-law, Judith Miller. You're the best!

Prologue

"Had laws not been, we never had been blamed;
For not to know we sin is innocence."
—William D'Avenant

"Stop!"

The broken cry shattered the silence of the night. He awoke abruptly, heart hammering, adrenaline surging. Disoriented, he sat upright on the sofa and blinked against the grainy dryness of his eyes, tried to focus. The cabin was dark, shadows blurring detail. Nothing moved save for the orgylike frenzy of snowflakes outside the window.

A dream, he told himself. Just another nightmare. They were stronger here in the cabin, where memories crowded in from every direction like ghosts in a desecrated cemetery.

He was a fool to keep coming back.

"D-don't kill him!"

This time there was no mistake. He was on his feet in

a heartbeat, running across the cold wood floor toward the hallway. She didn't belong here. *Not here.* But the snow-storm had turned vicious, rendering the roads too treach-erous for driving.

"S-stay away! Stay away from me!"

The pain in the voice he'd never forgotten, despite the passing of six long years, pierced deep.

"Don't touch me…"

He reached the closed door at a dead run, knew it was locked before he tried the knob. He pulled back, then rammed his body against the wood, crashed inside the room.

The sight greeting him almost sent him to his knees. The need to protect, to comfort, reared up from somewhere dark and forgotten and sent him toward the bed, where she fought the tangled sheets, lost in a nightmare he knew too well.

"My baby…"

He reached the bed and pulled her to his body, holding her against his chest. "It's just a dream," he assured roughly, running his hands along her back. She was thinner than he remembered. And she was trembling. "Just a dream."

Her arms twined around his waist, her soft palms sting-ing like ice against his bare back. "S-so real," she mur-mured as he held her, rocked her. "Just like before."

"It's this place," he reasoned, trying to ignore the feel of her soft breasts pressed against his chest. "Too many memories."

"S-so c-cold."

He pulled back to look at her and felt something deep inside splinter. Her sable hair was tangled, her devastated eyes an impossible shade of arctic blue, her skin like ice, the coral of her lips practically translucent. His threadbare black and blue flannel shirt had slipped over one shoulder, baring the curve he'd once loved to skim his mouth along.

A long time ago.

In the years since then, he'd lived without her. He hadn't touched her, seen her, talked to her for six long years. She'd come to him only during the long, dark hours of the night, when his defenses lay in tatters and desire made him weak.

He'd always felt things intensely, passionately. He'd never been able to walk away from a fight. Or from her.

Except when she told him to go, to never come back.

Clenching his jaw, he reached for the comforter and draped it around her shoulders. "You should be fine now. I'll be in the other room if you need me."

She reached for him, curled cool fingers around his wrist. "Don't go."

He went very still. "You don't know what—"

"I want to be warm again," she said, lifting her eyes to his. They were huge, dark. "Is that so very wrong?"

A hard sound broke from his throat. In some hazy corner of his mind, he knew it was a mistake even as he reached for her. It was like throwing a lit match into a pile of dried leaves and expecting nothing to happen. But too much emotion burned inside him. Too much need. That had always been the problem. He'd never been able to care about nasty things like consequences.

She didn't seem to care, either. She reached for him, pulled him to her.

"You're real," she murmured against his chest. "I never thought…"

Her words trickled off, but he didn't need to hear them. He knew. God help him, he knew. And he could no more stop touching her, wanting her, than he could change the past. Make it better. Write a new ending.

"Neither did I," he said hoarsely.

Outside, the temperature hovered just below freezing, but inside, the fire licking at the grate crackled and sizzled, filling the cabin with the scent of burning pine and times long past. But never forgotten. Memories hovered everywhere, slipping around him and slicing through him, se-

ducing even as they destroyed. The joy and the desperation, the smiles and the laughter, the tears. The cold, hard
truth.

Against his chest he felt the moisture, and knew that she
was remembering, too. He pulled back to wipe the silent
tears away, but instead of swiping a thumb beneath her
eyes, he put his mouth there. Very gently, he kissed away
her pain, though he could do nothing about the emotion
stinging his own eyes. He could only skim his mouth along
her cheekbone, the line of her jaw, finally finding her lips.

The onslaught of sensation stabbed deep. She tasted of
regret and longing, tomorrows that never came. Of hope
and possibility, dreams that never died. She tasted of the
hot chocolate he'd made shortly before midnight. Of the
tiny white marshmallows that had finally coaxed a smile
from her.

The first she'd given him in almost nine years.

Now her mouth moved against his with the same hunger, the same urgency, that drove him. And when at last
she pulled back and lifted her eyes, he saw the glaze of
mindless passion that had haunted him for a seeming eter-
nity.

"I...forgot," she whispered.

He pushed up on one arm. "Forgot what?"

"What it's like when you touch me, how everything else
just...fades to the background."

He told himself to quit touching her. Walk away, close
the door. And again, he wished he was a different man,
the kind who couldn't be lured into stepping off the side
of a cliff.

"It's been so long..." Her voice was soft, distant. Almost pained. "Did you forget, too?"

Yes was the smart answer. *Yes.* "No."

"Then help me remember," she murmured, tugging him
toward her. "Help me remember what I've forgotten."

That was all it took. He returned his mouth to hers, and
she came alive in his arms, touching him, running her

hands along his body like a benediction of cool spring water. Everywhere she touched, he burned. Wanting to touch her, too, all of her, he lifted a hand to the buttons, but his fingers were too big, too impatient. He pulled the fabric, sent the buttons popping.

And then there she was. Through the flickering light of the fire, he drank in the sight of her sprawled against the flannel sheets. Her skin was flawless, almost shimmering. Her breasts could make a grown man weep.

And her smile. Dear God, her smile. He *had* forgotten. It had been the only way to stay sane.

''Are you sure?'' he somehow managed to ask.

She answered not with words, but by skimming a hand down his chest, along his abdomen to his waistband. There she tugged.

On a low groan, he kicked off the ratty sweatpants. He told himself to go slow, to linger and savor, but the second the scrap of pink silk no longer separated them, she curled her legs around his and restlessly tilted her hips. And restraint shattered. He heard her name tear from his throat as he pushed inside, pushed home, nearly blinded by the rush of heat and pleasure. She was tight, almost virginal. But he knew this wasn't her first time. He'd taken care of that nine years before. And then the marriage—

''Hurt her, and I'll kill you.''

Six years hadn't lessened the punch of the vow he'd made to his cousin that starkly cold January morning, nor the emotion behind it, but as she twisted in his arms, murder was the last thing on his mind. He destroyed the memory, refusing to grant power to the past. It was over. Done. Meaningless. She was here now, gazing up at him with untold longing in the blue of her eyes. That was all that mattered.

Need took over, the raw, soul shattering kind that could send a strong man to an early grave. It burned and seared, demanded. He wanted to take away the pain, the sorrow. To prove once and for all that fire didn't always burn.

Past and present collided, melded, their bodies remembering what time couldn't fully erase. They moved together as one. She cried out when he brought her to the edge, a distorted gasp from deep within her throat. He answered, twining his fingers with hers and tumbling over after her.

Stranded there in the mountains, surrounded by a forest of the tallest, most beautiful old-growth pines in all of Oregon, the real world seemed a distant entity, a faraway place that didn't matter, couldn't harm.

In the hazy light of early morning, he awoke alone.

She was gone. He didn't need to leave the bed to know that. She'd been gone a long, long time. Years. Many of them. A snowstorm and a nightmare couldn't change that.

On a low oath, he ripped the tangled covers from his body and surged to his feet, crossed the braided rug to stand at the window. The ending never changed, not in real life, not in his dreams. No matter how hot the fire raged, in the end, only ashes remained. And no matter how beautiful the snowfall that had temporarily transformed the mountainside into a winter wonderland, it always, always faded into a cold, relentless drizzle.

A snow globe sat on the small pine table beside the bed, the foolishly romantic one he'd bought her so long ago, the one that contained a cabin nestled in the mountains.

"It's…beautiful."

"I thought you might like it."

She smiled. "What happened to fairy tales don't come true?"

"Maybe I was wrong."

Like hell he'd been wrong.

In one fluid motion he picked up the dome and hurled it across the room, taking obscene satisfaction in the way it smashed against the wall and fell to the floor, shattered just like all those pretenses he abhorred.

"Never again," he vowed in a voice shaking with an emotion he refused to call hurt. "Never the hell again."

Chapter 1

Six weeks later

The upper hand felt good.

With insulting detachment, Lance St. Croix studied the sunlight glinting through the cathedral window in a violent wash of light. Shadows stretched languidly across the white carpet of the opulent living room, one threatening, the other nearing the massive fireplace in retreat.

"You'll never get away with this," he warned with deliberate dismissal. "Not after what you've done."

The one who'd accused *him* of having a God complex laughed, not yet sensing the trap. "You can't just use people and discard them at will. Life doesn't work that way."

"Get off your high horse," he said with a cutting smile. "The shadow of innocence doesn't touch you any more than it touches me. Have you forgotten I know what you did?"

A glitter moved into blue eyes that invited trust and hid betrayal. "If my secret comes out, so will yours."

No, it wouldn't. He'd make damn sure of that, just like he made damn sure of everything else. Every action had an equal and opposite reaction, no matter how innocent, how misguided, the intentions.

"People will be hurt," he pointed out, changing tactics.

"You should have thought about that before!" the misguided one muttered with all the foolishness of the doomed. "It's too late now."

The shadows against the carpet blurred, the sudden absence of the sunlight leaving only an indistinguishable mass of darkness. It was impossible to discern predator from prey.

"Please," Lance added, playing the emotional card he'd fashioned into an art form during long years of marriage. "Just listen to me. I wasn't thinking clearly. I was careless, I let emotion take over. Trust me, it'll never happen again."

"Cut the innocent act!" his betrayer shouted, shattering the illusion of calm. "I'm not falling for it again. You knew exactly what you were doing, and I have the evidence to prove it. Soon, everybody in Portland will know what a gutless coward you are."

He attacked without thinking, swift, necessarily brutal. There was only a second to react. One second to grab the shiny fire poker before the violent impact of flesh to flesh. The ensuing scream was hideous, the blow shocking, the contrast of red on white horrifying.

The end came obscenely fast.

Dylan St. Croix was nearing the Portland art district when the scratchy report came across the police scanner.

Ten forty-nine at 1467 Lakeview Road confirmed. Requesting backup.

Everything inside him roared violently in protest. Blindly, he changed lanes and whipped his Bronco around, fighting the gnarled rush hour traffic like a living beast. His heart pounded as he slammed his foot down on the gas pedal and tore down crowded streets. Red lights meant nothing. Time seemed to crawl.

1467 Lakeview Road. He knew that address. Knew only one person lived there. One woman.

Ten forty-nine. He knew that code. *Fatal Injury.*

Something dark and primal tore through him. *No!* he thought savagely. *No.* He clenched the steering wheel as tightly as he could, determined not to let his hands shake. But he could do nothing about the adrenaline pooling in his gut like poison.

Never was supposed to last longer than six weeks.

Fatal Injury.

Questions battered him, but the scanner granted few answers. Crime scene technicians had been dispatched. The coroner. Possible homicide.

Dylan swerved off the highway and zipped through a Yield sign. And then he was there, the posh Portland neighborhood greeting him like a sleepy still life. He blinked hard, not sure how half an hour had raced by in the space of a heartbeat. He hardly remembered leaving downtown.

With no regard for the sanctity of the quiet community, he swerved around a slow-moving minivan, turned sharply onto Lakeview, then accelerated toward the house two blocks down. Against a crimson-streaked sky, pines towered high and the sun sank low, working in unison to obscure his view. Squinting, he barely saw the police cars that blocked his progress.

He jerked the Bronco to a stop against the curb and threw open the door. Then, God help him, he ran. Men and women and children blocked the sidewalk, crying and wringing their hands, staring. Dylan pushed past them, until he reached the line of yellow police tape. Then he stopped cold.

The fading light of early evening cast long shadows across the wooded lawn, while a tulip-lined walkway meandered toward the wide porch. Golden light spilled from the cathedral-style front door and arched windows. Bushy baskets of impatiens and petunias swayed in the breeze.

So this was where she lived, he thought morosely.

Perfect, was Dylan's first thought. Tranquil. Deceptively serene. Just like her. Except for the garishly flashing lights of the four squad cars. The two ambulances blocking the street. The cops swarming the yard like a freshly kicked anthill.

This was where she lived, he thought again. This was where she'd died.

Bethany.

His vision blurred, as an unwanted pain sliced through him. He should feel nothing, he knew. Not anymore. But he'd never learned how. He felt everything. Intensely. Always had. He called it passion. She'd called it out of control.

Shoving aside the memory, he forced his long legs to move up the driveway. Steady. Measured. He was a strong man. He'd seen a lot of ugliness in his life—crime scenes were nothing new to him. He'd visited many. He'd even caused a few.

But the cheerful flowers drove home the reality that this time was different.

This time was personal.

"You don't want to go in there, son."

Dylan glanced over his shoulder to see Detective Paul Zito break from a cluster of patrolmen and cut across the lawn. Dylan's work as a private investigator brought him in contact with the homicide veteran often enough that the two had formed an unlikely friendship.

On the third Tuesday of every month, they met by the river at Shady's for beer and cards. Nothing rattled Detective Paul Zito. Nothing fazed him. Dylan couldn't remember a single time when the irreverent cop had looked the least bit uneasy. Certainly not stricken.

Until now.

Dylan's heart rate accelerated. Dread twisted through

him. And for a moment, he wanted to turn and walk away. Walk far. Like she had. He wanted to get back in his car and drive, get on with his life. He wanted to pretend the only woman who'd ever crawled under his skin didn't lie dead inside.

But that was the coward's way out, and while Dylan had been called many names in his thirty-two years, coward wasn't one of them.

"Trust me," Dylan said when Zito joined him on the tulip-infested walkway. "This has nothing to do with what I want."

The homicide veteran frowned. "Technically, I can bar your sorry ass from taking another step. This is a crime scene. You have no right to be here."

"I'm family. That gives me every right."

"So that's what you're calling it these days?"

He ignored Zito, stared at the front door. It hung open, allowing light to spill like blood from a starkly white foyer. A wide staircase swept toward the second level. She was in there. He wondered where. If she'd suffered. If she'd known.

A primal emotion he didn't understand bled through the indifference he struggled to erect. The last time he'd seen her—Christ, he didn't want to think about that night. Until the scanner report, he'd done a damn fine job of blotting it from his mind. But now he had to wonder. If he'd known it was to be their last, would he have done things differently?

He didn't want to think about that, either.

Needing to do something, anything, he stooped and snapped off a bloodred tulip. Indifferent, he reminded himself. Objective.

At the sight of his cousin's white Ferrari parked in the street, his gut clenched. He could only imagine how Lance must feel, the shock and the grief. Lance and Bethany had long since gone their separate ways, but once, he'd pledged to love her forever.

"Where's Lance? Is he inside?"

"In the living room."

Dylan pushed past Zito. "How's he holding up? Is he okay—"

"Christ, Dylan. I thought you knew."

The tone, more than the actual words, stopped him cold. He'd heard that tone before, the sunny day eighteen years ago when the police chief had shown up on his grandfather's doorstep.

"I'm sorry, Sebastian. I don't want to be standing here any more than you want me to, but I didn't want you to hear from strangers. There's been a terrible accident…"

Adrenaline spewed nastily, prompting Dylan to turn toward Zito. The white porch rail and neatly trimmed hedges blurred, but the grim-faced detective looked carved of stone.

"Knew what?" Dylan bit out.

"There was some kind of struggle," Zito said. "Someone took a fire poker to the side of his head. He probably never even knew what hit him."

"Never knew what hit him?"

His friend frowned. "Looks like the end came pretty damn fast."

Horror slammed in, hard. Shock numbed the pain. Lance. His smooth, invincible cousin. The St. Croix prince. Dead. Just like so many St. Croixs before him.

"The ex called 911," Zito added. "She was pretty incoherent."

The point-blank statement jolted Dylan back from the whirring vortex like a frayed lifeline. "B-Bethany?"

"The first officers on the scene found her in the living room wearing a torn nightgown."

"She's alive?"

"Found the body…or so she says." Zito glanced at a small notebook in his hands and shook his head. "Story's got more holes than the ozone layer."

Dylan swore softly. For the past forty minutes, images

of Bethany hurt and bleeding, dead, had tortured him. Now…

Lance.

Jagged emotion cut in from all directions, but Dylan didn't miss Zito's insinuation.

"You think she did it?"

"It's her house, her fire poker, her ex. The blood was on her hands." Zito shrugged, shook his head. "I count my blessings when Pam was done with me, she was content to sign a few damn papers. Don't know why people have to complicate a good divorce with murder."

Blood on her hands.

The image formed before he could block it, turning everything inside him stone cold. Disbelief surged. Too well, he knew how misleading Bethany's porcelain-figurine exterior could be. Intimately, he knew there was nothing she couldn't accomplish, if she put her mind to it. Hell, she'd cut him out of her life with the ruthless precision of a heart surgeon. But murder?

"Where is she?" He needed to see her, to—

To nothing.

Zito flipped his notebook shut. "Out back, by the pool."

"Is she…hurt?"

"A nasty blow on the side of her head, but no concussion."

Dark spots clouded Dylan's vision. "Someone *hit* her?"

"Maybe. Or maybe she hit herself."

Revulsion knocked up against disbelief. He'd heard worse, a young woman slashing her throat with a steak knife to cover the fact she'd killed her lover, but Bethany…

"I want to talk to her."

"This is a crime scene. I can't have you contaminating—"

"*Her,* damn it! I want her."

Zito cocked an eyebrow.

"You've already taken her statement," Dylan reminded,

fighting a pounding urgency he didn't understand. "What do you think I'm going to do? Tell her how to change her story?"

Zito's dry smile said just that. "Stranger things have happened."

"Ten minutes, Zito. You can listen to every word. Just let me see her." He had to. God, he had to. He didn't know why, just knew that he needed to look into those languid blue eyes and see if he saw a murderer looking back at him.

Zito sighed, motioning for Dylan to follow him around the wide porch. "Five minutes."

The side of the house boasted a wall of windows, giving Dylan a distorted view into Bethany's world. The thick, beveled glass denied detail, but not impression. Everywhere he looked, shades of white glared back at him— flooring, furniture, art.

Near the back of the house, French doors hung open, revealing another room, where a sheet lay draped over a form near the fireplace. Three uniformed cops stood around talking, while two technicians examined the fire poker. A photographer busily recorded the scene.

"No matter how hard it is, boys, we go on. From now on, I'll be more like a father, than a grandfather. And you'll be more like brothers than cousins."

"But you're not my father!" eleven-year-old Dylan raged. *"And he's not my brother! We don't even like each other."*

"Then you'll just have to pretend, won't you?"

"It's the St. Croix way," thirteen-year-old Lance added, *earning his grandfather's approving smile. "It's not so bad once you get used to it."*

But there was no pretending now. Lance, the complicated cousin who'd never become a brother despite how hard Dylan tried, really did lie dead on the living room floor. And apparently Bethany had blood on her hands.

Remorse clogged Dylan's throat, the hopes and dreams

of two very different little boys who'd grown up to fall in love with the same woman. Somehow, he kept walking.

"She's just around the corner," Zito said.

Dylan stopped before turning, taking in the elaborate cabana and pool area. In the distance, the fading light of early evening cast the Cascades a giant, misshapen shadow against a horizon streaked with shades of crimson.

Even the sky seemed to be bleeding.

And then, for only the second time since that cold night on the mountain, when a snowstorm had shattered the preternatural indifference he'd lived with for six years, he saw her.

"She's all yours," Zito indicated with a sweep of his hand.

A hard sound of denial broke from Dylan's throat. Zito couldn't be more wrong. Bethany Rae Kincaid had never been all his. Never all anyone's.

But still, his heart kicked, hard. And the years between them crumbled, just like they had on the mountain.

The ice princess, they'd called her in high school. She held herself apart from the world, refusing to fully give, fully surrender herself to anyone, least of all Dylan. Except when they'd been in bed. Then, she'd literally come apart in his arms. But after, after she'd always sewn herself up a little tighter.

Some things never changed.

The sight of her sitting in a chaise lounge, holding a black-and-white cat and staring toward the mountains, stirred something he'd thought finally dead. Her long chestnut hair was tangled, her creamy skin alarmingly pale. Blood stained her slinky ivory robe. Her feet were bare.

"Pink or red?"

She looked at him, laughing. "What?"

"Your toenails," he said, running his hand along her high arch. "I want to paint them. Pink or red?"

The memory cut in from somewhere long forgotten,

prompting Dylan to swear softly. In the end, she'd chosen red. At her wedding, she'd worn pink.

That damning, defining night in the cabin, there'd been no color at all.

Dylan clenched his hands into tight fists. Damn her. Damn her for turning him into a gnarled mess, while his cousin lay dead inside and she sat there perfectly calm. Untouched.

Untouchable.

He wanted to tear across the patio and take her shoulders in his hands, put his mouth to hers, breathe some life into her. He wanted answers. He wanted to understand. He wanted—

He wanted to stop wanting.

A cool breeze drifted across the flagstone, bringing with it the scent of jasmine that was quintessential Bethany. Or maybe that was only his imagination. Slowly, he stepped into the shadows of twilight and started toward her. Birdseed crunched beneath his loafers, drawing the cat's attention, but not Bethany's. Big and scruffy and missing most of one ear, the black-and-white narrowed yellow eyes and watched Dylan approach.

His heart hammered cruelly. *Look at me,* he raged silently. He wanted her to turn to him, acknowledge him. He wanted to see those startling blue eyes rimmed by the darkest, thickest lashes he'd ever known, see what truths lurked in those deep, deep depths. What lies.

But classic Bethany, she didn't grant his wish. She just sat there, seemingly oblivious to the world around her, staring beyond the pool that looked more like a lagoon. The evening breeze sent ripples across the turquoise surface, while a stunning waterfall at the far corner babbled peacefully. The wall of rocks seemed to weep. Birds sang.

And deep inside Dylan, something twisted.

It was a damn peaceful scene for a murder.

Beth St. Croix stared blindly across the cabana. Nearly sunset, she knew shadows would be stretching across the pool, but she could bring nothing into focus. The world beyond was hazy, cold. Frozen.

Or maybe that was her.

Till death do us part rang with a finality she'd never expected on that cold day she and Lance had quit pretending theirs was a real marriage. Legal documents couldn't make up for the distance that had settled between them. She could still see the suitcases sitting against the white marble of the foyer, the empty shelf in the entertainment center where CDs and DVDs had once been stacked. She hadn't asked him to stay.

Hadn't wanted him to.

Ma'am, where's the body?

Horror surged, clogged. Bile backed up in her throat. Once, in a fit of rage, her mother had thrown an iron candlestick at a sliding door. The thick glass had cracked into thousands of misshapen pieces, but by some miracle remained intact. Fascinated by the sun streaming through the prism of color, a six-year-old Beth had put her hand to the surface, only to have the shards crumble, slicing her palm to the bone as they fell to the cold tile floor.

Now, with absolute certainty, Beth knew if she so much as moved, she'd shatter just like that door.

Wake up, she commanded herself fiercely. *Wake up!* It was time to leave this terrible dream behind, to claw her way out of the frozen cocoon where each breath stabbed like daggers. She had to make her legs work, so she could go back inside and make Lance wake up. Tell the police there'd been a terrible mistake.

Without warning, a low hum broke through the stillness, a sharp wind rushing through a narrow ravine.

"Bethany."

Her heart staggered, but in some faraway corner of her mind, she wondered what had taken him so long. He always invaded the shadowy realm of her dreams sooner or later, tall and strong, eyes burning, touch searing.

"I came as soon as I heard."

The hoarse voice settled around her like a steadying hand, a lifeline back from that frozen place she'd slipped into upon finding Lance. She wanted to turn to him, feel his arms close around her like they had one cold, desperate night. Instead, she held herself very still, acutely aware that if she so much as blinked, if she let go of that tight grip she held on herself, she risked losing hold of all those nasty sharp pieces she'd gathered up and shoved deep before the police arrived.

"Bethany," he said a little stronger, a lot harder. "Look at me."

No, she thought wildly. *No*. But slowly, she turned to face him. She'd never been able to deny him anything, at least not in her dreams. In real life the cost had been shattering, but she'd learned the importance of denying him everything. Fire burned. She knew that, couldn't afford to forget.

He towered over her, his big body blocking out the last fragile rays of the sun. Familiarity faded as well. In her dreams, her memories, he always, always touched her.

Now he just stared, his eyes hot and condemning. And she knew. God help her, she knew. Dylan was here. *Here!* Which meant she wasn't dreaming. She was awake. Horribly, vividly awake.

The past two hours came crashing back, breaking through the blanket of shock like a hideous rockslide. "Lance…"

Dylan swore softly. "I thought it was you."

The strangled words shattered the jagged pieces she'd been trying desperately to hold together. Everything fell away, the haze and the blur and the vertigo, leaving the cold hard truth.

And it destroyed.

For six years this man had stayed away. He hadn't touched her, spoken to her, even acknowledged her, except that one shattering night on the mountain, when loose ends had played them both like puppets. At a charity auction just two nights later, he'd walked right by her with a gorgeous woman hanging on his arm, looking through Bethany as though she didn't even exist.

But now, now that he thought she lay dead on the living room floor, he was first in line to view the body.

"Sorry to disappoint you," she managed through the broken glass in her throat.

The hard planes of his face were expressionless, but a pinprick of light glimmered in his eyes. "Rest assured," he said softly. "Of the many ways I've imagined you over the years, hurt, bleeding, or dead isn't even close. Not when I watched you marry my cousin, not when I woke up alone."

The pain was swift and immediate, forcing her to blink rapidly to hide it from him. She looked at him standing close enough to touch, but saw only a man bursting in through a closed door, running across the darkened room, shouting her name.

"What happened, Bethany? What the hell happened?"

The slow burn started deep inside, pushing aside the shock and giving her strength. She released Zorro and stood, welcoming the bite of cool flagstone beneath her bare feet.

Dylan St. Croix was not a man to take sitting down.

He loomed a good six inches over her five-foot-eight, bringing her first in contact with the wrinkled cotton of his gray button-down. He wore it open at the throat, revealing the dark curly hair she'd once loved to twirl on her finger.

Shaken, Beth looked up abruptly, only to have her breath catch all over again. It was bad enough facing him after the night on the mountain, but to do it here, now, like this, seemed crueler than cruel.

Time and maturity had served him well, hardening the lanky, reckless boy into a devastating man. Tall and broad-shouldered, he wore his thick dark hair neatly clipped, obliterating the curls he'd always hated. His green eyes were narrow and deep-set, his cheekbones shockingly high. There was a cleft in his chin. His jaw always needed a razor.

He looked like a million tainted bucks, her friend Janine had once said. The description fit.

"You don't belong here," she said, but the words cracked on the remembered smell of sandalwood and clove. "Please. Just go."

"So you can slip back into your pretend world where roses don't have thorns, we weren't lovers, and Lance isn't dead on the living room floor?" He paused, stepped closer. "Sorry, no can do."

"You don't know what you're talking about," she said, instinctively stepping back.

His gaze hardened. "Zito says you found him."

The memory speared in before she could stop it, Lance lying near the fireplace. So still. So cold. She'd lain there for a few minutes before opening her eyes, dizzy, disoriented. The sun cutting through the windows had blinded her at first, but after several moistening blinks, she'd brought him into focus.

Odd place for a nap, she remembered thinking. Odd time.

Then she'd become aware of the stain on the carpet. And the fire poker in her hand.

"What else did the good detective tell you?" Lance had been a prosecutor with the D.A.'s office; she knew how weak her story sounded. Murder was rarely random or anonymous. Spouses almost always topped the list of suspects.

"Did he tell you they don't believe me when I say I have no idea what happened? That they don't believe the gash on my head isn't self-inflicted? Did they tell you that?"

Dylan frowned. "Not in so many words."

But she didn't need words. Everything Dylan St. Croix believed, felt, wanted, burned in that dark primeval gaze.

He was a man driven by the kind of searing passion that incinerated everything in its path. Her included. Her especially. That he stood there now, so ominously still, so silent and expressionless, chilled in ways she didn't understand.

"I can see it in their eyes," she whispered, "just like I see it in yours."

"It's a logical assumption."

In another lifetime, she might have laughed. Logic and Dylan went together as well as fire and ice.

Needing to breathe without drawing in sandalwood, she turned and walked to the edge of the pool, where an empty blue raft floated near the waterfall.

"I came home and walked inside," she said, looking out over the pool. In the distance, jagged mountain peaks blended into sky, only the faint stars indicating where one world ended and another began.

"Someone grabbed me. I screamed, but…everything went dark." She lifted a hand to the back of her head, where a nasty knot throbbed. "When I came to, I was in the living room next to Lance. He was…" A sob lodged in her throat. "The blood…There was nothing I could do."

She stiffened when she felt a warm hand join hers at the base of her scalp. She hadn't even heard him approach. He circled the injury, making her acutely aware of his fingers in her tangled hair, gently exploring the wound the detectives wondered if she'd given herself.

"Does it hurt?"

"Not anymore." *Liar.*

Somewhere along the line, the birds had stopped singing. There was only the sound of cascading water and the hum of activity inside the house. The sound of their breathing. The crazy desire to lean back, to feel the solid strength of a hard male body.

"When did you change into your negligee, before or after?"

Cool evening air swirled around her bare legs, reminding her that beneath her robe, she wore only a white silk chemise. One she hated. One she'd never worn, though Lance had bought it for her over a year before.

"I—I didn't put it on," she said, stepping from Dylan and tightening her sash. "I was wearing a suit. It's hanging in the closet now."

"What was Lance doing here? I didn't think you two were even speaking. Had something changed?"

"No." *No way.* Their marriage had ended long before he had walked out the door, long before she took a drive one deceptively beautiful afternoon. Long before she learned truths that violated everything she'd ever believed.

"Then why was he here?"

"He called and said he had a few things to pick up, wanted to know when I'd be home. He sounded…strange."

"Strange how?"

"Just…strange. Upset." Very unLancelike.

"And?"

"And nothing."

Dylan swore softly. "Don't hold back from me," he said, turning her to face him. Inches separated their bodies, their faces, years their hearts. "I'm a private investigator, for God's sakes. I make a living finding what people don't want me to know. And I see secrets in your eyes. What, damn it? What are you hiding? Are you afraid? Is that it?"

Deep inside, she started to shake. He was too close. Much, much too close. The mere sight of him ripped her up in ways she hadn't known were possible, resurrected feelings and desires and dangers she'd tried to bury.

She didn't want to see him now.

She didn't want to see him ever, ever again.

"I came home to find Lance dead and the police think I did it. I had blood on my hands. How do you expect me to feel?"

Dylan frowned. "I learned a long time ago not to have

expectations when it comes to your feelings. Still waters run too deep for me. Too cold.''

She angled her chin. ''Only because you can't muddy them.''

''This isn't about *me!*'' he practically roared. He took her shoulders and pulled her closer, forcing her to tilt her head to see his eyes. ''This isn't about us or what happened on the mountain. It's about what went down in this house a few hours ago. It's about you. It's about a whole hell of a lot of questions, and too few answers.''

A hard, broken sound tore from her throat. ''You think I don't know that?'' she tried not to cry. The wind whipped up, sending tangled strands of hair into her face. Agitated, she lifted a hand to push them back, but Dylan did the same. Their fingers met against her cheekbone, hers cold, his thick and hot. She closed her eyes briefly, but the sound of a vicious curse shattered the moment. Heart pounding, she looked up just in time to see hot fury erupt in Dylan's eyes.

It was the only warning she got.

Chapter 2

Something inside Dylan snapped.

He stared at Bethany's wrists, at the smears of blue and black circling pale flesh like violent bracelets. She said she'd been hit on the head and the gash there bore testimony to her claim, but clearly she'd been grabbed by the wrists, as well. Grabbed hard. Crushed with more than casual force.

The picture formed before he could stop it, heinous, damning. Bethany as a cold-blooded murderer he couldn't see. But crimes of passion required neither forethought, nor intent. They simply exploded, destroying everything in their path.

Dylan knew that well.

"Did he do this to you?" he demanded, taking her cold hands and turning them palm up. Deep, crescent-shaped gouges in the fleshy part of her palm told him just how tight she was holding on. The discolored thumbprints on the inside of her wrists turned his blood to ice. "Did he hurt you?"

She gazed up at him, her eyes cloudy and confused, her mouth slightly open. She looked lost and alone standing there in nothing but the pale silk robe, like she'd just rolled from bed and found that while she slept, the whole world had slipped away.

"W-what?"

The thought of anyone getting rough with her, hurting her, chased everything else to the background.

"Lance. Did Lance put these bruises around your wrists?"

Slowly, she looked down, as though just now noticing the discoloration. But she said nothing.

His mind worked fast, reenacting the crime with a brutal precision learned from years as a private investigator. He could almost hear Lance and Bethany arguing, the elevated voices, the desperation. Hear her telling him to leave. See his cousin grabbing her wrists and squeezing. Hurting.

"Bethany." His voice broke on her name. "Did Lance do this to you?" *Tell me no,* he thought savagely. *Tell me no!*

She blinked at him. "Would you care if he did?"

Once, he would have killed. "Answer me, damn it!"

"Let go." The words were soft, but carried unmistakable strength. Strength the girl she'd been had not possessed. Strength that would have threatened the St. Croix prince.

"Maybe the two of you were arguing," he theorized ruthlessly. He needed to crack through her control, and a toothpick wouldn't cut it. "Things got out of hand and Lance lost his cool, got rough. Maybe he even found out about—"

"No!" She jerked her hands from his and backed away. "That's not how it happened." The wind whipped long locks of hair against her mouth, but this time neither of them moved to slide the silky strands back. "I told you— someone knocked me out when I walked in the door."

Dylan studied her standing there against the darkness,

that skimpy robe falling open at the chest and revealing too much cleavage. He didn't need to be a seasoned detective to see the secrets in her eyes. The fear. He didn't need to be a man practiced in seeing through pretenses to notice how badly she trembled.

But he did need Herculean strength to keep his hands off her.

Too damn well, too intimately, he knew how passion could blind and distort, make even the most rational person snap like a sapling in a gale force wind.

He'd just never thought passion played a role in Bethany and Lance's relationship. The thought, the reality that it might have, made him a little crazy.

"If it was self-defense, you need to tell me." He tried to speak casually now, to match calm with calm, but the horror was like a rusty stake driven through his core. "If he grabbed you, tossed you around—"

"No—"

"You wanted him to leave," he pushed on, needing to hear her denial as badly as he'd ever needed anything. Even her. "He wouldn't. Maybe he grabbed you. You only picked up the fire poker to protect yourself. You never meant to hurt—"

"Stop!" she shouted, lifting a hand as though to physically destroy his nasty scenario.

He caught her wrist, just barely resisting the crazy desire to pull her into his arms. He knew better than putting a snub-nose to his temple.

"I wish I *could* stop," he said as levelly as he could. "But I can't. Don't you understand what's going on here? Lance is dead and his blood is on your hands."

The change came over her visibly, the glacierlike wall she used to separate herself from the world slipping into place with eerie precision. "I don't owe you any explanations."

Come back, he wanted to shout, but for the first time Dylan could remember, he envied her the ability to isolate

herself from what she felt. He wanted to do that now, to
shut himself off from the horror and the rage and the fractured grief that splattered through him like vivid splashes
of color all mixed together until nothing was discernable
except for dark, jagged smudges.

But lack of feeling was her specialty, not his.

"You may not owe me anything," he said, "but the
cops are a different story." He glanced toward the door,
where Zito stood watching. "And their questions are going
to be a hell of a lot harder."

She lifted her chin in a masterful gesture of cool defiance that was pure Bethany. "If you're trying to reenact
the crime, it's not going to work. The fire poker is inside."

The words were soft, but they landed like crashing boulders. He looked down at his big hand manacling her slender wrist, the nasty bruises completely hidden. It was a
miracle whoever roughed her up hadn't snapped the small
bone in two. It wouldn't have taken much extra effort. Just
a little pressure—

He let go abruptly and stepped back.

Slowly, Bethany lifted her eyes to his. "Do you really
think I'm capable of murder?"

The night fell quiet, so silent he would have sworn he
heard the pounding of his heart, the rasp of his breathing.
Or maybe that was hers. Theirs.

Everything else faded to the background, Zito waiting
in the wings, the ugliness inside. There was no horror or
blind rage, no stabbing grief, no crime to be solved, no
betrayal to be forgotten. There was only a man and
woman, a silent communion he neither understood nor
wanted.

He drank in the sight of her standing there, finally allowing himself to look into eyes he'd relegated to the
darkest, coldest hours of the night. They were deep and
heavy-lidded, fathomless, liquid sapphire framed by full
dark lashes. A man could lose himself in those eyes, swirling and serene, but somehow, always, always, lost.

But they were dull now, huge and unfocused, her pupils dilated. Long, tangled brown hair concealed a portion of her face, but not the smear of blood on her left cheekbone. Nor the fact that no tear tracks marred her features.

Because he didn't want her to see how badly they'd started to shake, Dylan shoved his hands into his pockets. He tore his gaze from hers and let it slide lower, to the silk garment gaping to reveal the swell of her breasts, the indentation of her waist, the curve of her hips. He couldn't help but wonder about the negligee beneath, whether it would be pristine, as well, or if at least in the bedroom, she'd displayed a little warmth and creativity.

Like she had with him.

Before.

"Sweetheart," he drawled, "you're capable of anything you put your mind to."

Beth curled her fingers into her palms, digging deep. The lingering smell of stale cigarette smoke and scorched coffee burned her eyes and throat; the gash at the back of her head throbbed with every beat of her heart. She wasn't going to wake up. Two detectives really did sit across from her in the small interrogation room, tossing out one nasty scenario after another, as they'd been doing for over an hour.

"So you invited him over, slipped into that skimpy negligee, and tried to seduce him back into your bed."

"No."

"You didn't like being divorced. You wanted your fancy life back. You were a little desperate. Didn't enjoy being a has-been, the butt of town gossip, like your mama, is that it?"

"No!" The word burst from her with the force of a bullet. The fact they'd finally thrown her mother into the fray pushed Beth dangerously close to the edge. One way or another, everything always circled back to the notorious Sierra Rae.

They were trying to break her, she knew, rattle her, find some way to make her trip. It was their job.

Dylan didn't have the same excuse.

"This has nothing to do with Mrs. St. Croix's mother," Janine White bit out. A longtime friend of Lance's, then of Beth's, the attorney had met her at the station without hesitation. The women who'd laughed over martinis sat side by side in the small room, cups of bitter coffee and a tape recorder separating them from detectives Paul Zito and Harry Livingston.

Detective Zito picked up his pencil. "Just trying to establish motivation."

"There is no motivation," Janine shot back, "because you're talking to an innocent woman. Beth did not kill Lance."

Gratitude squeezed through the icy tightness in Beth's chest. Janine's sleek white evening gown made her look more like an Amazon priestess than a savvy attorney, but she had a reputation for being as tough as nails. Even now she appeared amazingly composed, the red rimming her eyes the only evidence of tears Beth knew she'd shed.

"Did you and Mr. St. Croix have intercourse today?"

The question might as well have been a knife. It sliced deep, robbing Beth of breath. Disgust bled through.

Janine recovered first. "This woman's ex-husband has been murdered!" she said, surging up and slamming her palms down on the table. "What the hell are you trying to prove?"

"You know damn well what I'm trying to do," Detective Livingston drawled, turning his stony eyes to Beth. "Did he take what you offered and walk away? You felt used and hurt and ran after him—"

"That's disgusting," Beth bit out.

The balding detective frowned. "Murder is."

Beth sucked in a sharp breath, trying not to splinter despite how effectively the detectives thrust the battering ram. For nine years she'd done her best to live a quiet,

simple life. She didn't want the spotlight Lance had de-
veloped a fondness for. She didn't want the passion that
propelled her mother from marriage to affair to marriage.
To affair. She didn't want the chaos Dylan created without
even trying.

*"A husband who loves me and a couple of kids, that's
all I want."*

"That's all?"

*"Well, maybe a house in the mountains, a couple of
dogs and cats, some goldfish."*

The innocence of that long ago day burned. At the time,
she would never have imagined how quickly things could
fall apart, that within a month she'd tell Dylan that she'd
never loved him, never wanted to see him again. That she
would lay her hand against the tiniest casket she'd ever
seen. That Lance would sit quietly beside her hour after
hour, listening to her cry her heart out. That Dylan would
leave town, but Lance would stay. That she wouldn't see
Dylan again for three long years, until the day she pledged
her life to his cousin.

That Lance would become blinded by ambition.

That she would be sterile.

That the marriage she'd been so determined to make
work would crumble.

That Dylan would suddenly reappear in her life.

That Lance would one day lie dead on the living room
floor.

That the fire poker would be in her hands.

"Beth?" Janine asked, touching her hand. "Are you
okay?"

She blinked, a steely resolve spreading through her.
Slowly, she looked up, meeting Detective Livingston's
hard gaze. "I didn't have sex with him today, this week,
this month, or even this year. And I didn't kill him."

The older man leaned forward and steepled his fingers.
"Then maybe you'd like to tell me why you were in a
negligee."

"She's already told you she doesn't know," Janine reminded.

"So she's said." This from Detective Zito, the tall, strikingly handsome man who'd stood in the shadows with Dylan.

"What about your wrists?" he asked, flipping through the pages of his small notebook. "Who put those bracelets there?"

Beth looked at the nasty purplish bruises, but saw only Dylan's hands curled around her flesh. "I don't know." The claim sounded weak, but she spoke the truth. "I had no reason to kill him. We were divorced. There were no hard feelings."

"You wouldn't be the first woman to strike out at the man who walked out on her," Livingston pointed out.

The pale green walls of the cramped room pushed closer. "That's not how it happened."

"Refill anyone?" Detective Zito asked, crossing to pick up the coffeepot.

Beth looked at the paper cup sitting in front of her, its contents long cold. She'd barely taken a sip. The mere smell of the burned coffee made her gag.

"Guess not." He filled his cup and returned to the table. "Did your husband have any enemies?"

"He worked for the district attorney's office," Janine answered for her, practically snarling at Zito. "You know that. He was a prosecutor." Just like Janine was. If Beth was arrested, Janine would be unable to help in an official capacity. "We all have enemies. It's a hazard of the job."

"Anyone in particular? Had he received any threatening phone calls or letters?"

"Not that I know of," Beth said, but then, she and Lance had rarely spoken of that kind of thing. Toward the end, they'd barely spoken at all. She'd lost herself in her work at Girls Unlimited, a center for underprivileged teenage girls, and Lance had worked ungodly hours as one of

Portland's leading prosecutors. His political future had never burned brighter.

"That's quite a security system you've got at the house," Zito went on. "Was he worried about someone coming after him?"

Obviously, the detective hadn't known the man whose murder he investigated. "Lance wasn't scared of anything or anyone. He was born a St. Croix. It never occurred to him that something bad could happen to him."

"And you?" Zito asked. "Did the thought occur to you?"

Icy fingers of certainty curled through her. "Bad times don't discriminate. They touch us all."

"Even the St. Croixs?"

"Yes, even the St. Croixs." Especially one in particular. But then, Dylan preferred it that way. He'd caused an uproar by dropping out of law school six months before graduation, opting for private investigations rather over the formal justice system. His grandfather the judge had been furious, and while Lance had put on a good show, she knew he'd secretly embraced the opportunity to outshine his black sheep cousin.

Beth stiffened, shaken by the direction of her thoughts. She had no business thinking of Dylan now. No business remembering. He was a living, breathing reminder of mistakes she'd give almost anything to erase. Fire burned. Fire always, always burned.

"I've told you everything I know," she said, and stood. The room spun like a tilt-a-whirl, prompting her to brace a hand against the chair. The two detectives looked at her oddly, Janine in concern.

"It's late, I'm tired and my head is pounding." And she was afraid she was going to be sick. Gingerly, she lifted a hand to the gash at the back of her head, but rather than feeling her fingers, she felt Dylan's. Gentle. Disturbing. "I'd like to go now."

"We're not done—" Livingston started, but Zito cut him off.

"Don't leave town without letting me know first."

She hardly recognized the woman in the mirror. Beth stared at the pale mouth and dark eyes in the reflection, and felt her throat tighten. Cupping her hands, she returned them to the stream of cold water running from the faucet, then lifted them to her face. Over. And over. Only when two female patrol officers strolled into the bathroom, laughing, did she stop.

Very quietly, very deliberately, she patted her face dry and slung her purse over her shoulder, walked out the door.

She saw him the second she stepped from the elevator. He stood not ten feet away, talking on his mobile phone and slicing a hand violently through the air. He had his back to her, but she didn't need to see the hard lines of his face to recognize him. She always felt him first, that low hum deep inside, followed by a tightening of her chest.

Somehow, she kept walking.

"No, damn it," she heard him bark. "Let me handle this."

Her heart revved and stalled. Handle what?, she couldn't help wondering. Her? It didn't matter. She'd—

"Beth, wait!"

She stiffened and, though she wanted to keep going, had no choice but to stop. "Janey," she said, turning to her friend. "I appreciate all you did for me. I hope I didn't pull you away from anything important."

"Don't think twice about it." Janine took Beth's hands and squeezed. "How are you holding up? I know things weren't great between the two of you, but this has to be hard."

Her throat tightened. Janine was Lance's friend first, but in her soft voice and expressive brown eyes, Beth found a concern that almost undid her. "I didn't do it," she whispered.

"Of course you didn't," came a rough masculine voice.

Beth barely had time to turn before the man was beside her, pulling her into his arms. "I just heard, Beth. I'm so sorry."

The hug caught her off guard. As district attorney, Kent English had been both Lance's mentor and friend. And though she and Kent had been cordial, the man whose place the media had speculated Lance would soon take had never touched her beyond a handshake. Now the embattled D.A. skimmed a hand along her back in a gesture that should have been comforting.

But wasn't.

Instantly, she looked across the hall and found Dylan watching her through the most scorched-earth eyes she'd ever seen. Her chest tightened, and her heart started to thrum. The breath stalled in her throat. The truth disturbed.

This hug. This embrace. It was what she'd wanted from Dylan the second she'd seen him standing on the patio, to feel his arms around her, his body against hers. To just lean against him and be held.

She'd be safer dancing naked in a bonfire.

"Thank you," she said against Kent's chest, struggling to free herself. His arms suddenly felt like a net, sending panic twisting through her. She needed to get away. Not from the cops or Kent, but from Dylan and those hard, penetrating eyes.

Kent, a shrewd politician with a well-earned reputation for cutting throats and breaking hearts, didn't try to stop her, just stepped back and frowned. For a man rumored to be on his way out, he still held himself with commanding presence.

"I'll have Livingston's badge for putting you through this. Anyone who knows you knows you couldn't hurt a flea."

Involuntarily, Beth looked toward the end of the hall, only to find Dylan gone.

"Thanks for coming down," she said, turning back to Lance's colleagues. "It means a lot to me."

Kent pulled her in for another quick hug and Janine did her best to smile. Beth bade them good-night, then crossed the lobby to the front door. A few uniformed cops lingered by a counter, talking in loud tones. A woman rushed inside, demanding to know where her Donny was. Across the room, a young girl with ratty hair and torn clothes yelled to anyone who would listen.

Pushing open the glass door, Beth welcomed the blast of cool night air.

"Mrs. St. Croix!" came a shouted voice, as a crowd of reporters rushed up the steps. "Mrs. St. Croix, can you tell us what happened?"

Flashbulbs exploded around her. Microphones were jammed toward her. "Do they have any suspects?"

"Was the murder weapon really a fire poker?"

Beth tried to turn away, but the swarm had circled her.

"Did you really find his body?"

Revulsion surged through her. She saw the collective gleam in the eyes of the reporters, the thirst for a story with no regard for the fact that the roadkill they picked apart was someone's world. She'd worked hard to keep her personal life private, but when Lance went to work for the district attorney's office, anonymity became a luxury of the past. He'd thrived on the adulation, fed off it. And the press had fallen in love. He was the grandson of a wealthy state judge, he was handsome, and everyone believed it only a matter of time before he capitalized on his popularity and ran for public office, starting with D.A. The press had been having a field day with rumors about English stepping down, Lance taking over.

No one was quite sure why.

But now the golden boy was dead; murdered, she thought with a sharp stab, and the media he'd used so shamelessly wanted to know why.

"I have no comment," Beth said. No intention of telling

them anything. Even words of innocence could be twisted into stones of condemnation.

"If you'll excuse me," she said, trying to push through the tight circle of reporters.

"Did you kill him?"

The question stopped Beth cold. Yvonne Kelly, an investigative reporter whose love of going for the jugular Lance had always admired, pushed her way to the front. The wind blew pale hair into her face. Her eyes glittered.

"Was it a crime of passion?" she asked icily. "Is that how you ended up with blood on your hands?"

Control shattered. "You'd like that, wouldn't you—" she started, but the crowd erupted into a frenzy of shouts and curses and shoving before she could finish. Someone screamed. Flashes of light ricocheted through the darkness. She heard a low roar, then the sound of something smashing violently to the concrete.

"You can't do that!" a reporter shouted.

"Watch me." Dylan broke from the throng and pushed to her side, hooked an arm around her waist without breaking his stride. "Sorry, folks, but this feeding frenzy is over. Ms. St. Croix has no comment."

Disappointment tittered through the reporters, but the swarm instantly loosened, obeying Dylan's command like he was some fallen deity and the price of going against him was eternal damnation. He led her down the steps, his stride long and purposeful. Determined. She almost had to run to keep up with him. He never looked back, just kept his arm around her waist and guided her to the dark SUV at the curb.

He opened the passenger door and grabbed a bulging file from the bucket seat. "Get in."

Beth hesitated. The interior of the black Bronco looked as dark and isolating as a cave, and once inside, they'd be completely alone. Just the two of them. No outside interference. Just like that cold night at the cabin, the terrible mistake that still had her jerking awake in the middle of

the night, heart hammering, chest tight, body burning from
his touch.

She didn't want that. Lance was dead. She was a suspect. There was no room for the chaos that was Dylan in
her world. Hadn't been for a long time. She'd worked hard
to carve him from her life, her dreams. But God help her,
because of one mindless slip, he'd stepped out of those
shadowy, forbidden images and into the worst nightmare
of her life.

And Yvonne Kelly was closing in fast.

"We don't have all night," Dylan prompted.

Beth cut him a sharp look then slipped into the Bronco.
In a heartbeat he had the door closed and was sliding into
the driver's seat, effectively shutting them off from the
world. Through the tinted windows, Beth saw Yvonne
Kelly hit the sidewalk at a run, but the engine purred to
life and they tore from the curb with a shriek of tires.

Her heart raced as fast as the blur of buildings and cars
they passed. He took a right curve too fast, then another,
then swerved onto the side of the deserted road and threw
the gear into park. A few cars lined the street, but no activity, and very little light. They were behind the police
station, she realized. Not far away, but completely out of
sight.

"You sure do know how to attract a crowd, sweetheart."

The insolent words brought her back to familiar territory. Or at least, remembered territory. For a few dizzying
minutes, Dylan had seemed more stranger than one-man
wrecking crew. In his touch, she'd felt a protectiveness she
didn't remember. In his rough-hewn voice, she'd heard a
strain she hadn't understood. This bold, in-your-face proc-
lamation was much more suited to the man she'd foolishly
given her heart so long ago.

Little light made its way from the street lamp through
the tinted windows, leaving only the blue glow from the
dashboard to cast his face in shadow. He watched her in-

tently, his six-foot-two frame dominating the front seat. She could hardly move without touching him.

She didn't want to touch him.

She hadn't wanted to spend the night at the cabin with him, either. She'd driven to the mountains after an emotional appointment with her doctor, in search of peace and quiet, to clear her mind. Instead, she'd found Dylan. She hadn't realized he spent weekends there, at the St. Croix retreat. She hadn't known the snow would make the roads impassable. She hadn't anticipated all the memories closing in on her, the nightmare that had pinned her to the bed, waking up to find Dylan by her side, so big and strong, so…gentle. That had been new. Or maybe just an illusion. A dream. A wish. Regardless, it had shredded every remaining particle of her defenses.

Until she'd awoken just before sunrise, sprawled over his big hot body, their legs tangled, his arm draped possessively over her waist.

She'd wanted to cry.

Even now, weeks later, she could hardly believe the gravity of her mistake. She should have been able to tell him no. Tell herself no. She should have been able to resist that keening deep inside, the acute longing to feel his arms around her. It was tempting to make up some excuse like she'd been confused, hadn't realized what she was doing. But that was a lie, and she knew it. She'd known. And she'd wanted. Badly. That was the problem. Being with Dylan went against everything she believed in, violated the life she'd built. And still, she'd given herself to him.

Still, she'd given.

Never again, she'd promised herself on the cold, slick drive down the mountain. Never, never again would she let herself give in to the kind of desire that burned everything in its path. Passion was intoxicating, but it never, never lasted.

Believing otherwise only led to pain.

She had to focus on Lance now, couldn't let her irrational reaction to Dylan blur her focus all over again.

"Thirsty?" he asked.

She blinked. "What?"

"Good old-fashioned H_2O," he said, offering her the plastic bottle from his cup holder. "It's nothing fancy and a little warm now, but it's better than you passing out on me."

She stared at his big, scarred hand, but rather than seeing those capable fingers wrapped around clear plastic, she saw them closed around her wrist. She'd felt the strength of his grip, but an unmistakable tenderness, as well.

It had been the tenderness that made her lash out.

Now she forced herself to look from the hand that could play her body like a song, to the hard line of his mouth and those eyes so deep and dark. And for a shattering moment, she didn't see the uncompromising man who wanted to know if she'd killed the cousin who shared his last name but not his life.

She saw what she'd remembered on the mountain, the reckless boy he'd been, the one who'd coaxed her from her safe little world and made her want to be a little bad. Daring. To take chances she'd never even considered. And from that mirage came the crazy desire to lean closer and soak up the warmth of his body, to feel his arms close around her and hear his rough-hewn voice promise everything would be okay.

But that was impossible, and she knew it.

With Dylan St. Croix, nothing was ever okay.

"No, thanks," she said, reaching for the door. "I don't need you charging in and playing hero." She'd learned the hard way that leaning on Dylan St. Croix was like leaning on a volcano ready to blow. And if she forgot, she had only to drive thirty minutes south of town, where two cold tombstones stood in silent reminder. "I can take care of myself."

Curling her fingers around the handle, she pulled.

But the door didn't budge.

"This isn't a game," came Dylan's dangerously quiet voice from behind her. He reached across the passenger's seat and pulled her hand from the door. "And I'm sure as hell not doing this for fun."

"Then let me go."

"I can't."

She turned to face him. Only inches separated them, making her painfully aware of the whiskers shadowing the uncompromising line of his mouth. "Yes, you can."

"Lance is *dead,* Bethany, and you're just barely hanging on. Queen Cutthroat was ready to crucify you. What kind of man would I be if I just melted into the shadows?"

The breath stalled in her throat. His words were soft, silky, but the warning rang clear. She sat there crowded against the seat, stunned, struggling to breathe without drawing the drugging scent of sandalwood and clove deep within her. Not only was he still holding her hand, but his body was pressed to hers, seemingly absorbing every heartbeat, every breath.

"It's a little late," she said slowly, deliberately, "to pretend you care what anyone else thinks about you."

The light in his eyes went dark. "I'll say it one more time." He let go of her hand, but didn't ease away. "I don't do games. I don't do hero. And I sure as hell don't pretend. That was always your specialty."

The pain was swift and immediate, driving home the truth. Dylan St. Croix had a penchant for streaking into her life like a shooting star, big and blazing and beautiful, but he'd never really known her. Never understood her. Never loved her. He'd just wanted her. In his arms and in his bed, but not in his heart.

"No," she said, hoping he couldn't hear the ragged edge to her breathing. "You just blaze along seeing how many applecarts you can knock over."

He didn't retreat as she'd hoped, didn't pull back to his

side of the car. "Sometimes that's the only way to separate the good fruit from the bad."

"And what am I?" she asked before she could stop herself.

"It's not for me to decide."

"Then why won't you let me go?"

His lips thinned. "I've already told you, Bethany, I'm not into standing on the sidelines and watching someone get raked over the coals. Not even you. I'm not that cold."

There was a rough edge to his voice, a hoarseness that hadn't been there before. "I never thought you were cold."

"What about Lance?" he asked, leaning closer. "Did you think he was cold?"

The urge to pull away engulfed her, but with her back against the locked door, she had nowhere to go. Instead, she reached for the blanket of numbness.

"I don't want to talk about Lance."

Dylan lifted a hand to her face, violating the space she'd put between them by skimming his index finger beneath her eyes. "You haven't cried."

She swallowed against the tightness in her throat. No way would she tell him she was all cried out, that before that ill-fated night on the mountain, the last tear had spilled from her eyes the night before she married Lance, when she'd awoken with the remembered touch of Dylan's hands on her body.

"Crying doesn't help, Dylan. Crying doesn't change a damn thing." She squeezed her eyes shut, not wanting Dylan to see truths she couldn't hide. Not even from herself.

She realized her mistake too late. A woman should never close her eyes on Dylan St. Croix. Never turn her back to him. Never give him an advantage to press. Because he would.

Dylan St. Croix never turned down the killing blow.

Out of the darkness his mouth came down on hers, and just like that explosive, snowbound night in the cabin, the bottom fell out from her world.

Chapter 3

She could retreat from the world, build ice palaces where no one could touch her, hurt her, but by God, Dylan refused to let her slip away from him. Not again. Pretenses made him crazy. Lies destroyed.

Sex, Dylan. It was just sex. Nothing more, nothing less.

The words tore in from the past, dark. Tortured. After all this time, he still didn't know if she'd spoken the truth when she'd told him she loved him, or when she'd told him she didn't.

And he knew if Bethany had her way, he never would.

He felt her stiffen beneath his hands, his mouth, heard the sharp intake of breath. But she didn't lift a hand to his face like she'd done that night in the mountains, didn't sigh, didn't open for him.

Frustration twisted with something darker, something he'd tried to destroy, but that had lain dormant instead. He'd hoped to slice through the remote facade she wore like a tight-fitting bodysuit, to see if he could still reach

her or if after that night she'd traveled so far away, sewn
herself up so tightly, that she was beyond even his touch.

He might as well have lifted a goblet of arsenic to his
own mouth and drunk greedily.

Bethany wrenched away from his kiss and stared at him
through huge, bruised eyes. The breath tore in and out of
her.

"Does that change anything?" he asked darkly, buying
time to bring himself under control.

She wiped the back of her hand across her mouth. "I'm
not a naive, passion-drunk little girl anymore," she whispered, "I'm not my mother. It takes more than a kiss in
the dark to break me."

Like he'd done before. She didn't say the words, but
they reverberated through him. He looked at her sitting
inches from him, her hair loose around her face, the mutinous line of the mouth that could set his body to fire.
She no longer wore that slinky robe, and for that, he found
himself grateful. But somehow, even in the severe black
pantsuit, she still managed to look shockingly vulnerable,
wary, but beautiful all the same.

"Who said I was trying to break you?" Maybe he'd
been trying to break himself.

A hard sound broke from her throat. He refused to label
it pain.

"You forget," she said. "I know you, Dylan. I know
how you operate. But it's not going to work. You can't
rattle a confession out of me—you lost that ability long
ago."

The words sounded tough, but he'd felt the tremor race
through that lithe body of hers. Who was she trying to
convince? he wondered. Him? Or herself.

"Careful, Bethany. Some men might mistake that as a
challenge."

She pulled his hand away from her face. "Let me go."

He should, he knew. A smart man would unlock the
door and let her vanish into the night all over again. But

he couldn't do that. Lance was dead, and Bethany had bruises around her wrists. He didn't want to think about what other, less visible, wounds she hid. But did.

"You always thought you'd break if you showed emotion. But the truth is you'll break if you don't. There's honesty in feeling things deeply. Not shame."

Through the glow of the dashboard, her eyes darkened. At the house, he'd seen the wall of ice slide into place, but this time her expression remained naked and raw, like she was bleeding from the inside out and couldn't make it stop.

"Maybe I don't feel anything." The words were soft, brittle, surprisingly candid. "Maybe everything inside me is cold. Frozen."

And maybe he was a fool. He never should have come to the police station, never should have left his grandfather's house. He'd gone there to tell the judge about Lance, but afterward, the silence had been suffocating. The older man had retreated, not showing a flicker of the grief Dylan knew he felt.

"It's called shock," he said and knew, "but someone who doesn't know you could mistake lack of emotion for lack of feeling."

"And you, Dylan? Is that what you think?"

"I know you're capable of feeling. At least you used to be." Earlier, the years between them had fallen away; now they stacked right back up. "But I don't know you anymore, and I don't have a damn clue how you felt about Lance."

He never had, either. Part of him wanted to hear her express pure, undying love for his cousin. No matter how badly that would sting, at least it would help assure him Zito's suspicions were as crazy as Dylan wanted them to be. Without that sentiment, he was left standing on the razor fine edge of doubt, and it was slicing him to the bone.

"Did you love him?" he asked point-blank.

She didn't look away like he expected her to, like she

once would have. Through the darkness, she just stared at him.

"Well?" he asked. "It's not that tough of a question."

Bethany looked down at the hands clasped severely in her lap, where the gaudy two-carat, emerald-cut solitaire Lance had given her no longer overwhelmed her slender finger.

"Lance and I had a…complicated relationship."

"I thought it looked pretty simple." Though he'd tried not to look at all. Not to know. "He went his way, and you went yours."

She looked up abruptly. "Not every relationship has to be fire and brimstone. Sometimes they can be quiet and simple, undemanding. That doesn't mean they don't exist."

"Relationship? It looked more like a photo-op to me."

Pain flickered in her eyes, and yet she lifted her chin like a queen. "You have no right to pass judgment on me, Dylan. Not you, of all people. You and Lance were hardly the devoted cousins your grandfather wanted everyone to think you were."

"How could we be?" Sebastian St. Croix had done his best to raise Dylan and Lance as brothers, but they'd been as different as fire and ice. Lance had thrived in the posh world of the Portland elite, old money and timeless hypocrisy.

Dylan had felt like he'd been sent to prison.

"The only thing we had in common was something two men should never share." And now Lance was dead, leaving Dylan to pick up the pieces, like his cousin had done for him so long ago.

"I'm not doing this," Bethany said, reaching for the door.

But he didn't release the locks, wasn't ready to let her go. "I'm just calling a spade a spade, sweetheart."

She turned back toward him. "But that doesn't change anything, does it? Lance is still dead. And no matter what went down between the two of you, the two of us for that matter, he didn't deserve to die."

She'd yet to say she loved him. He wondered if she realized that. Worse, he wondered why he cared.

"No," he agreed, "he didn't." But too well, Dylan knew people didn't always get what they deserved. Or wanted.

Once, a long time ago, Dylan's grandmother had given him a bag of marbles. He'd loved playing with the small, colorful glass balls, had spent hours organizing and sorting them. Then Prince Lance had come over, yanked the bag from Dylan's hands, and dumped them on the sloping driveway. The marbles had scattered everywhere, and no matter how quickly Dylan tried to scoop them up, they just kept rolling away from him. With sickening clarity, he remembered the sound of Lance's laughter.

But when his grandfather had caught them fighting, it had been Dylan who got the belt.

Now he studied Bethany through the blue glow of the dashboard lights, the shadows playing against the soft lines of her face. Silky hair cascaded down her shoulders, looking more sable than brown. She'd brushed it, he noted, and wondered if Lance had ever done the task for her. Like he had.

A long time ago.

"Where will you go?" he asked.

"Home," she started, but he saw the second awareness dawned. Her home was a crime scene. "Maybe a hotel."

"The media will be crawling all over you there," he said. "You'll be safer at my house."

Her eyes flared. "*Your* house?"

He didn't stop to think. "It's isolated, secure. No one would find you there."

And he really was out of his mind.

She just stared at him. And when she spoke, her voice was soft but cutting, classic Bethany. "That was me on the patio this evening. That was me you practically accused of killing your cousin. It's too late to pretend you're on my side.''

No matter where he stepped, they always landed in the same place. "I'm not the one pretending, Bethany.''

She didn't defend herself as he wanted, didn't take the bait. She just frowned. "It's late, I'm tired, and I don't have the energy for your games right now. Please. Let me go.''

"My God," he said in a deceptively quiet voice, the one that masked all those sharp edges slicing him up inside. "You're really just going to sit there and act like that night on the mountain didn't happen?" He'd told himself he wasn't going to bring it up, but the fact she was pretending it never happened pushed him over the edge. It happened. She'd come alive in his arms, twisted and turned, begged. "We didn't even use birth control, for crissakes. I could have gotten you pregnant. Would you have even told me?"

The car was dark, but he saw the color fade from her face, saw her wince.

"I can't have children," she said. "You know that.''

The pain in her voice almost made him turn back. Almost. "Are you sure about that?''

She stared at him a long moment before answering. He waited for one of her ice walls to slide in place, but her expression remained naked, bleeding. He could hear the edge to her breathing. And slowly, slowly, fire came back into her eyes.

"Do you enjoy being cruel?" she asked in a cracked voice.

"It's a legitimate question. We had sex. If there's any chance—"

"It was a mistake!" she surprised him by shouting. "It was one of those heat of the moment—"

He went coldly still. "Don't.''

He didn't know whether it was the edge to his voice or the fury he knew hardened his expression, but something dangerously close to fear flashed in her eyes. "Don't what?"

"Don't sit there and insinuate you didn't know what you were doing. You wanted me every bit as much as I wanted you."

For a moment he saw the same heat in her gaze, that glaze of passion that had haunted him for so long. But then, finally, at last, a Bethany ice wall slid into place, and she angled her chin. "That doesn't make it right."

He wasn't going to let her do it. Wasn't going to let her use the heat between them as a weapon against him. "Quit trying to make everything black or white," he bit out. "It wasn't premeditated. It just…happened. We were stranded. You needed someone, and I was there."

A shadow crossed her face. "It was *wrong*."

It took effort, but somehow he resisted the urge to reach across the seat and put his mouth to hers, prove what she tried to deny.

Instead, he let an insolent smile curve his lips. "I thought it was pretty damn right."

"Dylan—"

"But don't worry, angel, when I think of that night…" which he tried not to "…I don't see you naked or hear the way you cried out my name, I see the morning after, waking up alone in that big cold bed. I may be a slow learner, but sledgehammers like that usually do the trick."

"Then there's nothing left to say, is there?" she asked in a voice devoid of all emotion.

Because he wanted to crush her in his arms, he released the locks. "Go."

She did. Without looking back, she pushed open the door and let in a blast of cold, then stepped into the night and vanished in the darkness.

Just like always.

B. B. King belted out the blues, but with only ten minutes until Shady's called it a night, few remained to listen. Two of the three pool tables stood deserted. Only one poor soul remained at the bar. The smoke was actually beginning to clear.

"You know this breaks every rule in the book," Zito said, running a hand over his scruffy face.

Dylan polished off his scotch and dropped the empty glass on top of a heart carved into the battered wood table. "Depends upon whose book you're talking about."

"Since when have I given a damn about any book but my own?"

That's exactly what Dylan was counting on. After he'd followed Bethany to a hotel, he'd tried to go home and put her out of his mind, but quickly realized climbing Mount Hood blindfolded would be easier.

He needed to know what had gone down in that interrogation room. He knew Zito's partner, knew the man's knack for going for the jugular. And it had killed him to wait outside, to not know, to imagine. Had they broken her? Had they made her hurt?

"No one's making you stay," he reminded the detective.

Zito made a show of picking up his microbrew and drinking deeply of the local favorite, all the while his speculative, too-seeing gaze trained on Dylan. "Don't tell me the champion of the underdog is standing by the woman who killed your cousin? Beauty doesn't equate innocence, son."

"You think she did it?" he asked as blandly as he could. Zito shrugged. "Chances are."

"Evidence?"

Zito reached for a cigarette. "Mostly circumstantial at this point, but the divorce makes a nice motive. She lost a lot when he walked out on her."

"Money never mattered to her." Just stability. Peace. Solitude. The kind of lifestyle Dylan could never offer.

"People change."

Dylan eyed the half-empty pack of cigarettes. He hadn't put one to his mouth in over a year, hadn't craved the pungent bite in months. Until now. Sure people changed, but deep down, needs and desires stayed the same.

The daughter of a woman who thrived on grabbing the spotlight any way she could, who upgraded husbands and lovers more frequently than most people did cars, Bethany had always dreamed of a life straight out of a fifties sitcom. She wanted to be June Cleaver. She wanted to marry Ward.

Instead, she'd married Lance.

Dylan had always wondered what went down when Lance decided to enter public service, rather than the private sector he'd always promised he would serve. If she'd been angry, betrayed, she'd never let it show. While Lance's star soared, she'd devoted herself to a nonprofit organization for underprivileged teenage girls.

The blade of sorrow caught him by surprise. Prince Lance was dead now. Gone forever. And Bethany was left standing in the spotlight, alone. With blood on her hands.

"It doesn't add up," he muttered. Despite the circumstantial evidence and apparent motivation, Dylan couldn't see Bethany doing anything to draw attention to herself, much less place herself in the heart of a scandal.

"Not all crimes are premeditated," Zito pointed out. "Passion can lead to murder as easily as a one-night stand. You don't know what went down today. You don't know what was going on between her and Lance. She might have just snapped."

A hard sound broke from Dylan's throat. "You don't know Bethany." She never snapped, never came unglued. Never. Except—

Don't go there, he warned himself. *Don't even acknowledge there existed.*

"I hate to spoil the party," Loretta Myers said as she picked up their empties, "but some of us have homes to go to."

Dylan glanced around the darkened bar and saw that only he and Zito remained. "Come on, Lori, cut us some slack."

"Five minutes, saint. Five minutes."

He winked, earning a glower before she strolled away.

"You can't let that pretty face fool you, son."

Dylan jerked his attention back to Zito, the cigarettes begging him from the table. Sometimes, restraint came at a high cost. "Come on, man, even I'm not that hard up."

"Not Loretta. Bethany. I saw the way you were looking at her, the way she was looking at you."

"And what way would that be?"

"I'm not a poet, son, but for a minute there I thought I was going to have a second crime to clean up." Zito stood. "One of the hardest lessons a cop learns is to remain objective, no matter what. That's what makes Bethany St. Croix so dangerous. I know it's hard to look into those sexy blue eyes and see a murderer, not a woman you'd love to have underneath you, but facts don't lie. And right now, the facts say she probably killed Lance. It's my job to prove it."

Everything inside Dylan hardened. He wanted to hit something. Someone. Hit hard. He wanted to turn his back on Bethany like she'd done him, but couldn't. Not until he knew what really went down in that house.

"What the hell happened to innocent until proven guilty?" he barked.

Zito's gaze sharpened. "There you go again, defending her. Is there something going on I should know about?"

Dylan almost laughed. Almost. It was either that or slam his fist against the table. The good detective had no idea. None. And if Dylan was going to get to the bottom of this mess, he needed to put all that boiling emotion aside and keep it that way.

"Chill out," he said, standing. "I'm not defending her,

and I'm sure as hell not getting suckered by a pretty face and killer body.'' Not again. ''Just considering all possibilities.''

''The cops are going after a crime of passion angle.''

Passion. The word made Beth cringe. ''Lighting a wet match would be more likely,'' she told Janine, looking out the window of her seventeenth-story hotel room. Early morning sun streamed through low clouds, the eerie backlighting making the vista look more like a dreamscape than a landscape.

Through the phone line, her friend sighed. ''I know, but I also know how quickly things can spiral out of control. One moment is all it takes to change a lifetime.'' She paused, seemed to hesitate. ''Listen, Beth. If I'm going to help you, I need to be sure you've told me everything. About when you got home, when you came to, everything. I need to make sure there's nothing the police can discover that you've held back.''

A chill cut through her. Too easily she could see the fire poker, feel its cold, deadly shape in her hands. ''I didn't kill him,'' she said with absolute conviction.

''What about motive? Is there anything—*anything*—that could spark an argument? Lies? Betrayals?''

Deep inside, she started to bleed. ''We didn't argue.'' Not even about the betrayals.

A few minutes later Beth hung up the phone. Fatigue pulled at her, but restless energy kept her from the bed. How could she slip between crisp sheets and close her eyes, when all she wanted was to wake up? Go back to before. Yes, she'd wanted Lance out of her life, but not like this. Dear God, not like this.

The numbness spread. She should feel something, she thought. She should feel something other than this icy chill whenever she thought about Lance. But the second she'd stepped from Dylan's Bronco, the cold fog had returned, settling deep into her bones.

Sorrow squeezed her chest. Instinctively she clenched

the lapel of the thick terrycloth robe tighter, as though in doing so she could hold the seams of her life together, as well. She had to find a way to stop the bleeding. To warm up. She couldn't break down. She had to be strong.

Not just because of Lance, but because of Dylan.

She drew a hand to her mouth and tried to forget the feel of his lips on hers, the shock and the dizziness. His kiss hadn't been hard like the words volleying between them, but unbearably soft. Seeking. Almost…desperate.

It was as though when he'd put his mouth to hers, he'd breathed life into her, a piece of himself. Just like before. The memory burned through her heart and her soul, and everywhere in between, searing and scorching. Tempting.

She couldn't let him do that to her. Couldn't let him overwhelm her through physical or sexual prowess. Couldn't let him slip in and play her like a never-ending song. The coming days and weeks promised to be hard enough. She had no idea how she'd move past the horror of finding Lance dead, but knew Dylan St. Croix wasn't the answer.

Turning, she headed for the bathroom, but saw the TV first.

"No stone will be left unturned," Judge Sebastian St. Croix was vowing. The imposing patriarch's face was pale, his brooding eyes red-rimmed, his white hair mussed. "No avenue unexplored. We will find my grandson's murderer and exact swift justice."

Beth froze.

"Have you talked to his wife?" Yvonne Kelley asked.

"That's a family matter."

The steely-eyed reporter didn't back down. "Judge, a source tells me evidence at the scene suggests she might be involved. Is the family standing by her?"

His smile turned cutting. "The St. Croixs stand by justice, Evy, pure and simple. There'll be an investigation—"

The sound of a loud knock overrode the rest of the

judge's rant. Beth swung toward the door, but didn't move. No one knew she was here. She'd driven around for over an hour last night before losing the last of the journalists following her. She'd checked in under an assumed name. She'd paid in cash.

Another knock, this one more forceful. "Room service."

Beth edged closer to the door, again tightening the sash of the bulky white robe provided by the hotel. All her clothes remained at the house that had never quite been a home, but was now a crime scene.

Through the peephole, she saw nothing, not even light, and her heart started to pound even harder.

"I didn't order room service," she said, keeping her eye to the opening.

"Damn it, Bethany, let me in."

Her hands fell away from the door, as though the man outside had infused the cool wood with the power to burn her palms.

Dylan.

Her heart slowed and thrummed, then started to hammer. Swearing softly, she looked more closely. Clearly he hadn't slept much, but not even fatigue interfered with Dylan St. Croix. It enhanced. He stood there in an olive button-down and black jeans, a knapsack over his shoulder, a silver tray on one of his hands. His dark hair was mussed, his deep-set eyes deceptively benign. Whiskers shadowed his jaw.

Deep inside, the icy wall started to fissure, and her pulse kicked up. Resentment came next, alarm, because therein lay the danger.

Despite everything she knew about the man—his penchant for muddying the waters and wreaking havoc—he possessed the disturbing ability to make the rest of the world fade away. When he walked into a room, everything else slipped to the background. Bethany could see only him. Feel only him.

She didn't want that kind of intensity now, couldn't trust something that spun out of control so easily. She didn't want that kind of mindless, blinding blur ever, ever again. With absolute certainty, she knew if she let the man standing in the hall anywhere near the fractured glass door of her emotions, the shards would more than slice to the bone.

They would cut clear through to the core of who she was.

Months had passed, but somewhere deep inside, the little girl still lived, the one who'd stood barefoot in the cold hallway, clutching a well-worn, much-loved stuffed rabbit while her mother laughed at her father, telling him this time she'd found a real man. An exciting man. A man who could satisfy her. Her father had fired back that some day she'd learn the difference between passion and love, he only hoped it wasn't too late for them all.

Too late had come a long time ago.

"Now isn't the time for games, Bethany. You took a nasty blow to your head yesterday. Don't make me—"

She didn't need to hear the rest of his threat. She knew. Dylan St. Croix wouldn't hesitate to use force to have his way, including persuading the manager to use his passkey.

"I'm not hungry," she announced, pulling open the door.

His smile said he didn't care. "Sure you are." Without waiting for a response, he invaded the room just like he invaded her dreams, striding in and setting the tray on a small table.

Beth closed the door, but didn't move, just watched him. Tried to breathe. He moved with incredible grace for such a large, destructive man, pouring coffee into a small demitasse cup that made his hands look even bigger, adding just the right amount of milk and sugar.

She didn't want to think about the fact he remembered.

He wanted something. That's what she had to remember. Dylan St. Croix wouldn't show up at her hotel room with a tray of breakfast unless he had an angle to play.

"How did you find me?" she asked.

He took a bite from a flaky croissant and chewed thoroughly before answering. "I'm a private investigator. I find what people hide." His gaze met hers. "Even themselves."

The words were soft, matter-of-fact, but they left her feeling as exposed as though the robe had fallen from her shoulders. "I wasn't hiding."

An odd light glinted in his eyes, undeniably hot, but unbearably cold. "It wouldn't matter if you were."

Chapter 4

Because he would find her. He didn't say the words, but Beth heard the warning loud and clear. Dylan St. Croix had earned a reputation for unearthing deeply buried secrets. Because of him, companies had been made to pay, people cry.

"Nothing has changed since last night, Dylan. I walked away for a reason."

"Nothing has changed for far longer than just last night," he said in a deceptively quiet voice. "But that doesn't mean I'm going to stand by and watch you suffer."

The fierce words curled through her like a warm mist, giving birth to a temptation she knew better than indulging. Yes, fire burned. But first, it warmed.

And she so very desperately wanted to be warm.

"Why not?" she asked. "You're a St. Croix. The family prince is dead and the cops can't wait to sink their teeth into me. You're the last person I should turn to."

"But I'm also the only one here." The words were soft, devastating. He gestured toward the plate of scrambled eggs and thick strips of bacon. "Quit looking for hidden agendas and nasty motives. Just eat. Please."

Her stomach rolled. "Eating's not a good idea right now," she said, drawing a hand to her mouth. Just the sight of all that rich food, the warring scents, almost did her in.

Dylan looked at her like she'd suddenly turned ten shades of green. "Are you okay?" In three long strides he was by her side. "Is it your head? Do you need a doctor?"

She drew a hand to her stomach, but the fight drained out of her. She was tired of pretending, of fighting. Because no, she wasn't okay. Every time she closed her eyes, she saw Lance on the living room floor. And every time she opened them, she saw her bloodstained fingers curled around the fire poker.

"I've always been able to pull myself out of a nightmare before the knife touched my throat or the water got too deep, but this time…" She hesitated. "I can't make this one end."

Dylan lifted a hand to her face and smoothed the hair behind her ear. "Because you never even went to sleep, did you?"

His touch, the gentle question, sent the room spinning. She reached toward the wall, hoping Dylan wouldn't notice. The vertigo was getting worse. She'd been battling it all morning, a strange, disconnected feeling, like she'd been yanked from her life and could only watch it happen.

"It shows?" she asked, and immediately regretted.

His gaze dipped from her face down her chest, where her robe gaped. He lingered a moment, then continued his perusal to the sash at her waist, on down to where terry cloth gave way to calves and bare feet.

Unwanted sensation whispered through her, as though Dylan skimmed a feather along her flesh, and not just his gaze. For a moment there, a dangerous, insane moment, she forgot what she had seen in the mirror a little over an hour before—the dull tangled hair, the pale skin and dark rings under her eyes, the chapped lips. *The faded, jagged line along her hairline.* For a moment, the look on Dylan's face made her feel beautiful. Desirable.

It had been a long time.

"Most people wouldn't notice," he said.

An emotion she didn't understand jammed into her throat. "What?"

"You asked if your sleeplessness showed—I said most people wouldn't notice."

But he did.

"You look beautiful even when you're ready to drop," he added, tracing a finger down her face, dangerously close to the scar that served as a reminder of that long-ago night.

This time Bethany did back away. Turned away, too. She didn't need to hear words like that. Didn't want to. Not from him. Not now. With anger and sarcasm the man was dangerous.

With tenderness, he destroyed.

"A good investigator draws conclusions from multiple sources," he continued, and she could tell he was moving from her. "And even if I couldn't see through you, I'd still know."

She turned to find him by the king-size bed.

"It hasn't been slept in," he said, running a hand over the pillow. "You haven't even laid down."

Hadn't sat either. She'd stood at the window for a long, long time, before taking a shower until the water ran cold. Then she'd returned to the window.

"Sleeping didn't seem appropriate."

"Maybe not appropriate, but necessary." Dylan eased back the thick down comforter. "If you're not going to eat, you at least need to sleep. You need your strength."

Who was this man? she wondered in some faraway corner of her mind. No way was she walking across the room and joining him anywhere near that big bed. Just seeing him running his hand along the crisp white sheets was bad enough. "I don't need you to tuck me in, Dylan."

"Who said anything about tucking you in?"

Beth closed her eyes and counted to ten. She'd been right before. The past twenty-four hours had left her defenses in tatters. And being in the same room as Dylan St. Croix without defenses was like going to the equator without sunblock.

"You should go," she told him, reaching for the numbness that always dissolved around him. "I'm a big girl, I can take care of myself." Had to, even if the way the room swayed made her wonder if stepping into Dylan's arms would make it stop. "I have a lot of calls to make."

He frowned. "I've already taken care of it."

"Taken care of what?" she asked more sharply than she intended.

"The funeral."

The two words brought every horrific second of the past sixteen hours barreling back. The darkened house and the blow to her head, waking up on the floor, the blood on her hands. The accusations. The brutal finality of it all. A funeral. Of course there had to be a funeral. But...

"You shouldn't have done that, Dylan. Lance was *my...*" *Husband.* The word lodged in her throat. No, he wasn't her husband. Somehow, after six years, it was still hard to remember. Old habits, she figured.

Before she could blink, Dylan was across the room and taking her shoulders in his hands. "He wasn't your husband anymore, Bethany."

She lifted her chin. "Don't call me Bethany."

"Would you rather I call you *sweetheart?*" he asked softly.

Memories tumbled forward, dusty and threadbare, completely unwanted. "I go by Beth."

"You pretend to be Beth," he countered. "You want to be Beth. Beth is nice and safe. Beth fits in. But deep inside, the passionate woman named Bethany still lives." He slid a hand to the back of her head, gently skimming the gash.

"You and I both know that, just like we know your marriage had been over a lot longer than you're admitting."

A fact the cops wanted to use against her. "You don't know what you're talking about."

"Don't I?" he asked in a dangerously quiet voice. "When was the last time you and Lance made love? Do you even remember?"

She stiffened. "You have no right—"

"Since when has that stopped me?"

Words of denial formed, but emotion clogged her throat. Dylan was right. She'd called Lance husband for six years, but they'd quit living as man and wife long before he'd walked out. She didn't know the last time they'd shared breakfast, a joke, a bed.

"What happened, Bethany? Tell me."

The sharp stab of longing was ridiculous, that she could accept his concern at face value. But she also knew silence opened the door for him to form his own conclusions, conclusions more dangerous than the truth.

"Nothing happened," she said woodenly. "That's just it. Lance and I worked long hours, and after a while, being alone seemed normal. It wasn't until he moved out that I realized what a farce our marriage had become."

"Is that why you never became parents?"

She pulled from him and put distance between them, drew a few deep breaths, tried to ignore the subtle aroma of clove and sandalwood that was all Dylan.

"I wanted children," she said, and felt the ache in her heart. "Right up to the end. Call me a fool, but I always thought children would fill the gap somehow. Give us something to love."

Dylan frowned, but his eyes gentled. "Because you didn't love Lance."

The truth lay at her feet, but acknowledging it seemed wrong. Because she *had* loved Lance. Once. A long time ago. But it had been a different kind of love, one a man like Dylan would never understand.

"You don't trust me, do you?" he asked.

She looked at him standing there and cursed the way her pulse thrummed low and deep. Too well, she remembered the last time she opened herself to this man, the fallout. It wasn't his fault, she knew. He was who he was. But he wasn't the kind of man she could let into her life. A few kind gestures could no more erase the hard words from last night, than they could overshadow the fundamental differences that stood between them. She wanted simple. He thrived on chaos.

And no matter how exciting that kind of mind-numbing passion could be, Beth had learned it was dangerous. Passion led to pain. It wasn't sustaining. It always, always burned out.

"Last night you asked if I killed your cousin," she reminded. "How *can* I trust you?"

"Damn it, Bethany." His gaze seared into hers for a punishing heartbeat. Earlier, the low light in his eyes had made her feel beautiful. This time, his scrutiny ran over her like a black crayon obscuring something that didn't quite measure up.

"You see only what you want to see, don't you? Just like before."

An immediate defense vaulted through her, but she bit the words back. She didn't need to defend herself to Dylan St. Croix. Instead, she stood silently and watched him stoop down and violently snag the knapsack he'd carried into the room.

"I don't know why I even bothered," he muttered, handing her the large satchel as he strode to the door.

The sudden jolt of panic made no sense. If she didn't know better, she would have sworn she'd hurt him.

Quickly, she looked at the bag—it didn't weigh much, and when she squeezed, she found the contents soft. "What's this?"

He jerked open the door before turning back to her.

Those dark green eyes of his blazed with an emotion she couldn't even begin to name. "Open it."

Curiosity nudged against caution. She couldn't imagine what he would give her, knew that sooner or later a Dylan-bomb had to detonate. One always did.

"It's not a bomb, Bethany."

She winced, wondering for a second there if she'd spoken aloud. But of course she hadn't. That was just Dylan.

Beth didn't consider herself a brave woman—she rolled her eyes at movies where a scantily clad, defenseless woman investigated a noise late at night. But she wasn't a coward, either. Instinct may have warned not to open the bag, but determination demanded she not give Dylan any indication that he could rattle her. Whatever he had squished up inside, she could handle.

Or so she thought.

She unfastened the two buckles and pulled back the flap, just stared. "Clothes?" she asked, looking up at him. "You brought me clothes?"

He leaned against the door frame, crossing his legs at the ankles and folding his arms across his chest. A slow heat lit his gaze as it dipped down over her body. "Bastard that I am, I didn't think you'd want to wear a robe to the funeral."

Everything inside her went very still. She felt as though she'd just been given a pop quiz, and not only did she not understand the subject, she couldn't even make out the language.

"What's the matter?" His voice was lower now, thicker. "Scared to look?"

Terrified. What a man bought for a woman said a lot about how he thought about her. How he felt.

"Do you really think I'm capable of murder?"

"You're capable of anything you put your mind to."

She didn't want to look inside that bag. She didn't want to know what Dylan really thought about her. Too easily she could see him in some trendy store, running his hands over short skirts and sheer blouses, leopard prints and crotchless underwear.

But she wasn't a coward. Fire with fire, she reminded herself, then scooped a hand down into the knapsack.

For the second time in twelve hours, Dylan saw Bethany's eyes go wide and dark, her mouth tumble open. He heard the sharp intake of breath. Her hand came out of the bag slowly, carrying with it the items he'd picked up on his way over.

He wanted to feel anger. He wanted to resent her for the heartlessness she so clearly expected of him. He'd seen the wariness in her every move, her every look, knew she expected him to supply her with the kind of sleazy clothes a woman like Bethany would never wear.

She didn't need clothes to send a man to his knees.

Hell, even exhausted and frightened, she took his breath away. The sight of her when she'd opened the door in that bulky white robe had almost wiped out everything he'd told himself on the way over. To just play it cool. To stick to the facts, the matter at hand. See if he could detect any hint of a vital secret she might be keeping. Tell her he'd already planned the funeral, then leave. Breakfast was a mere necessity—he couldn't have her passing out while they stood graveside. And the clothes, well, she had to wear something.

But then he'd seen her standing there, bare-legged and barefoot, looking lost and alone despite the fact she stood in an opulent hotel room, and self-defense had gone to hell in a handbasket. Those eyes of hers, he knew. Those damn swirling blue eyes, fringed by lashes long and dark without even the aid of mascara. They'd looked especially provocative against skin a few shades too pale. And her lips, that lush mouth of hers that looked startlingly like a dewy rose petal, had been dry, cracked.

Like an idiot, he'd wanted to moisten it himself.

Thank God he was a strong man. Thank God he knew

that even if he couldn't count on himself to keep his hands off, with a few well-aimed words, he could count on Bethany. With most women, a smile or wink, a suggestive word here and there, and they came running. Not Bethany. She recoiled from heat and honesty. She preferred impersonal. Telling her she looked beautiful was tantamount to telling her he never wanted to see her again. So he had. Because like an idiot, he did. But knew he shouldn't.

She may well have killed his cousin.

Everything inside him rebelled violently at the thought.

"They're…" She looked from the garments in her hands and met his gaze. Her dilated pupils overrode the blue of her eyes, making them look dark, almost dazed.

"Perfect," he finished for her. Classy. Elegant. Just like her. He'd picked the clothes out with great care, linen slacks and cotton blouses, silk pajamas, the muted tones she preferred. A black suit.

She fingered the fabrics gently. All but the underwear. She didn't touch the slip or bra, the panties.

"You knew my size," she whispered.

"A good guess." Like hell. He knew everything about her, every exquisite, damning detail. He knew how her mouth felt, tasted. He knew how her eyes glazed over when he touched her breasts. He knew the soft little whimpers that rasped from her throat when he drove deep.

He knew what it felt like to wake up alone.

But last night he hadn't slept. Every time he closed his eyes, he saw the white sheet draped over Lance's body. And then he saw Bethany. But rather than holding the fire poker, she held a child.

The disturbing image had kept him standing at the window until the first red rays of the sun streaked over the mountains.

Now she just kept looking at him, like the secrets to the universe might suddenly appear on a face he worked hard to keep impassive. He stayed where he was, kept his arms crossed over his chest, knowing if he moved so much as a muscle, he'd end up across the room and smoothing the hair from her face, pulling her into his arms. It was distracting enough seeing her in that bulky robe that kept falling open, revealing far too much creamy flesh.

Under no circumstances did he trust himself to touch.

She drew a soft blue blouse to her chest, blessedly obscuring his view of the swell of her breasts. "Why are you doing this, Dylan? Why are you helping me?"

Because he knew Lance's secret, and she did not, damn it. Because he had to learn how far-reaching the consequences would be. He had to know just how radically he'd altered the course of his life. If fate had a good laugh and she went to prison—

He broke off the thought, not willing to travel down a treacherous road that would forever change everything.

"The St. Croixs stick together," he told her, "if not in life, then in death."

The light in her eyes dimmed. "I don't understand you," she whispered.

"No, Bethany," he said, pushing free of the doorjamb and walking into the hall. "You never did." That said, he turned and walked away.

Fire and ice just didn't mix.

"To everything there is a season, and a time to every purpose under the heaven: a time to be born and a time to die."

A time to die. Beth lowered her eyes and studied the freshly mowed grass of the cemetery. The crisp scent reminded her of times long ago, of laughter and skinned knees, simplicity and innocence.

"...a time to mourn and a time to dance...a time to love and a time to hate..."

The four days since Lance's death were little more than a blur. She stared numbly at the polished white coffin, the green skirt hiding the gaping hole in the ground. By her side stood Dylan, so close she could feel the sleeve of his black suit brushing against her arm. Propriety dictated that she put some space between them, but she couldn't bring herself to step from the warm hand at the small of her back. The feel of his palm helped keep her steady. Standing. She found gratitude in his silent gesture, uneasiness in her response.

"Lance St. Croix, grandson of the esteemed Judge Sebastian St. Croix, was a man to look up to and respect...."

The vertigo pushed closer, grew stronger. The midmorning sun was unusually hot, blazing from its perch in a cloudless blue sky. Spring. The season of rebirth. Burying a man seemed wrong.

Beth swallowed hard and concentrated on a Norfolk pine stretching against the horizon like an ill-placed Christmas tree. Still, she felt the expectant gazes on her, hostile and accusing.

You haven't cried.

That would help, she knew. Openly grieving. Like her mother. Sierra Rae Kincaid Barton Winston Landaiche had returned from her Russian honeymoon the night before, and now made quite the picture of a grieving mother-in-law, black veil and all. Beth couldn't help but wonder for what her mother mourned—the former son-in-law she'd spent little time with, or the severance of her link to one of Oregon's most prominent families.

Next to Dylan, Judge St. Croix sat stoically in his wheelchair, presiding over the graveside service like a patriarch who'd endured one too many tragedy. He'd been bluster and invincibility on the evening news, but here, now, signs of age and grief made his face appear even more weathered than usual. The judge had attended too many funerals, Beth knew. Two wives and two sons, and now his cherished grandson.

There'd been no funeral for the great-grandchild.

Her throat convulsed and her chest tightened, but again, no tears slipped free. She wished they would. A few impulsive decisions, a few desperate measures, and so many lives suffered the consequences. The innocent always paid the highest.

Beth was far from innocent.

Dylan's fingers stiffened against her back, and ever so slightly, he urged her closer to him. He stood there so tall and somber, solid. She could feel strength emitting from him, just as she could detect the scent of sandalwood mingling with that of pine. The urge to lean closer, to sink against his side and feel his arm curl around her, hold her, made her stand straighter.

On the other side of the casket, Detective Zito stood next to Yvonne Kelly, while Janine, the grim-faced D.A., and other members of his staff stood clustered together. The irony didn't escape Beth, the divide between her and the prosecutor's office. If charges were filed, she'd face Lance's colleagues across another divide, that of a courtroom.

"Lance St. Croix will be deeply missed," the minister concluded, giving way to the sound of "Taps" filling the cemetery. The effect was peaceful in a haunting way, the high-pitched wail drifting among the pines, the wind rustling a patch of wildflowers.

Beth drew a distracting sandalwood-laden breath and watched Janine crying. She envied her friend that ability, that free display of emotion. She wanted to cry. To yell. To throw something. But she'd sewn everything up so tight she wondered if even a knife could cut through the stitches.

Beneath the glare of the sun, the truth grew hotter, more punishing. And the cemetery started to spin.

Dylan felt Bethany sway and pulled her closer to his side. She looked disturbingly pale, her eyes too dark against skin that looked like porcelain. The wind whipped long sable hair around her face, obscuring and hiding, making him itch to loosen the strands clinging to her dry lips. Normally, black became her, but the suit he'd picked out looked too stark, too big. The tailored jacket practically hung off her shoulders. He would have sworn she'd lost five pounds in four days.

Alarm shot through him. Clearly she wasn't eating, and the shadows beneath her eyes told him she hadn't slept much, either. Why? What did she see in the darkness that disturbed her so? What did she remember? What did she fear?

Stop it, he admonished himself. Stop it. He didn't want to think about the toll the past several days had taken on her. He couldn't think of her as one of the underdogs he made a career of championing. Bethany Rae Kincaid was nobody's underdog. She made her own choices, her own beds.

But still, the urge to pull her to his side, to slip his arm around the curve of her waist, almost undid him.

The spectacle raced on around them, the pomp and posturing and celebrity his family thrived upon. His grandfather had public grieving down to an art form.

Against the palm of his hand, he felt Bethany's breathing change, grow more shallow. He looked down to see her gaze fixated on a lone pine beyond the crowd of mourners. Her pupils were huge, dilated.

"Bethany?" he asked, leaning closer. "You okay?"

She glanced up, her eyes blinking too rapidly. "D-Dylan?"

Her voice was strained, raspy, as though she'd been running, not standing completely still. Maybe that was it. She'd been standing too straight, the sun glaring too hot.

"Don't lock your knees," he whispered.

Beth gazed up at Dylan. He stood out from the crowd of mourners, a tall man in a black suit, eyes as dark and fierce as a primeval forest. She remembered thinking that before, couldn't quite recall when. Those eyes were narrow now, focused on her. And his mouth, she saw those distractingly full lips moving, heard the low rumble of his voice, but the never-ending trumpet drowned out the words. Spots clouded her vision. She blinked, but the dis-

tortion grew. She tried to draw in that dangerously soothing aroma of sandalwood, but found herself gasping instead.

Lance.

The darkness.

The blood.

The screams.

Dylan.

Her knees buckled.

It was a hell of a time for the past four days to catch
up with her.

From that hazy, faraway place she'd inhabited since
Lance's death, she saw Dylan reaching for her, but then
the world again went black, and she saw nothing at all.

Chapter 5

Dylan saw everything. He saw her eyes go blank and her pale mouth go slack. He saw her lift a hand, saw it fall back to her side. He saw her body go limp. "Bethany!"

She slumped against him and would have melted to the ground had his hand not been at her back. He slid his arm around her waist like he'd wanted to all along, and held her to his side.

She didn't protest, didn't move.

The trumpet stopped. A collective gasp rose from the mourners as they turned to stare at the inert woman in his arms.

Only then did he realize he'd roared her name, rather than the whisper he'd thought.

"What happened?" her mother asked, rushing over. "Is she okay?"

He eased Bethany to the crisp grass and kneeled beside her, resting her head in his lap. She didn't move. She just lay there, still save for her chest rising and falling with each shallow breath. Strands of sable hair fanned over her face, prompting him to lift a hand to smooth them back. He didn't have time to steel himself. He didn't have time to fight off the memories that immediately clobbered him. And he hurt.

His heart started to pound, so hard, the echoes reverberated through the heavy silence. Nine years dissolved into nothing. Bethany may have cut his heart out, but she hadn't escaped without scars. And where there were scars, there was pain.

The pale, jagged line running down the right side of her face bore silent testimony to that.

Something inside him started to break. Damn it, he hadn't known.

"She's exhausted," he told her mother, skimming a finger along Bethany's cheekbone. Her eyes were closed, her features relaxed, her skin pale aside from the shadows. She felt sinuous in his arms, liquid, not tense and on guard like she'd been for the past several days. Years. Nine.

"She's too warm," he gritted out, going to work on the buttons of the black blazer. Guilt stabbed deep. He'd bought the long-sleeved, long-skirted outfit for her, selecting a tailored style like she preferred.

He hadn't thought about the sun and the humidity, the heat.

"Bethany Rae?" Sierra went down on her knees and took her daughter's hand. "Can you hear me, sweet thing?"

She didn't move, didn't stir.

"Give her a minute." Dylan eased back her jacket, exposing the soft swell of her chest. She wore no jewelry around her neck, just a few fading bruises that made his blood run cold. He didn't open the jacket further, was in no frame of mind to see the black lace bra he'd purchased for her. "Let her cool off."

"What the hell is wrong with her?" barked his grandfather, who'd rolled his wheelchair closer. "Hasn't she made enough trouble as it is? Doesn't she know this is a funeral?''

Dylan cut him a sharp look. ''I'm quite sure she didn't mean to offend you, Grandfather.''

The older man snorted. ''She should have thought of that before she killed my grandson.''

Dylan just stared. He wanted to push to his feet and steer his grandfather beneath a cluster of pines, make it clear this was neither the time nor the place. And he would have, too. He didn't give a damn about Yvonne Kelly and her cohorts gathered like vultures just beyond the trees, the swarm of friends and family and political allies. It would serve them right, give them something to talk about for months to come. Years.

The thought almost made him grin. Almost.

But Bethany lay unmoving in his arms, his cousin lay dead in that shiny coffin, and everything he'd ever believed was tearing at the seams. ''The facts aren't all in yet, Grandfather.''

''Are you defending her?''

''I'm stating the law.''

His grandfather eyed him a long moment, the St. Croix eyes he'd shared with the grandson he'd never understood on fire. ''She's not one of your lost causes,'' he warned, then turned and wheeled toward the minister.

Dylan returned his attention to the woman sprawled in his lap. The sun glared hotter, the cooling breeze suddenly gone. He'd feared it was only a matter of time before the past few days toppled her. He just hadn't expected the crush to be literal, and he hadn't expected the fall to be at the funeral.

But he was glad he'd been there to catch her.

''Bethany, sweetheart, can you hear me?''

Her eyelids fluttered, and she shifted, her shoulders moving against his thighs, her face coming to rest against his waist. A soft little wisp of a sound eased past her dry lips.

"Should I call an ambulance?" Janine White asked.

"Not yet," Dylan said, not even sparing a glance for the woman Lance had tried to set him up with. Dylan had taken her out a time or two, but fresh from a nasty divorce, she'd carried more baggage than he cared to explore. He'd steered clear of her bed, an insult she'd never forgotten. "Just clear everyone back and give us some breathing room."

Bethany shifted again, forcing Dylan to bite back a groan. And a curse. What kind of man was aware of a woman sliding against his groin when she was completely out of it?

"Bethany?" he asked, and slowly those long lashes lifted, revealing the cloudy blue of her eyes.

"D-Dylan?"

Something inside him loosened. "I've got you."

"W-what happened?"

"You fainted."

Abruptly, the color returned to her cheeks, the wariness to her gaze. She struggled to sit.

Dylan helped her out of his lap. "Take it easy, sweetheart. Just breathe nice and deep for me."

She glanced to her left, where the casket remained perched over a gaping hole, where Janine had herded many of the mourners. Zito and Yvonne Kelly watched with near rabid interest, while others milled about.

"Oh, God," Bethany whispered, and he saw the second awareness hit. She was one of those rare women who hated drawing attention to herself, unlike her mother, who did everything humanly imaginable to gobble up the spotlight, no matter who she humiliated or hurt in the process.

Once, Bethany had told him she dreaded her own wedding, because everyone would stare at her. To this day, Dylan had never been able to forget the sight of her walking down the aisle, toward Lance. Everything inside him had systematically shut down, leaving only a concern as raw and elemental as the concern he felt right now. She'd been so pale. Mechanical, almost. Much like the evening in the mountains, when she'd realized they were stranded. Together.

"It's okay," he told her, brushing the back of his hand against the side of her face. "You've been through a tough couple of days. Everyone understands."

She gazed up at him. "I don't."

The moment of pure honesty stabbed deep. "How do you feel? Dizzy?"

She drew a hand to her stomach. "A little."

Dylan stared at her pale, fine-boned fingers pressed against the stark black suit, and a bad feeling twisted through him. "I'm taking you to the hospital."

"Hospital?" She frowned. "There's no need for that."

"Humor me." He stood and reached for her. "Can you stand, or do you need me to carry you?"

The wind whipped at her long brown hair, sending it into a frenzy around the soft lines of her face. Her fingers tightened against his palm. And just like he'd known she would, she stood.

"I can walk on my own," she said, but swayed.

"Of course you can," he murmured, but kept his hand at the small of her back as he led her to his Bronco.

She didn't swat it away.

Beth sat on the small hospital bed, arms in her lap, bare feet dangling. She no longer wore the gorgeous black suit Dylan had picked out for her, but rather, a formless hospital gown. The light blue cotton hung from her shoulders, extending down above her knees. Thank God panty hose no longer encased her legs. That's why she'd fainted, she told herself. Because of the sheer silk constricting the lower half of her body, while the sun beat down on her. She hadn't been able to breathe.

That was all. That was why.

But classic no-holds-barred Dylan, he refused to accept the easy answer. He'd barely said a word on the way to the hospital, just looked straight ahead, his fingers curled too tight around the steering wheel. He hadn't turned on the jazz he preferred, hadn't drank from the bottle of water in his cup holder.

And now, standing across the small cubicle in his black suit, he looked to be bracing himself.

In almost any other circumstance, with any other man, Beth would have laughed. Dylan St. Croix didn't flinch when he investigated the dirty dealings of a prominent congressman or brought down a well-respected import/export company. Threats of bodily harm didn't faze the man. But escorting a woman who'd fainted to a hospital totally undid him.

"I really am fine," she told him. "There's no reason to hang around." In fact, she'd prefer him to leave. Then she might be able to breathe. As it was, his tall form made the cubicle feel like a shoebox.

"When the doctor says you're fine, I'll leave. Until then, we wait."

She glanced at the small table beside the bed, where medical instruments sat helter-skelter. The nurse had checked her pulse and her heart rate, taken her temperature, felt her glands, even drawn blood and collected urine. Through it all, Beth had insisted she was fine. Just tired. Under a lot of stress. That's why she hadn't been eating right, why the thought of food turned her stomach.

But, of course, no one listened to her.

"Why?" she asked.

Dylan's gaze met hers. "Why what?"

"Why won't you leave?" And God help her, why did the sight of him leaning against the wall make time fall away?

He glanced out beyond the cubicle. "Would you rather I send in Detective Zito or your mother?"

She sat up a little straighter. "No." At least Dylan for the most part was leaving her alone, not grilling her with questions or smothering her with melodrama.

"How bad was it?" she asked. "When I fainted? Mom didn't make a scene, did she?"

A strange light glinted in Dylan's eyes. It almost looked like amusement. "Not too bad."

Beth drew a deep breath, let it out slowly. "I wish I could believe that." But couldn't. She knew her mother too well. Sierra Winston—no, make that Landaiche—lived for the spotlight. She thrived on it. Craved it. A small town southern girl, she'd gone west to make a name for herself in Hollywood, but through marriage had ended up in Portland instead. Her acting talents being what they were, or rather, weren't, she'd stayed in Oregon, and made a name for herself in other ways, trading one man for another, each more exciting than the last. Often younger, too.

"You didn't answer my question," she reminded Dylan. There was something dark and disturbing in his gaze, a jagged emotion she neither recognized nor understood. "Why are you here?"

"I bought the suit."

She glanced at the folded skirt and jacket sitting on a chair, the bra and panties beneath, the hose in the garbage can. Putting the garments on that morning had felt uncomfortably intimate, as though in letting the fabric Dylan had picked out slide against her body, the man himself was touching her.

"You think that's why I fainted?"

"I don't know why you fainted. That's why we're here."

Frustration pushed closer. Harder. She no more understood Dylan St. Croix now than she had nine years before. Whereas Lance had been predictable, trying to predict Dylan, or understand his motivation, was like chasing earthquakes.

With the exception of that one ill-fated night, for nine years he'd acted like she no longer existed in his world, and she'd done the same. But now he would barely let her out of his sight. She understood his presence at the house the night of Lance's death—blood bound the two men, and even though Lance had complained about Dylan's muckraking, an odd kinship linked the cousins. That's why Dylan had stood up for Lance at the wedding.

The memory scraped. Lance with his sandy hair neatly combed, his blue eyes glowing, his hands behind his back. Smiling. Dylan with his dark hair cut brutally short, his green eyes burning, his hands balled into tight fists, his body rigid. He'd looked more like a man facing a firing squad than a man waiting for his cousin's bride.

Now Lance was dead. Murdered, she amended, lowering her head to her hands. No matter how hard she tried, she couldn't scrape away the cold horror of it all. Couldn't chase away the ice in her blood. It was like someone had taken a knife and carved every second of that afternoon into the core of who she was.

"Bethany?"

Dylan's voice was sharp, concerned, prompting her to look up abruptly. "It's never going to go away, is it?"

He didn't pretend to misunderstand. "You've been through a terrible ordeal. Give it time. Eventually everything fades."

But that wasn't true and Beth knew it. Everything didn't fade. Some things just changed forms, twisted and contorted, slipping into different corners of your soul. But they were always, always there.

Just like Dylan since this whole ordeal had begun. Why? she wondered. Because of his penchant for diving into mysteries and shredding secrets? Because of family loyalty? Because he wanted to be there when she fell?

He hadn't let her fall at the police station, a small part of her pointed out. He'd stepped in like some menacing force when Yvonne Kelly had gone for the jugular. Of course, he'd plied her with questions of his own after that. Maybe that had been his goal all along, catch her off guard and see what secrets he could unearth. No one believed she didn't harbor any.

In truth, she harbored only one.

The fire poker. It had been in *her* hands.

"Mrs. St. Croix?" Dr. Audrey Lyons, the attending physician who'd spoken with her earlier, entered the cubicle with a file in her hand, several pages on top. "We have the results back."

Beth started to smile, but then caught the odd expression on the older woman's face. "I'm fine, right?"

Dr. Lyons glanced at Dylan. "Is he your husband?"

"No," they answered in unison.

"Then perhaps he should leave for a few minutes."

Beth went very still. She recognized the look on the doctor's face, the caution in her voice. She'd heard it before, that cold night so long ago, when she'd lost Dylan's baby. Now, panic backed up into her throat, making it impossible to breathe.

Something was wrong.

"Don't ask me to walk away now," Dylan said, striding toward the hospital bed. "I have a right to know what's wrong."

Beth looked at him standing beside her, noticed the tension in his body. His eyes were somber, his mouth a grim line. He looked somewhere between fierce and alarmed.

But he also looked solid, steady, and with him standing there, she didn't feel quite so alone.

"He can stay." The words came out strong, but deep inside, she started to shake. Looking back, she'd been feeling off-kilter for a few weeks, but had attributed it to the stress of the divorce. "What's wrong with me?"

Dr. Lyons glanced at the folder in her hand, and her brow furrowed. "When was your last period?"

Beth's heart started to pound. Hard. "Just a couple of—" she started, but stopped abruptly. She thought back on the whirlwind of the last several weeks and months, and realized that for the first time in three years, she didn't know the date of her last period.

"I've spotted off and on," she said, "but I've been

under a lot of stress and haven't had a full period for a while. That's happened before."

By her side, Dylan tensed.

"It's not stress," Dr. Lyons said.

The blade of fear was ridiculous. "Endometriosis?" she asked. She'd battled the nasty condition before.

The older woman smiled, and finally the bomb Beth had been waiting for ever since Dylan blazed back into her life exploded. Except he didn't detonate it.

Dr. Audrey Lyons did. "You're pregnant."

Chapter 6

Once, a long time ago, while hiking along the Rogue River, Beth stepped too close to the edge. The ground crumbled from beneath her, sending her scraping down the rocky embankment and splashing into the racing current. Icy water cut into her like knives and sucked the breath from her lungs. She thrashed for something to hold on to, a boulder, a stick, anything, but the current ran too swift. Unusually hot weather was melting the snowcaps off the mountains at a faster than normal pace. The runoff literally raced down the mountainside.

And Beth didn't know how to swim.

Panic welled within her. She remembered opening her mouth to call out, but numbness took over with brutal quickness, and the words froze in her throat. The water turned rougher. White water, they called it. Perfect for rafting.

Deadly for anything else.

Her body started shutting down with terrifying speed,

and darkness pushed closer. Her arms and legs grew leaden. The effort to breathe choked her.

Much as she felt now. Shock crashed in from all directions, paralyzing as it went. Irony tortured. She could barely move a muscle, not even her heart.

You're pregnant.

The words reverberated through her with the punishing force of the raging mountain river. She'd heard them before. Once. A long time ago. For years she'd dreamed of hearing them again, rejoicing in them. To hear the words now, and know they weren't true, amounted to cruelty.

She started to shake, from the inside out. "That's not funny," she whispered.

Dr. Lyons frowned. "Pardon?"

"I can't have children," Beth said, grasping on to a rock and bracing herself against the current. "I'm...infertile."

"Not according to these tests," the physician said, looking at the file in her hands. "You're most definitely pregnant."

The current knocked her free and slammed her further downstream. Debris cut into her. Coldness permeated her heart.

But then she saw him. Dylan. Running along the riverbank, shouting out her name. The roar of the water stole his words, but in the ferocity of his eyes, she found strength, and calm.

He towered over her now, tall and strong and uncompromising. But he didn't touch. "How far along is she?"

The doctor cut him a curious look, then glanced at Beth, clearly seeking permission to discuss her condition with a man other than her husband.

"I can't be pregnant," she whispered. "I would have felt something." But then it hit her, the dizziness she'd attributed to fatigue, the nausea she'd attributed to shock. The light, irregular period she'd blamed on stress.

"Why did she faint?" Dylan asked, diving into the boiling stream and swimming toward her. A hand, on her shoulder. Steady. Strong. "Is everything okay?"

Beth looked up abruptly, saw the doctor nod. "Everything's fine. It's not uncommon for pregnant women to black out, particularly if they've not been sleeping or eating properly."

"My God," Beth whispered, but then Dylan was there, wrapping an arm around her waist and swimming against the current, bringing her with him. She quit fighting and wrapped her arms around him, let him pull her from the water. They collapsed on the muddy bank, soaking wet and breathing heavy. But alive. The sun fought with the wind, one to warm, the other to chill.

Reality overrode both.

Dylan filled her line of vision now, dominating the cubicle and obscuring her view of the doctor. His eyes were dark and more than a little wild. His breathing was as hard as it had been that day by the rapids. And his expression...the intensity glittering in his eyes.

It was as though she'd betrayed him all over again.

She felt the stab of pain deep, the regret, but knew history could not be rewritten.

"Lance moved out months ago," he said. His normally commanding voice was so tight she barely recognized it. "Has there been someone else since then? Has someone else been in your bed?"

Beth struggled to breathe. Jagged emotion jostled around inside her. Once, she would have thrilled to the possessiveness underlying his questions. Once, she would have hurt at the pain. Now, she could only find confusion.

"Nobody," she whispered. "Nobody."

Dylan swore softly. He looked like he wanted to touch her, put his hands to her shoulders. But he didn't move. She wasn't sure he could.

"Lance? Did you let him into your bed after he walked out?"

"No." The mere thought sickened her.

"Then—"

"No!" she said, realizing he was trying to link her pregnancy with the night in the mountains. The thought rocked her even harder. "No. I can't conceive naturally. If I'm pregnant, it's from artificial insemination."

His expression hardened. "What are you talking about? You and Lance are divorced, for crissakes."

"Not Lance," she whispered, emotion ripping through her. "I...I saw no reason to quit trying just because I was suddenly single. I—I wanted a child."

"Whose?"

She put her hands to her stomach. "Donor." She hadn't really expected it to work, not after all the years trying, but her doctor had encouraged her. The memory of that day cut deep, how alone she'd felt. How bittersweet and nostalgic. That's why she'd driven to the mountain retreat.

And found Dylan.

He stepped from the bed, as though he'd been standing too close to the edge of some place deep and dark. The planes of his face tightened, paled. His body was tense, his hands balled into tight fists. He looked angry, shocked, like she'd just confessed to killing Lance in cold blood.

"Why?" he asked in an oddly hoarse voice.

"Why what?"

"Why didn't you tell me you might be pregnant?"

Her throat thickened. "Why would I?"

"Because it changes everything."

She couldn't dispute that. For days now she'd been suspended in an alternate world where time held no meaning and feeling brought only pain. But now a few rays of sun had broken through the clouds, and whispers of warmth overrode the chill.

"It changes *my* life," she said softly. "Not yours."

She might as well have slapped him. He recoiled visibly, his eyes going even harder.

"I had no idea," she added. Had long since given up

hope. "I took a test after the last procedure. It came back negative. And then I started to bleed."

"Many women spot during their first trimester," Dr. Lyons put in. "It's just the body's way of adjusting."

Dylan stood back from the bed, but he'd yet to look away from her. It felt odd having him there, listening to her and the doctor discuss intimacies such as bleeding, but the look on his face made it clear Special Forces would be required to make him leave.

After issuing a few more instructions, including the recommendation that Beth see her ob-gyn, the physician left.

There was just her and Dylan now, but the cubicle seemed smaller with the two of them than it had with three.

Silence pushed in from all directions. Her throat and chest were tight, breathing hurt. So did looking at Dylan. Looking at him crushed nine years into nine minutes, and too easily she saw him staggering out of the bathroom, pale and dark-eyed, holding the plastic wand of the home pregnancy test in his hand.

"Bethany?"

She looked from his trembling hand to the hard line of his mouth. "Oh, God. Dylan."

"When were you going to tell me?"

His expression mirrored that of so long ago, prompting her to draw her hands to her stomach. "Don't look at me like that," she whispered.

He didn't move, didn't change expressions. "How?"

"Like I've—" betrayed you "—done something wrong."

Swearing softly, he crossed the room and with a simple touch, shattered her. "You're crying."

She blinked rapidly, but the tears kept coming, spilling over her lashes from eyes long dry. She hadn't been able to cry for years now, not after all the failed attempts to become pregnant, not when she realized Lance was involved with another woman, not when he moved out, not when she realized she really didn't care. Not when she found him dead.

But God help her, the tears wouldn't stop now. And more than anything, she wanted Dylan to pull her into his arms and hold her. Just hold her.

"I'm pregnant," she whispered. "I'm going to have a baby." Her throat closed up on the words.

"Bethany. It could be mine."

"No," she said again, and this time the word came out sharper. Harder. Then came the blade of sorrow. "I can't conceive spontaneously. This child is someone else's."

Dylan's hand fell away. "I don't understand," he ground out. "Why would you do this alone?"

She drew a deep breath. His tone, the hardness of his eyes, told her exactly what he thought of her decision. "The divorce didn't change my desire for children," she told him. Actually, it had increased her sense of urgency, the awareness of the time sweeping by. "Lance and I tried for years, but never could. Intimacy," if it could be called that, "turned into clinical procedures." The mere thought of making love had turned painful, and gradually, Lance quit coming to her bed.

She'd never invited him back.

But she didn't tell Dylan that, didn't want him to figure out the shameful secret that drove home she really was her mother's daughter. That sometimes when she lay in the darkness, she'd closed her eyes only to find images of Dylan awaiting her.

"We tried artificial insemination twice," she revealed, sticking to facts and ignoring lingering feelings. "When my period came after the second, Lance fell apart. Said he couldn't make me happy, was tired of pretending he could. Said he couldn't live with a wife he couldn't make smile. Then he walked out the door."

Emotion clogged her throat. She'd always known irony had a cruel sense of humor, but this went beyond mere cruelty. In less than a week she'd gone from a childless divorcée to a pregnant woman facing charges of murder.

"If I'd conceived, he might not be dead."

Dylan's gaze sharpened, signifying the return of the investigator. "Why not? What are you saying?"

"I'm not confessing, if that's what you're asking." His willingness to believe the worst shouldn't have hurt. But did. "I didn't kill Lance in a fit of rage. I didn't kill him, period."

"Then what?"

"I don't know," she said honestly, trying to fit the pieces together. "I can't stop thinking that Lance moving out tipped something into motion, something dark, something that cost him his life.

"But I have no idea what went on in his life after he moved out." Longer than that, if she was honest. "I don't know why he was at the house that day." Didn't understand what she saw in Dylan's eyes—she refused to label it longing, but for the first time, she wondered what his life was like. *Really* like. Dylan the man, not the whirlwind. What went on when no one else was around? What did he think about? What did he want? How did he feel? Did the shadow of regret follow him like it did her?

No way, she answered silently. A man like Dylan St. Croix didn't have regrets. He had causes. He had crusades. And for him, that was all that mattered.

"I don't know why I'm pregnant now," she whispered, with the child of a man she would never know, when God had taken Dylan's. "After all these years. It doesn't seem real."

He lifted a hand as though to touch her, but didn't. "Life has a strange sense of humor."

And an even worse sense of timing. "Don't tell anyone."

"It's hardly a secret."

"About the baby. Don't tell anyone about the baby."

The small muscle in the hollow of his cheek began to thump. "This isn't a secret you can hide."

"But I can protect. I can protect my child." In the midst of a nightmare, she'd been granted a dream. No way would she let anything happen to this child.

His gaze dipped to her stomach, where her hand remained splayed. "Protect from what?"

"Everything." From the horror of the past few days, the frightening possibilities that loomed ahead of her. The truth about the fire poker. Standing trial. Prison. "I feel like there are dark storm clouds on the horizon. Gathering. Boiling. That if I'm not careful, the sky will crack open and all hell will break loose."

He cocked a brow. "You'd hit me, wouldn't you, if I said you sound like your mother?"

Beth just stared. Her breath caught. She didn't know how the man did it, made her want to laugh when minutes before she'd been crying. "Yes," she said. "I would."

"That's what I thought."

She looked at him for a long moment, marveling at the strange paths life took. Their child would have been eight years old now. She tried to imagine Dylan as a father, and though she didn't want to see the image, she knew he would have made a great dad. The kind of man to play with his children, spend time with them. Laugh. Make messes. Teach. Raise. Love.

The wash of longing swirled deep, way deep, journeying beyond her heart to that place she'd walled off. She had no business thinking of Dylan St. Croix as a father.

She had no business thinking of Dylan St. Croix, period.

"Take me back to the hotel, Dylan. Please." Before she did something she'd regret, like ask him to hold her.

Fire and ice, she reminded herself, never mixed.

"You've got everything you need, right?"

Standing in the open doorway of her hotel room, Bethany glanced in the bag in her right hand. "Prenatal vitamins, yogurt, five books on pregnancy." She rustled a little deeper. "And bubble bath." Looking up, she attempted to smile. "What more could a girl need?"

A whole hell of a lot, Dylan answered silently. Like a father for her child. "And you're going to take a nap, right? The doctor said you should get some rest."

Her smile slipped. "I'll try."

Dylan hesitated. He knew he should turn around and walk away. Walk far. He had no business lingering over Bethany like she'd suddenly become a delicate flower, fragile and in need of care. Fire burned flowers. Fire destroyed. And anyway, if he knew anything about Bethany St. Croix, he knew she was no fragile flower. She was strong and enduring, like the perennials growing wild at the base of Mount Hood. The ones that came back every year, bolder and prettier than ever. Bethany didn't need anyone—him, especially—hovering over her like a mother hen.

And yet, he didn't know how to walk away.

Despite the path he'd chosen, he'd never been a man to shuck responsibility. He'd never been a man to turn his back on trouble. He'd never been a man to pretend.

That was Bethany's modus operandi.

She watched him expectantly, her long glossy hair loose and sweeping across her face, hiding the pale scar and making her dark blue eyes look even more mysterious than usual. She wore little makeup, but there was a glow to her cheeks. He wondered if she realized she had a hand against her stomach, her fingers splayed against the cotton of her dress, gently caressing.

Damn the urge to put his hand there, too.

Bethany was pregnant. Pregnant. *Pregnant.*

And she might be going to jail.

The thought, the truth, burned. And for the first time in Dylan's life, he flat didn't know what to do. Decisions had always come easily to him. Something was black, or it was white. He turned left, or he went right. He never waffled.

He never wavered. But now…he didn't trust himself to be around her right now. Didn't know how to tell her the truth that would destroy that slumberous, serene look in her eyes. The words that would shatter the calm they'd stumbled upon.

He would confirm first, he decided. Then he would shatter.

"You should go," Bethany said, moving to close the door.

"Yes," he agreed, backing away. "I should."

So he did.

"How is she?"

"Give me that," Dylan growled, taking the freshly lit cigarette from Zito before the detective could draw it to his mouth. He brought it to his lips and took a long, long drag, savored the bite. Years had passed since he'd kicked the habit, but damn, a man could only deny himself for so long.

"That bad?" Zito asked.

Dylan exhaled a plume of smoke, took another drag. He wanted to draw the whole damn thing into his lungs. He wanted the burn. The blur.

"How the hell do you think she is?" he asked.

The detective stopped in front of a retro art gallery. "If I knew, I wouldn't ask."

Dylan dropped the cigarette and with his foot, ground it into the concrete. The late afternoon sun bore down on him. He knew what Zito was asking, what any good detective would. Had Bethany cracked? Had she slipped up and revealed anything?

"She's fine." The words aiding and abetting jeered him on. "Must have been standing a little too straight, that's all."

"That's all?"

"That's all." Bitterness seared through him. Irony laughed. He'd steered clear of Bethany for nine years, but in only a matter of days, she had him keeping secrets for her. Him, the man who abhorred pretenses. Keeping secrets. For Bethany.

It didn't take long, did it?

That was always the hell of the matter, how quickly he could slip into her world. Fall. Plummet. Because of those damn slumberous eyes.

She had no reason to kill Lance, he reasoned. Not unless she discovered his extracurricular activities and horrifying lies. The shock, the betrayal, could have sent her over the edge.

But she showed no signs.

Then again, Bethany never did. It was impossible to know what dwelled beneath that beautiful, placid surface. Still waters, he reminded himself. They ran too deep.

"I hear you've been poking around." Letting him off one hook, Zito snared him with another. The detective lit another cigarette. "You're not trying to do my job for me, are you?"

"Would I do that?" Dylan asked.

"In a New York minute."

"He was my cousin."

"And she used to be your lover."

Dylan plucked the cigarette from Zito's fingers and dropped it to the ground. This time, when his boot came down, he didn't just grind, he destroyed.

"Nasty habit," he said. "Could kill you, if you're not careful. You really ought to kick it."

Pregnant.

Five hours after Dr. Audrey Lyons dropped her bomb, the word still echoed through Beth. Pounded. Drilled. Floored.

Elated.

She stood in a small dressing room at a local department store and stared in the full-length mirror. Wearing only the bra and matching panties Dylan had purchased for her, she pressed a hand to her stomach, marveling at the pooch she hadn't noticed just that morning. The smile started in her heart, but quickly spread through her like liquid sunshine, curving her lips.

A child. She was carrying a child.

The ache came next, a sweet ache, one of melancholy and irony. Of regret. Destiny. Bone-chilling fear.

For years she'd longed to be a mother, mourning each month when her period came. The doctors never could find anything clinically wrong with her. Stress, one decided. Just one of those things, another said.

But Beth never accepted those answers. She'd conceived once—Dylan's child—and longed to carry another child, not just in her body, but in her arms. Her heart. She tried everything, starting with charting her temperature, ovulation kits, then graduating to hormone pills, followed by injections and artificial insemination. Romance and dreams had given way to medical science.

By the last year of her marriage, she and Lance had become more like lab partners, than lovers.

As Beth's sorrow grew, Lance withdrew from her emotionally, physically and every other way imaginable. Passion had never been their hallmark, but in the early days, a genuine fondness had flowed between them, an easy, undemanding friendship that helped her heal after Dylan. But Lance didn't understand her sadness, didn't understand her pain. He told her to quit obsessing. He told her maybe she wasn't meant to be a mother.

She should have seen the writing on the wall then. She should have realized the marriage really was over, that Lance, her friend, had become a stranger.

Instead, she'd convinced him to try one last time. For her. For their future. And Lance had reluctantly agreed.

When she began spotting twelve days after the artificial insemination, Lance caught her crying. And he'd exploded. He said he'd tried to warn her, but she just didn't listen. He told her he couldn't live with a woman who lived in a pretend world. He couldn't live with a woman who wouldn't accept reality.

And with that, he'd moved out.

The pain, the sense of failure, had been blinding. At first. But as the shock receded, she'd realized living without her politically ambitious, workaholic husband wasn't much different than living with him. Somewhere along the line they'd gone their separate ways, but neither of them had noticed. Beth hadn't seen Lance since, until five days ago, when she came to on the living room floor, next to his body. Whether she'd loved him anymore or not, the horror of that would never leave her.

Tears burned the backs of her eyes. She spread her fingers wider against the warm skin of her stomach, letting her pinkie touch her panties, her thumb her bra. It felt uncomfortably intimate wearing underwear Dylan had purchased, touched. Picked out just for her. For nine years she'd worked to keep him and his out-of-control passion from scorching her life, if not her dreams, but now she was wearing lingerie he'd chosen.

And he knew her most precious secret.

The cramped dressing room closed in on her. Breathing hollowed out. There could be no more secrets between her and Dylan St. Croix. No more intimacies. She had to forget about that alarming night in the mountains, the intensity in his dark green eyes just that morning when she'd come to in his arms. She had to forget the feel of his fingers drifting through her hair, the fleeting awareness that she wasn't alone. His insistence that she see a doctor. She had to forget all of that, and remember only the way he'd retreated when the doctor made her announcement. The way Dylan's eyes had hardened. The way he'd looked at her as though she'd somehow betrayed him.

With one last, awed glance at her stomach, Beth finished trying on clothes, selecting several loose-fitting outfits to purchase. She didn't want anything that remained at the house she'd shared with Lance. She wanted to start new.

And that included underwear, bras and panties she could slide onto her body without thinking of Dylan.

The baby clothes stopped her cold. She was heading to the checkout when she saw them, and warmth immediately flooded her. Her throat burned. Her heart thudded erratically. She stood there a long moment, just touching the soft little onesies. Closing her eyes. Imagining. And again, a hand found her stomach.

But then the hair on the back of her neck prickled, and the rhythm of her heart changed. Accelerated. She'd had the feeling since leaving the hotel, but when she turned, she found only two pregnant women, laughing over a miniature designer dress.

Paranoia, she reasoned. Shock.

Twenty minutes later, she stepped into the blinding sunlight and headed for her car. Heat radiated from the asphalt, but the chill hit her again, the sensation of being watched. She stopped, looked around. Nothing. Just a sea of cars and SUVs, mothers pushing strollers toward the mall, laughing teenage girls.

Uneasy, Beth found her car, slung her purchases in the back seat, and eased in with traffic. But when the turn came for her hotel, she didn't take it. Nor did she take the exit to the exclusive neighborhood she'd once called home. Instead, she headed north on I-5, checking her rearview mirror every few minutes to see if someone followed her.

Until she reached the gorge. The second she turned east on I-84, she realized where she'd been headed all along. It was impossible to think dark thoughts while driving through the verdant valley of the Columbia Gorge. Between dark basalt cliffs, the winding river sparkled in the midafternoon sun. As always, rainbows greeted her, stretching over the highway in a shimmering array of colors.

Beth smiled, started to hum ''Somewhere Over The Rainbow,'' and headed toward starkly beautiful Mount Hood. Snow still blanketed the higher elevations like a melting ice cream cone, but springtime wildflowers tangled across the foothills.

The craziness of the day caught up with her just before four o'clock. She blinked rapidly and inhaled, but the fatigue crawled deeper, and when she saw the crowded truck stop, she counted her blessings. After a quick trip to the not-so-clean ladies' room, she wandered over to the refrigerated section, and wondered just what a pregnant woman drank to stay awake. She'd have to read those baby books Dylan insisted she pick up, but figured caffeine was not an option. Maybe orange juice, she thought, opening the door and absorbing the blast of cold air, then reaching for a chilled bottle.

"What in God's name are you doing?"

The angry voice sent her heart jackhammering through her chest. Adrenaline surged. She spun around, found him blocking the aisle. Late afternoon sun glinted in through the store windows and distorted his features, but she didn't need details to recognize him. Not when the hum rumbled, deep, deep inside.

"Dylan."

He stood there, as bold and unmovable as Mount Hood, staring at her through eyes as hard and cold as the snow-capped peaks. "Running, Bethany?"

She thought about telling him not to call her that, but realized that would only guarantee he continued to do so. "Following me?" she asked instead.

"I'm sure as hell not out for a Sunday drive."

The sense of freedom she'd found on the scenic highway crumbled, reminding her why she'd started driving in the first place. She'd been right all along. Someone had been following her. "I don't need an escort."

He stepped closer. "You're a suspect in a high-profile murder investigation. I'm sure Zito told you not to leave town."

God help her, for a few hours there, she'd actually forgotten. "I'm not going anywhere."

"You're seventy miles from Portland."

He had her there. "I'm just taking a drive."

"Straight toward Canada."

Warning signs flared everywhere. Just a few hours before, when he'd dropped her off at the hotel, he'd been...tentative. Now mistrust emanated from every pore of his body.

"You think I'm running?"

"You stocked up on clothes at the mall. You didn't go back to your hotel room. You're pregnant and scared and you told me yourself you'd do what it took to protect your child."

Shock stole her breath. "You've got it all wrong."

"Do I?"

"I don't owe you any explanations," she said, and started to push past him.

She might as well have tried to move a prehistoric boulder. Dylan's hand closed around her upper arm. And his eyes caught fire. "If you think I'm going to let you walk out of here by yourself, you're out of your mind. I can't risk you driving up into those mountains and never coming back."

Beth gaped at him. She heard the warning in his voice, saw it in every rigid muscle in his body. She just didn't understand. "Why? You really think I killed Lance?"

The thought pierced deep, proving that the man she'd once loved with every corner of her heart didn't know her at all.

"You're pregnant," he said.

The memory came, hard and fast, of the only other time she'd carried a child. His. The one she'd lost. "I appreciate your concern, Dylan, but I'm not some fragile flower, and I don't need you playing bodyguard or bounty hunter or whatever it is you think you're doing."

Even if for a few dangerous moments, only a few hours before, she'd wanted to feel his arms close around her more than she'd ever wanted anything.

His expression darkened. "I'm not playing anything."

"Then what would you call it?"

"Father. I'd call it father."

Everything inside Beth went very still. Even her heart. She stared at Dylan, trying to understand the gravity in his eyes, the hard line of his mouth. "W-what?"

He released his hold on her arm and slid his hand to her stomach, where his fingers splayed wide. "This child you're carrying, Bethany. This child *is* mine."

Chapter 7

The bottle of orange juice slipped from her fingers and shattered against the dirty tile floor. Cold liquid splashed against her legs, but Beth didn't move, didn't look down.

"What did you say?" she asked in a thready voice she barely recognized as her own.

Dylan grabbed a wad of napkins from the coffee bar by his side. "You're bleeding."

Beth looked at the feathery cuts on her calves, the streaks of orange juice and blood racing toward her ankle. They were nothing compared to the gash left by his words.

He went down on a knee. "Here let me—"

"Don't touch me!" she practically shrieked, knowing she'd come unglued if he did. "I don't care about my legs. I care about my baby, and what you just said."

Slowly, Dylan pushed to his full height, towering over her by a good six inches. His eyes were hard. Hot. "Not here," he said, reaching for her. "Come on—"

"No." She yanked her hand from his and backed away,

her sandals crunching on shards of glass. "I'm not going anywhere until you tell me what you meant."

His jaw tightened. "Damn it—"

"Excuse me," the clerk said, pushing past them with a bucket of water and a mop. "Let me just—"

"Go away," Dylan said, but didn't move, didn't look away from Beth.

The clerk scurried away, not needing to be told twice that the tall man with the angry jaw meant business.

Beth swallowed hard. She wanted to scurry away, too. At least part of her. The rest of her, the dominant part, wanted to put her hands to Dylan's impossibly wide chest and shove. Hard. He'd always rocked her world, but this time he'd gone too far.

"I mean it," she said. "Tell me what you meant."

A small muscle in the hollow of his cheek began to thump. "I meant what I said. The child you're carrying is mine."

Beth swayed, reaching a hand behind her to brace herself against the refrigerated glass. "That's not possible."

"I'm afraid it's more than possible, sweetheart. Don't tell me you've forgotten about that night in the mountains, how we—"

"Stop it," she practically shouted, then tried to shove past him.

He didn't move. "Just asking an innocent question," he said with a grim smile.

She glared at him. "You haven't been innocent since the day you were born."

"Be that as it may, I took biology and went to law school. I know how to put facts together, and the cold hard truth is that Lance was sterile."

The busy minimart started to spin. Beyond Dylan, the cartons and cans along the cluttered aisle blurred and fused, whirled away. "W-what are you talking about?"

"How many years did you try to have a baby? How

many years did the doctors tell you they found nothing wrong with you?''

She just stared at him. ''They never found anything wrong with Lance, either.''

''Did the doctor tell you that himself, Bethany? Or is that what Lance told you?''

Memories came crashing down like towering spruce snapping in a thunderstorm, all the different times they'd been tested, the procedures they had done. Lance had always gone to his own doctor. A guy's doctor, he'd said. She couldn't expect a man to feel comfortable seeing a woman's doctor. She remembered laughing at the time...

Now an entirely different emotion clogged her throat. Betrayal cut like a fine-edged paring knife, slicing clear to her bones. ''No,'' she whispered. ''No.''

Dylan stepped closer, practically pinning her between his very hard, very angry, very hot body, and the cold glass behind her. ''Why would I lie?'' he asked in a dangerously quiet voice. ''What do I have to gain?''

Her hand slid protectively to her stomach. ''My child.''

His expression twisted. ''Funny, that's exactly what Lance said.''

The sense of vertigo accelerated, dipping wildly like a roller coaster out of control and carrying her to an alternate universe she didn't understand. ''W-what are you talking about?''

Dylan gestured to the next aisle over, where a trio of ponytailed and bearded truckers watched the two of them like a tennis match. ''This isn't the time or the place, Bethany.''

''I don't give a damn,'' she said, and realized she didn't. For the past six years she'd lived in a carefully constructed world, working hard to make sure her life never blew up around her like her mother's did on a regular basis. That's all she wanted. Normalcy. Simplicity. A husband she loved, who loved her back. A few kids. A couple of dogs and cats. Goldfish.

But that life, that illusion, was gone now. Shredded. She could never go back.

And for the first time in her life, she flat didn't care. "Tell me what you know about Lance, and tell me now."

Dylan stepped closer. "He was scared," he said. "Ashamed. For the first time in his life, the St. Croix prince had come up against an opponent, a challenge, he couldn't defeat. He couldn't make his own wife smile. He couldn't make you pregnant."

"How do you know this?"

"He told me."

"You?"

"Me."

"But…why didn't he tell *me?* We could have adopted—"

"And shatter that pretend world the two of you lived in? Lance? You must not have known the man you married as well as you thought you did. He was a St. Croix, for God's sake. Appearances were everything to him. It was bad enough that he knew he couldn't fulfill a basic, human function. He'd have sooner cut off both his hands than admit the truth to you."

"Even if what you're saying is true, which I'm not sure it is, this child has nothing to do with Lance. I did the insemination on my own."

"Ah, Bethany. Do you really think Lance would let you get pregnant mere months after he walked out on you? Do you really think he'd let you emasculate him like that?"

"It wasn't his decision."

"Once you step foot in his house of cards, you can never leave. I know this is my child, Bethany, because I know Lance made damn sure your artificial insemination wouldn't work."

Horror shuddered through her, leaving a chill in its wake. "I'm not listening to this," she said and tried to shove past him, but he easily caught her wrist.

"Running away won't change anything."

She glared up at him, slowly shaking her head. "You don't know what you're talking about," she insisted, but deep, deep inside, she was very afraid that he did.

Dylan looked at Bethany standing there, her eyes wide and dark, her skin flushed, her mouth mutinous, and wished to hell and back he *didn't* know what he was talking about. But he did. Painfully so. In excruciating detail.

"Hate to shatter your illusions, sweetheart, but I know exactly what I'm talking about. A man. A man I grew up with. A man who broke down in front of me and cried. A desperate man. A man who couldn't accept his own failings and didn't think his wife would, either."

Bethany winced.

"The truth ate him up inside," Dylan told her. "Messed him up bad." The lies Lance had told were hideous and indefensible, but she deserved to at least understand why. "Failure wasn't an option for Lance. Success meant everything to him. And that included giving you a child." Dylan could only imagine what it had cost his cousin to approach him, the horrendous proposition he'd outlined, the humiliating admission that Dylan could give Bethany what Lance couldn't. No one would ever know, he'd promised. Lance would love the child as his own. Dylan would be nothing but a sperm donor.

The suggestion still made Dylan cringe.

"He couldn't look at you without knowing he couldn't function as a man."

Bethany wrapped her arms around her waist and cradled her child. *Their* child. Her loose, light blue shift concealed all traces of her pregnancy, except a slight fullness at her breasts.

"You're saying he admitted this to you?" she asked. "The two of you barely spoke."

Dylan had been surprised, as well. "We're genetically close," he said, repeating his cousin's rationale.

"Genetically close?" she repeated, and her voice cracked.

Dylan hated what he had to say, but he wouldn't lie. "He wanted me to be a sperm donor."

Beth just stared at him. "He what?"

"I told him no." Had exercised every molecule of restraint he possessed not to lunge across the table and slam his fist into his cousin's jaw. "I told him I wasn't playing in his house of cards, and if he wasn't careful, he wouldn't be for much longer, either."

Now, the memory, the obscene prediction, chilled.

Slowly, Bethany's eyes met his. "You threatened him?"

"I warned him."

She lifted a hand to her forehead. "But...that was before the divorce. This child had nothing to do with him!"

Clearly she hadn't really known the man she married. "Lance's penchant for playing God didn't end with legal documents, Bethany. I went to the fertility clinic this afternoon." Being a St. Croix definitely had its advantages. So did being a private investigator. Especially when a murder hung on the line. "Our boy Lance paid a technician there twenty-five thousand dollars to make sure you didn't get pregnant."

She looked alarmingly pale. "Dear God, I...this is just...how could Lance do this?"

That, Dylan could answer too well. "He would have done anything, Bethany. Anything to present the image he wanted the world to see." It had never occurred to him that he would be caught, that his lies would catch up with him. That he would one day lie dead on his living room floor.

And it hadn't occurred to Dylan that he'd be the one left to pick up the pieces.

But he wasn't a man to walk way from responsibility, even if that responsibility seared him like a hot poker into a fresh wound. Playing hero wasn't his shtick, and fatherhood hadn't been in his immediate plans.

But as he looked at Bethany standing there so rigidly, her chin lifted in defiance, her arms wrapped protectively around her waist, he saw only the trusting girl she'd been, the future she'd once dreamed of. And he knew his greatest battle still lay ahead. This woman who'd been betrayed in the most heinous way imaginable was suspected of murder. She might be going to jail.

He could well be raising his child alone.

Or, if she slipped across the border and into Canada, not raising his child at all.

"Come on," he said, reaching for her hand. "Let's get out of here."

She stepped back. "I'm not going anywhere with you."

"Sure you are," he drawled. "Just think of it as an early family vacation." That had a much better ring to it than abduction.

She wouldn't give him her hand, so he draped an arm around her stiff shoulders and steered her toward the front of the store. More customers stood watching now, not just truck drivers, but the clerk and the manager and a family of four wearing T-shirts extolling the virtues of Idaho.

A warm breeze lifted the ends of her silky hair the second they walked outside. The sky was darker, more ominous. The sun had slipped behind a bank of heavy clouds, only a few meager rays slipping free. A storm threatened to break soon.

Bethany headed toward her car, but Dylan caught her wrist.

"You can't keep me here against my will," she gritted out.

"I can't let you walk away and drive into the sunset, either."

She lifted her chin. "Pregnancy doesn't make a woman unable to drive."

"You're a suspect in a high-profile murder case," he reminded. "You're carrying my child, and you're scared. If ever anyone had the motivation to slip across the border into the wilds of Canada and conveniently get lost, it's you.''

Her eyes flared. ''I'm not running.''

''I know you're not,'' he said, taking her hand and leading her to his Bronco. ''I'm not letting you.''

Opening the door, he gestured for her to slide in. Instead, she looked up at him, the strangest look swirling in her eyes. Wisdom and understanding and sorrow. Regret. Acceptance. ''This is why you followed me to the police station and showed up at my hotel, isn't it? This is why you've been pretending to care.''

He'd be a fool to think he heard hurt in her raspy voice. He'd be an even bigger fool to remind her that pretenses were her forte, not his.

''I had to know,'' he said simply.

Those fabulous eyes of hers darkened, blue turning black. ''You should have told me the truth all along,'' she said, and though the words were soft, almost broken, they cut to the bone.

Because they were true.

A distorted laugh broke from his throat. ''I should have done a lot of things. But it's too late for second-guessing.''

''It was too late a long time ago,'' she corrected, then slid into the Bronco and closed the door.

Beth gazed out the window, watching the darkened landscape of towering trees rush by in a blur of shadows. Slowly, to the sound of mournful blues, her eyes drifted shut and she began to drift. A warm fire awaited her, the oddest sensation of homecoming. She stretched out before the flames, sure there was some reason she shouldn't relax so completely, but unable to remember why. The fire maybe. The heat. But rather than burning, they beckoned.

A long time had passed since she slept so soundly.

''Bethany?''

The low voice drifted over her like a warm caress. She sighed and snuggled closer, not ready to be disturbed.

"Sweetheart, we're here."

Where? she thought in some hazy corner of her mind. She didn't want to be anywhere other than where she was.

"Come on," the voice encouraged.

She didn't move, didn't want to leave the warmth of the cozy fire, the feel of hands gliding over her body. She shifted to allow better access and nuzzled closer to the warm chest.

Warm chest.

Reality jarred her out of the dream and back into the Bronco. Or rather, Dylan's arms. He'd eased her from the front seat and now carried her as he walked across what sounded like gravel. Her eyes opened abruptly, but through the darkness she could see little more than the glow of his gaze. The air was cool, the night quiet, save for an owl somewhere in the distance. Around them, trees stretched up toward the star-dappled sky like shadowy guards. The night obscured detail, but the strong scent of pine identified them as spruce or fir.

"Where are we?" she asked, but the gauzy light of the moon answered before Dylan could. The massive structure sprawled out from her memory and loomed straight ahead. "No," she whispered.

Not here. Not now.

Dylan had always been wild and unpredictable, but he'd never been cruel. Until now. The St. Croix cabin. He'd brought her to the St. Croix cabin. Or rather, retreat.

Her heart started to pound. Hard. She squirmed against him, but his arms were like steel bands, his chest as hard as the rock on the side of the mountain.

"Put me down," she tried to command, but the words broke on the way out, just like everything else that came in contact with Dylan St. Croix.

He kept right on going. "What's the matter? Don't want me to carry you over the threshold?"

The memory lashed in, shockingly vivid despite the passing of nine long years. The laughter and teasing. The make-believe game she'd naively believed would translate into reality.

"No," she whispered.

He took the four steps to the rustic porch in two, then strode toward the door. A light came on as though by magic, flooding the expanse of weathered wood with a golden glow.

Dylan stopped and shifted her in his arms, easing her down the length of his body until her feet settled against the doormat. She stood there in the chilly night breeze, not trusting herself to move without stepping on a land mine.

"Bethany?"

She swallowed against the tightness, but couldn't look away from the empty hanging baskets, swaying quietly in the breeze.

Dylan swore softly. "There's a commercial greenhouse ten or so miles down the mountain," he said. "We can swing by tomorrow, if you like."

She absorbed the impact of the words, wondering how a man who thrived on upsetting the applecart also knew how to restore it with punishing gentleness. "That's not necessary."

He didn't say anything, but she would have sworn she heard him frown. He turned back to the door and with a quick flick of his wrist ushered her inside.

Memories greeted her, not threadbare as she expected, hoped, but strong and enduring like the man behind her. Shadows of times gone by crouched in every corner, echoes of laughter and tears reverberated through the rafters. They washed over her just like they had that night almost seven weeks before, but rather than the chill she expected, she found only warmth.

Stepping onto the old braided rug, she wrapped her arms around her waist and wondered how this cabin where no one lived could feel so alive.

"It's computerized," he answered before she asked. "I programmed the heater on a few hours back."

Beth shook her head. She should have known. Lots of people kept mountain getaways, ramshackle structures where they escaped civilization for a few days. Not so with the St. Croixs. One of Oregon's most prominent families, they never did anything halfway, from politics to scandal to mountain retreats.

The so-called cabin featured a stunning display of glass and wood, modern yet rustic at the same time. The entry sprawled into an expansive great room, with wood floors and a wood-beamed ceiling, wood paneling. The two matching sofas were ivory, the easy chair slate blue. In the far corner a distressed pine armoire stood closed, but Beth knew a TV hid within its doors.

And then there was the fireplace.

"I keep meaning to update it," Dylan said. "Grandfather mentioned installing those gas logs controlled by a remote, but..." He hesitated. "That seems like cheating."

And God knew Dylan St. Croix, crusader of truth and justice and all that was right in this world, would never succumb to a make-believe fire.

Her throat tight, Beth glanced toward the wall of windows dominating the back side of the room. Darkness hid the vista, but in the morning, sunlight would glint through hundreds of Douglas fir, preserved here on the St. Croix land, safe from the intrusion of loggers and modern man.

The vastness drew her, just like the night not so long ago, when she'd learned all over again why she had to steer clear of Dylan. She crossed the room and put a palm to the cold glass, breathed in deeply of smoke and pine and sandalwood. Night had always fascinated her, brought peace even when the world exploded around her. Night gave her courage. The stillness, she supposed. The quiet. It was easier to forget. To pretend.

"Bethany?"

His voice was rougher than before, almost hoarse. His breath whispered across the back of her neck.

She closed her eyes, not wanting to look at him. She

didn't want to see his tired eyes, blazing with heated emotion she didn't understand.

Fatigue dulled her senses, but the shock of learning she and Dylan had created a child continued to burn. She'd worked hard to keep the chaos that was Dylan out of her life. Like a shooting star, he was exciting and sexy and stirred something deep inside, but he wasn't the kind of man with whom to build a future. A family. He wasn't the kind of man to provide stability and guidance to a child's life. She'd learned that the hard way. That's why she'd walked away, even when doing so felt like ripping her heart out. That's why she'd stayed away.

Opening her eyes, Beth looked toward the darkness, but found Dylan waiting for her there, as well. The light from the great room cast his reflection into the glass, forcing her to see him even when she did not look.

There was no running when it came to Dylan St. Croix.

He looked tired, she thought absently. Like one of the Douglas firs outside, that had been standing and enduring and weathering for far too long. His thick hair was rumpled, his jaw dark with whiskers. Shadows ringed eyes that reminded her of a soldier surveying a grisly battlefield.

The temptation to pretend was strong. To pretend they were friends and turn to him, reach out to him. To pretend being here didn't jar her, that she could stand in the room where they'd made love so many times and feel nothing.

"Why, Dylan?" she asked into the window. "Why did you bring me here?"

His reflected gaze darkened. He looked at her a long moment, his gaze skimming as intimately as his hands had the night they'd crossed the line. "I thought privacy might do you good."

This time she did hold back. He didn't need to know that she could have no privacy here, where ghosts and memories awaited at every turn, filled her every breath. They whirred around her and towered above her, preventing her from seeing anything beyond the past. The man.

"You're tired," he said, and almost sounded like he cared. "You should get some rest," he added, lifting a hand to her shoulder.

Beth sidestepped his touch.

"Damn it, Bethany," he swore softly, "quit looking at me like that."

She turned to face him, lifted her chin. She knew better than stepping into a game of chicken with Dylan, but like so many times, knowledge didn't stop her. "Like how?"

His gaze met hers. "Like I'm about to rip your heart out."

Everything inside her went very still, all but the organ in question. It strummed low and deep. Hard. Thin ice surrounded them, but Dylan didn't let something petty like risk stand in his way. He just charged full steam ahead, venturing out beyond the realm of safety, toward the point of no return.

Beth did not. She wasn't a coward, but she'd fallen into icy water before, felt the icy pinpricks slash at her, felt her body slow and the current pull her under.

She had no desire for a repeat performance, even if the way Dylan watched her conjured the fantasy that this time, he'd catch her before she fell.

"You're right," she said. Less than fourteen hours had passed since they'd stood at the cemetery, saying goodbye to Lance. Already, it seemed a different lifetime. "It's been a long day and I'm tired."

His gaze dipped from her face to her stomach, where her hand rested. Protected. When his eyes met hers again, an unfamiliar light glinted there. "I think there's still some hot cocoa. Would you like—"

"No." God no. That's how it had started before.

"Then let's get you into bed."

The words arced through her like live electricity, but Dylan merely took her hand and led her across the great room, as though oblivious to any sexual connotation. To the right lay the kitchen and a spiral staircase twirling to a loft. To the left, a short hall led to the three bedrooms.

They stopped at the first. "You can stay in here this time," he said, pushing open the door and flicking on the light.

She'd not let herself look inside this room seven weeks before, but now, Beth could only stare. The big bed, it was still there, massive and dominating, turning everything inside her liquid. She knew that big bed made of pine and shaped like a sleigh. More than knew it, she'd lost her virginity there.

And conceived her first child.

Emotion welled up like a swollen mountain stream. Her throat tightened. Her chest ached. Angry, with herself for the reaction, with Dylan for bringing her here, with Lance for being such a coward, she did the only thing she could. She tacked up a shield of bravado to hide the pain.

"If this were a movie," she said with an air of breeziness that both pleased and surprised her, "this is when you'd announce you have to stay with me, to make sure I don't try anything stupid."

Something odd flashed in Dylan's eyes. He leaned against the door frame and arched a brow. "Now don't take this the wrong way, sweetheart, but I can't think of anything more stupid than me crawling into that bed with you."

Heat sluiced through her. Hurt. "Touché."

"And anyway," he added lazily. "We both know movies are just fantasy. Real life rarely works out as neatly."

True enough. In the movies, in fantasies, they'd find a way to turn this mess into a happy ending.

Uncomfortable with the way Dylan lounged against the frame and watched her, she glanced into the large room. Across from the bed stood a huge wood-burning fireplace, while a wall of windows looked out on the darkness.

The swirl of longing caught her by surprise.

Nine years had passed since she'd stood in this room,

loved in that bed. And during that time, to her knowledge, Lance had never come here, either. The judge, in his wheelchair, could barely get around his estate—and he was hardly the outdoors type.

But the cabin was far from deserted.

"How often do you come here?" she asked before she could stop herself.

"Often enough."

"Do you come…alone?"

Beside her, she felt him stiffen. "Is that what you think I am, Bethany? A man who comes alone?"

The jolt was instantaneous, the heat searing. "Dylan—"

"If you must know," he said, tucking a finger under her chin and turning her to face him. Not until her reluctant eyes met his did he finish. "Yes, most of the time I come alone."

Surprise flared through her, igniting a dangerous curiosity that stoked deep. No, he couldn't mean…not a man like Dylan St. Croix. But the other possibility…it unsettled her, as well, but on an entirely different level. Deeper. Darker.

"But not always?" she managed.

His dark gaze held hers. "Not always."

Something deep inside went very cold. No matter how he'd intended his early statement, his answer meant the same thing. He didn't always come alone.

God help her, she could barely breathe. "And when you're here…where do you sleep?"

He nodded toward the bed. "Right here."

Beth followed his gaze to the bed. The image formed before she could stop it, of Dylan stretched out in that big bed, naked. With another woman.

The sense of violation was swift and immediate. Her throat tightened. And that place deep inside, the one that had gone cold, started to bleed.

She turned from the truth, the past, and headed down

the hall. "I'll take the guest room." She didn't really want that bed, either, where she'd faced both demon and desire one snowy night she could no longer pretend hadn't happened.

"What's the matter?" Dylan asked from behind her. "Scared of ghosts?"

She stopped abruptly, turned to face him. "The past can't hurt me, Dylan. Not anymore." It was the here and now that concerned her, the choices and challenges that still lay ahead.

A moment passed while she waited for him to fire back a cutting retort, to challenge her or goad her or insist upon tucking her in bed. But he did none of that, just stood there watching her, as still and unmoving as the night around them.

Discomfort pulsed through her. Stillness and Dylan St. Croix went together as well as meditation and one of those coyotes she heard howling in the distance.

"Good night," she said, and turned away from him.

"Bethany."

Hand on the knob, she stopped, smiling despite herself. Now this was more like it. This was Dylan. He always had to have the last word.

"I'm sorry."

Those weren't the words she was expecting. The huskiness of his voice wrapped around her, but she knew better than looking at him. Instead, she walked into the darkened room and closed the door behind her.

Somewhere in the distance, an owl called to a mate who didn't answer. A spotted owl, Dylan figured, glad that at least here on St. Croix land, they survived. He stood at the massive wall of windows, much as Bethany had earlier. But he didn't touch, didn't need to feel the cold sting of the glass.

What the hell had he done?

He didn't know why he'd brought her here; they'd long

since crossed the point of no return. The cabin couldn't change that.

Maybe he shouldn't have told her the truth. Maybe he should have let the pretense continue, let her give birth to a child she believed to be from an anonymous donor. Let her raise the child alone. Love the child.

But damn it, he couldn't live a lie like that. He couldn't stand in the background and watch Bethany raise his child. Watch her smile and laugh and love, and never step forward. And Christ, what if she went to prison for killing Lance? What then? The child would be taken from her, given to strangers.

Dylan couldn't allow that. Not his child. Not his and Bethany's. They'd already lost one. No way in hell could he let another child be taken from them.

Sleep hovered out of reach, seductive but illusive. Beth lay in the big guest bed for a long while, just listening to an owl screech into the night. In answer, a coyote howled.

Hours had passed. Two, she thought. Maybe three. The light slipping under her door had vanished some time back, and the sound of Dylan moving restlessly about the cabin ceased. She hoped he slept.

Careful to maintain silence, Beth eased from bed and dressed, grabbed her purse and slowly opened the door. As she'd expected, no light greeted her. No signs of wakefulness. She tiptoed down the hall, acutely aware of how the floorboards liked to creak.

Outside the master suite, she paused. She didn't really want to look inside, didn't want to see Dylan's big body sprawled out in that bed, the sheets tangled at his hips, but she had to know.

Easing the door open, she peered in and instantly found the big sleigh bed. The big, *empty* sleigh bed. The room looked totally undisturbed, showing no signs of man or life.

Sighing, Beth carefully closed the door and eased toward the great room. No sounds destroyed the silence, leaving two possibilities. Either Dylan slept, or he'd gone outside.

The second she saw the clothes strewn on the floor she had her answer. His faded jeans lay in a heap, his button-down strewn over them. Socks sprawled off to the side.

Thank God she didn't see his boxers.

Heart pounding, she stepped deeper into the room. She didn't want to get too close to him, knew the wisdom of letting a sleeping dog lie. But she had to know.

And then there he was. Glancing over the back of the sofa, she saw the tartan plaid blanket draped over the expanse of his body. Silently, she whispered a prayer of thanks for the cold. Otherwise, he would have slept with no covers, and instead of the blanket, moonlight would be glinting off a chest that went on forever, an enticing trail of dark hair leading down a flat stomach, powerful thighs she didn't need to remember.

But she didn't see any of that, just a soft old blanket covering a soundly sleeping man.

Whispering another prayer of thanks, Beth crossed to his clothes and picked up his jeans. They were soft, she thought, just a trace of body heat lingering. Slipping her hand in his pocket felt oddly intimate, but she knew of no other way to get his keys. Shaking them to the ground would surely wake him.

Her fingers closed around the cool metal, and she slowly withdrew them. Knowing better than opening the front door, she quietly moved through the kitchen to the alternate route outside. The cold slapped at her immediately, but determination provided all the buffer she needed.

From there, it was shockingly easy. She rounded the house on the porch, trusting the wood more than the gravel. Regret tugged at her when she climbed into the Bronco and slid the key into the ignition, but she squelched the ridiculous emotion.

She couldn't worry about stranding Dylan here. There

was a phone. He would call someone. She could only think about her child, a child Dylan could easily try to take from her. She couldn't stay there with him, alone with nothing but a forest of pine and memory.

Her heart pounded as she turned the key. This was the riskiest part. But the motor hummed softly, and Beth wasted no time putting the SUV into gear and driving away. Using the moon as her guide, she carefully navigated the twisting mountain roads. Adrenaline kept her alert.

The darkly amused voice from the back seat shocked her senseless.

"Bethany, sweetheart, you missed the turn."

Chapter 8

"And here I thought you said you weren't running away."

Beth's heart rate exploded into a staccato rhythm, and her breath froze. Her hands started to shake. She glanced sharply into the rearview mirror, where she found Dylan maneuvering that big body of his from the cargo section into the back seat. He wore all black, making him appear more shadow than man. He moved with incredible grace for his size, wide shoulders dominating the small opening. And then came his legs. So big. So powerful. She remembered those thighs—

"Keep your eyes on the road," he said with all the nonchalance of a walk in the park. "These turns can be treacherous."

"What in God's name are you doing?" she demanded.

The whites of his eyes gleamed in the darkness. "Funny, I was going to ask you the same question."

"I—"

"Watch out!" he shouted, vaulting between the seats

and grabbing the steering wheel. The Bronco swung wildly, skidding across the road and bouncing along the gravel-covered shoulder.

There was no guardrail.

Beth slammed the brake against the floor, sending the Bronco into a rocky slide. Tires squealed. Headlights slashed wildly through the darkness. Time slowed to a punishing crawl as Dylan fought momentum and gravity. She heard him curse, the scream that ripped from her own throat, the insidious echo of the past.

The Bronco stopped abruptly, violently, the seat belt cutting into her chest and abdomen.

She sat there, stunned. Adrenaline surged and crashed, right along with the knowledge of how close they'd come to plummeting over the edge.

"What am I doing?" Dylan growled. He crammed the gear into park and crawled next to her in the driver's seat. "Looks to me like I'm saving your life so you can find a way to kill me without hurting yourself in the process."

The ironic edge to his voice cut deep, but she refused to give him the reaction he obviously wanted. She didn't look at him either. Couldn't. Didn't need use of her eyes when he sat so close her other senses hummed and screamed in protest. Thigh to thigh. Shoulder to shoulder. The heat of his body made the cool mountain night feel warm.

Staring straight ahead, Beth focused on the headlights cutting garishly through the darkness. Towering pines obscured the light of the moon and the stars, but through the shadows, a sheer drop-off yawned not five feet away.

The truth rose up from that darkness, and deep inside, she started to shake. If Dylan hadn't grabbed the wheel, they would have gone straight over the edge.

"Bethany?" Warmth. Of flesh. Against her cheek. "Are you okay?"

Breathe in, she told herself. Breathe out. Deep. Slow. Focus, she reminded, ignoring the heat streaking from his fingertips down to her toes. She had to focus. Protect. Defend.

"Do you have to make a joke out of everything?" she asked, still stung by his earlier taunt.

"Who's joking?"

Now she did look at him. "You can't take credit for preventing an accident you almost caused."

His gaze bored into her, the fingers of one hand against the side of her face. With his other hand, he reached across and unfastened her seat belt. "You're pale, sweetheart. Are you sure you're okay?"

"You deliberately tricked me," she said, refusing to let him off the hook.

The soft blue lights of the dashboard revealed an unsettling glow in his eyes. "Tricked you how, Bethany? Be clear. What are we talking about here?"

"You made it look like you were sleeping on the sofa, when you were hiding in the back all along."

"You're a survivor, Bethany Rae. I knew you'd try something—you're not a woman to let life steamroll you." The hard lines of his face softened. "I always admired you for that."

She curled her fingers around his wrist and pulled his hand from her face. "I don't want your admiration."

"What *do* you want?"

The question was thick, dark, unbearable. She looked at him sitting inches away, all big and strong, at the hard line of his jaw and the dark whiskers just begging to be touched. At the shoulders she'd once leaned on.

Then, he'd promised to do anything, be anyone, give everything.

Words, she now knew, meant nothing without actions to support them.

"Nothing, Dylan. I just want to be left alone."

He frowned. "I'm afraid I can't do that, Bethany. I can't just let you walk out of my life."

The words, the ferocity behind them, did cruel, cruel

things to her heart. Every woman longed for a man to speak to her so possessively. So protectively. Every woman longed to believe there was a man who'd walk across hot coals for her.

But Dylan St. Croix didn't mean the words romantically. He meant them as a dare, a threat, a warning, reminding her that where Dylan St. Croix walked, wreckage always lay strewn behind. Not even fantasies or fairy tales survived the fallout.

"We could have died," she said softly, but with damning precision. "Because you had to prove a point."

Something hard flashed through his eyes. She refused to label it pain. "You're carrying my child," he said quietly. "That means something to me. I'm not going to let anything happen to either of you."

Instinctively, her hand slid to her stomach. *Her* child. The stab was sharp, the outflow of joy overwhelming. *His* child. The thought still jarred her, didn't seem real. *Their child.*

God in Heaven, she would never be free of Dylan St. Croix, not so long as their son or daughter lived and breathed. There would be birthdays and holidays, first days of school and graduations. A wedding.

They would share grandchildren.

"You sure you're okay?" His hand still lingered against the side of her face.

"Damn you," she whispered.

A dark grin tugged at his lips. "You can try," he said, "but I can tell you right now it won't work. I seem to be one of the few St. Croixs immune to the curse."

The St. Croix curse. She hadn't heard the term in years, not since Lance had jokingly talked about his family's doomed fate. Both his and Dylan's parents—brothers and their wives—had met early deaths through a boating accident. Dylan called it the price of living a privileged life, but Lance laughed it off.

Now Lance was dead, just like so many St. Croixs before him, passing away before hairlines receded and wrinkles set in.

"Scoot over, honey, and let me get us out of here."

She looked from the door to her left to his big body next to hers. The only way to scoot would be to crawl across his lap.

"I can drive," she said, meeting his gaze.

Gentleness burned in his eyes. "I know you can, but it's a long drop. If we're going to take the plunge, you don't need another murder suspicion hanging over your memory."

A protest rose to her throat, an automatic refusal to yield to this man. But then came common sense and the knowledge that he spoke the truth. The night was dark, the narrow ledge dropping off into nothingness. Dylan knew these roads. She did not. Dylan knew his Bronco. She did not.

Dylan thrived in chaos.

She did not.

Wrenching open the door, she stepped into the chill of the night.

"I wouldn't do that," Dylan said.

"Why not?"

"There's no shoulder on the other side."

Keeping a hand on the hood, she walked to the front of the SUV and saw the truth of his words. The front right tire sat inches from a sheer drop-off.

The sight, the reality, chilled her to the bone.

"Come on," Dylan said from behind her. He took her hand and led her to the front seat. "Climb in."

She did as he instructed, refusing to dwell on the fact that he'd spared her the discomfort of crawling over him.

"The next time you slide over my body," he said as he eased into the driver's seat and slammed the door behind him, "it will be because you want to, not because you don't have a choice."

Ponderosa pines stretched toward the night sky, where pinpricks of light glimmered like an enchanted kingdom.

Beth groggily blinked, trying to bring the world into focus. Adrenaline and emotion still sloshed around inside her, but somehow she'd managed to nod off.

The glow of the dashboard clock said she'd slept for close to an hour.

She shifted restlessly, realizing she'd gravitated away from the chill of the window and toward the warmth of the man.

"This isn't the way to the cabin," she realized aloud.

Dylan accelerated out of a hairpin curve. "No, it's not."

Up in the distance, the road opened to a parking area. Just beyond sprawled a gorgeous rustic lodge. Lights glowed in the windows, promising warmth.

But Dylan kept driving.

And her heart started to pound. Hard. She recognized the road now, the lodge, the destination. She remembered the profusion of elk from her last visit, right in the heart of mating season, when their bugled mating calls echoed on crisp mountain air. She saw no elk now, just shadows.

Turn around. Go back. Now.

The words vaulted to her throat, but made it no further. They would be futile, she knew. Dylan St. Croix would not listen to her. And deep inside, she knew she didn't want him to.

Nine years had passed since she'd traveled this road. Nine years since she'd seen the impressive renovated lodge, the elk grazing and playing, the studs keeping a close, possessive watch on their herds. Nine years since she'd seen the otherworldly Crater Lake. Oregon's only state park, the remnants of an extinct volcano fed Beth's soul like no other place. The unspoiled beauty, she figured. The serenity.

She pushed open the door the second he stopped the car, and practically ran to the crater's edge. Cool night air whipped around her, but she didn't care. The lake. All she could think was the lake.

At the edge of the steep crater, she stopped. And stared. Her breath caught. The lake, over one thousand feet below, glistened a vivid shade of blue during the day, pure and deep. Dylan had once compared the color to her eyes.

But when the night sky took over, the blue faded, leaving only the mercurial light of the moon and the stars reflected on the ominously still, ominously dark surface.

Once, she and Dylan had picked out constellations without ever lifting their eyes to the sky.

"Cold?" Dylan asked from behind her, and only then did she realize she'd wrapped her arms around her waist.

She smiled into the darkness. "No. Just drinking it all in."

"I thought you might." He moved beside her and spread something over the ground. "Come sit for a few minutes."

She looked at the thick blanket spread beside her, and knew a smart woman would turn and walk back to the Bronco, crawl into the warmth of the front seat and demand Dylan take her back to the cabin. A smart woman would resist the lure of lowering herself to the ground and absorbing the night around her, the sound of an owl hooting in the distance, the wind rustling through the pines. A smart woman would not gaze down at the pristine lake of her youth and see the past she'd worked hard to forget. But never had.

"Just for a few," Beth said, and took Dylan's hand as he helped her down. The warmth was immediate, the strength. The security. She let go as she sat and drew her knees to her chest, wrapping her arms around them. The night was remarkably quiet, remarkably dark. Unmistakably pure. Up here in the mountains, away from the glare of city lights and the blare of traffic, she could breathe a little deeper. Dream a little fuller.

Her thoughts had a way of clearing here, much like the water of the lake. Her grandfather had said you could submerge a book six feet into the cold, cold water and still read the words plain as day.

She'd never taken him up on his offer to demonstrate.

The books of her youth, the fairy tales of her heart, had been too precious to sacrifice to a dare.

A smile slipped from her heart and found her lips. She breathed deeply of the crisp night air, savoring the aroma of pine and smoke from the lodge. With each breath, she felt a little more of the tension leave her body on the cool breeze. She'd always loved it here, the sights and sounds and textures. The serenity. The remoteness. It was a pretend land, where the profusion of pines created a forest of Christmas trees. The modern world had yet to intrude, the one hotel limiting the number of tourists. Of those who visited the lodge, few were brave enough, resilient enough, to make the trek down the crater to the lake's edge.

Beth had. With Dylan.

The memory flowed in, the laughter and the freedom, the brilliant sense of adventure that had seduced her so completely. A cone of land rose up almost mystically from the center of the water. Wizard Island. During the day, a small boat made hourly trips, allowing tourists an up close look.

Beth and Dylan had spent the night.

She'd always wondered how he'd wrangled that, but figured a combination of cold hard cash and the St. Croix name could secure just about anything.

Lance had proven that in the most hideous way imaginable.

"Can you see Orion?"

The question, his voice, overrode the moment of darkness, washing over her like a warm summer breeze on a cold winter day. She looked from the lake below to the sky above. "Isn't it a little late for Orion? I thought he was only visible during winter."

"It is late," he acknowledged. "But not too late."

She scavenged the array of stars, looking for the three pinpricks in a row.

"Lay back," Dylan said. "You can see better that way."

She did, and he was right. "There's the belt!"

"Just a little faded," Dylan said, lowering himself beside her. He stretched out on his back with one hand behind his head, not touching her, but still, she felt his warmth.

"Do you think the moon looks sad?" she asked, remembering the legend behind the constellation.

"The moon just is," Dylan said. "It's neither happy nor sad."

"I think she still mourns him."

Dylan rolled to his side, one hand reaching out to finger the ends of her hair. "She killed him."

Beth looked at him, and her heart took on a low strum. Her whole body heated, even though a chill blew through the night air. Dylan looked dangerously sexy stretched out on the comforter, one arm crooked with his hand supporting his head, while his free hand lazily played with her hair. His eyes weren't hard like before, and yet, still they glowed.

"She didn't mean to kill him," Beth defended, like she always did. "It was just one of those things. She was doomed from the moment she laid eyes on him."

"I don't believe in fate, Bethany. That's a cop-out. We each create our own destiny."

The tightness of her throat became an ache in her chest. "Orion distracted Artemis," she said, referring to the legend from Greek mythology, where Artemis was the goddess of the moon and the hunt. "When she was with him, she neglected her responsibilities. The night sky went completely dark."

"When she was with him, she lived for the very first time," Dylan countered. "Everything would have balanced out if she'd given it a chance."

''Killing him killed her.'' That's why she placed his body and those of his hunting dogs in the sky. ''That's why the moon looks so sad and cold.''

An odd glitter moved into Dylan's eyes. ''And who said you weren't a romantic?''

She had. There was no room for romance in her life. No room for passion. Like Artemis, she knew the price, and while she didn't worry about herself, on the cold day she'd buried her unborn baby and her father, she'd vowed to never again hurt someone she loved.

Dylan watched her speculatively, prompting her to return her attention to the sky. For the first time in longer than she could remember, peace flowed through her. She didn't want to jeopardize that by looking too long at Dylan. Just being close to him was hard enough. Her body tingled with awareness of his presence, as though some mind-numbing tonic pulsed to every nerve ending.

''Did you come here with him?''

The question zinged in from the darkness and pierced the blanket of serenity. Somehow, it seemed a violation of something sacred to bring up Lance in this place where happy memories dwelled.

''No,'' she whispered. ''Never.'' He hadn't offered, and she hadn't asked.

Dylan swore softly. ''Jesus, Bethany, what happened?''

''Not now,'' she whispered, rolling to her side to look at him. ''Please. Don't dirty this place with what happened between me and Lance.''

''I wasn't talking about Lance.''

The ache in her chest shifted, deepened. ''Earlier you asked what I wanted,'' she said. ''Then I said nothing, but that's not true. I want tonight, Dylan. I want a night without having to think about the nightmare waiting back in Portland. A night without thinking about what the future holds. A night of just being. Can you give me that?''

The hand playing with her hair stilled. ''Is that all you want?''

She didn't dare think beyond the simple request, to the hum deep inside. "Yes."

"Then close your eyes and let go."

He made it sound so easy. Just close her eyes and let go. But Beth knew what happened when she quit looking, knew the fantasies that shimmied close. Knew the vulnerability. Too vividly she remembered the night in the car, when she'd closed her eyes and Dylan had put his mouth to hers.

The memory should have stopped her.

"Behave," she said, doing as he instructed. Part of her wanted to hold on to her dismay, at herself for being so weak and betraying her self-respect that night on the mountain, at him for just being there, but negative feelings seemed a desecration of the pristine beauty. And how could she be angry, upset, when the night she'd considered the greatest mistake of her life had resulted in the most precious gift imaginable?

Time passed. The night crawled around them, deeper. Darker. Somewhere out there, coyotes and elk and owls prowled the world, their howls and bugles and hoots mixing into a soothing rhythm.

"May I?"

The question was soft, uncertain. Opening her eyes, Beth glanced at Dylan, not at all prepared for the way the moon-cast shadows played across his face. "May you what?"

He nodded toward her stomach, where her right hand rested. "I've been lying here watching you," he said, his voice surprisingly hoarse. "Seeing your hand there, spread wide, so protective. Right or wrong, it's my child, too." His eyes met hers. "And I'd like to touch my son or daughter."

No, Beth thought wildly. *No.* Having Dylan so close she could feel the heat of his body was hard enough. Having his hand on her stomach...

"Okay," she said. It was a small thing to ask, after all.

Nothing compared to what lay ahead. How could she deny a father the right to touch his child?

Dylan scooted closer, bringing with him more warmth, the subtle aroma of clove and sandalwood overriding pine. He lifted his hand slowly, brought it to rest on top of hers with equal finesse. His palm was wide and square, his fingers thick and warm.

Talented, she remembered, and shivered.

"Thank you," he surprised her by rasping, then surprised her even more. He smiled. Full and sensuous, the curl of his lips curled something like inside her. She felt the tug, the melting, clear down to her toes.

"You're welcome," she whispered, then looked back toward the star-filled sky.

Quiet settled between them, peace lapping at her like the gentle waters of a lazy lake on a warm summer day. Gradually, she felt herself letting go of the fierce control she had to retain around Dylan, and her limbs turned heavy, leaden. She should ask him to take her back to the cabin, she thought in some hazy corner of her mind. But she wasn't ready. Didn't want to leave. Didn't want the night to end.

Just a few minutes longer, she told herself. She'd just close her eyes…

Dylan watched her sleep. She looked surprisingly peaceful, considering the tension she'd worn like armor for the past week. Just that morning he'd worried over the pale hue to her skin, the dark circles shadowing her eyes, the strain coiling her body so tight. Now, however, now she lay on the comforter beneath the stars, as still and serene as the lake below.

He'd give just about anything to know what really dwelled beneath the surface.

Frustration drilled through him, and again, he didn't have a damn clue what to do. He didn't know what had possessed him to bring her here, either. Her, of all people.

Here, of all places. Here, where he was destined to see a smile light her face, rather than the frown he'd seen entirely too much of this past week.

Smiles were dangerous, he knew. From Bethany, they were downright lethal.

Maybe his grandfather and Lance had been right. Maybe he really was out of his mind. The woman sleeping next to him was carrying his child, the result of a night she would give anything to take back. She might be going to prison. For murdering his cousin. Yet here he lay like he hadn't a care in the world, idly stroking her abdomen, where their baby grew.

God help him, he wanted to touch her elsewhere.

She sighed in her sleep, shifting closer, and Dylan almost groaned out loud. He wanted to believe he'd brought her here, away from the glare of the world, because of the baby. Because something had gone a little crazy inside him when he'd followed her from the hotel to the department store, then onto the highway north. When he'd realized how easily she could slip across the border to Canada and vanish forever. With his child.

That's what he wanted to believe, all he could allow himself to believe. Anything else was crazy.

A man of passion and fire couldn't live in a palace of ice.

But he'd sure as hell tried.

With damning clarity he remembered the first time he saw her, back when she'd been only sixteen. She'd been sitting on a bench at school, by herself, so closed, so tightly sewn up, that Dylan had wondered if anyone could reach her. Doing so became a quest for him, to find a way to touch the untouchable. To bring a smile to those sad lips. To make those fathomless eyes sparkle.

Three long years passed before she let him in.

Lance called him a fool.

But she'd been so damn lost, and for some stupid reason, Dylan had wanted to help her find herself, trust herself. Later, as she'd gradually opened to him, he'd realized Bethany would never be free to live and laugh and love, until she realized she wasn't like her mother. She wasn't shallow, didn't use and discard people at will. She didn't hurt others for kicks.

He'd tried to prove that to her. He'd dedicated himself to the task with more conviction than he'd ever approached anything.

In the end, he'd failed.

Left alone so much as a child, Bethany had taken her cues on how life should be, how a relationship should be, from television. She wanted to be June Cleaver.

Dylan didn't come close to being Ward.

But he'd tried. He'd tried to fit into her make-believe world of how life should be, tried to prove passion and stability, serenity, could live in harmony. Obstacles, he'd always believed, were made to be overcome. But then there'd been the baby, and then the ambush. Then she'd turned her back on him. And then she'd cut out his heart by marrying the St. Croix prince. Lance had been better for her in so many ways, Dylan knew. More suited. Able to give her the stability she craved.

Now he realized his cousin had only deepened the wounds left by Dylan. If the son of a bitch wasn't already dead, Dylan would have killed him.

Bethany sighed in her sleep, snuggled closer. So close her breasts teased his chest. He tensed, reminding himself of all the reasons he shouldn't do what he'd wanted to since the moment he saw her sitting on the chaise lounge, staring vacantly toward the Cascades.

Her eyes drifted open and saved him from himself. She gazed at him, the blur of longing and desire piercing as mortally as the arrow with which Artemis killed Orion. Something inside him stirred. Something ancient. Something more powerful than common sense or self-preservation.

Need. Need stirred inside him. And only one woman

had ever truly satisfied the thirst. He lifted a hand to the side of her face and cupped the curve of her cheek, stroked her soft skin.

Her eyes grew softer, her lids heavier.

The need that had been liquid hardened, and he lowered his face toward hers.

Something hot and fierce and wild flashed in her gaze. He felt her tense, but couldn't stop her from rolling away. He stared at her rigid back and shoulders, trying like hell to destroy the urge to pull her to him, show her she didn't need to be afraid.

"Don't turn away from me, Bethany."

A deep breath shuddered out of her, but she said nothing, just stared over the crater, the gorgeous body that had been soft and sinuous moments before, now unyielding.

"Bethany?"

"Why are you doing this?" she asked, turning to look at him. An unexpected note of frustration tightened her words. "Why can't you leave well enough alone?"

Because he was a fool in every sense of the word. "Old habits die hard," he said by way of answer, knowing that was no answer at all.

"Dylan—"

"Sh-h-h," he soothed, reaching out to feather the ends of her hair. He saw the alarm flare into her eyes, the way her body braced itself for battle. He saw, and he hated. "It's just you and me now, sweetheart. You don't need to pretend anymore."

Her gaze met his. "Who says I'm pretending?"

"Your eyes."

Just like that she shuttered the naked longing away, securing it behind the wall of indifference she'd fashioned to an art form.

"You're wrong," she rasped, but didn't pull away. Though she lay on her side, he could see her standing tall. "You don't know me as well as you think you do. Maybe you were right earlier. Maybe I *was* trying to kill you. Maybe I killed Lance.''

Through the darkness, he tried not to smile. The bravado in her voice replaced frustration with admiration. He knew what she was doing. He saw the barrier she was trying to erect as plainly as though she'd slapped bricks and mortar between them.

Selecting a hammer, Dylan began to chip away. He lifted his hand to her face, gently stroked. ''Why would you want to kill me?''

Her lips twitched. ''Where do I start?''

''Not everything has to start,'' he whispered, as always speaking on one level, communicating on another. ''Some things just are.''

''And some things just end,'' she countered, but didn't pull away.

''It's a chance I have to take.''

Her eyes met his. ''Still the tough guy, aren't you?''

He slid his thumb toward her lower lip. So full. So soft. ''You'd be surprised.''

''Oh?''

He watched the way she watched him, the defiance and challenge and curiosity. The courage. She talked a good game, but she wasn't turning from him. Nothing was stopping her from surging to her feet and marching back to the Bronco. Nothing stopped her from putting an end to this before they reached the point of no return.

The knowledge speared through him, and just like that, his body hardened. God help him, despite everything, the pain of the past and the lies of the present, the uncertainty of the future, he wanted her. To hold her and taste her, to be inside her once again. To feel her skin welcome him, her thighs bracket him. Even if she killed him in the process. Which she very likely would. Maybe not physically, but a man needed more than a body to live. A man needed a heart and a soul. A man needed passion.

Those Bethany could shred in a heartbeat.

"You won't kill me," he said, fingering her mouth. His words were purposefully silky. "I won't let you."

"How are you going to stop me?" she asked with a strained bravado he had to admire.

"Like this," he said, and lowered his mouth to hers.

Chapter 9

Nothing prepared her. She saw his eyes glaze over too late, the hum in her blood drowning out common sense. A protest leapt through her, but before she could voice it, Dylan put his mouth to hers and laid siege to her soul. He leaned over her, his big body blanketing out the chill of the night, his warm hand settling against the side of her face in a feathery caress.

The stream of longing caught her by surprise. Thick and heady, the dangerous desire welled up from deep inside and pulsed to every nerve ending. Her heart strummed low and hard, pounding a rhythm as old and provocative as time itself.

He changed the angle of the kiss, deepened it, tentative exploration giving way to a full-scale invasion. His whiskers scratched the side of her face, soft as she remembered.

Tendrils of heat licked hotter. She'd forgotten how quickly a flash fire could consume everything in its path.

The feel of his mouth against hers seared the walls she'd tacked up between them. What her mind had struggled to forget, her body remembered. But this was no teenage boy's kiss, no fumbling in the dark. This was a man's kiss, full and deep and demanding. Just like that night in the cabin.

She lifted a hand to cup his cheek, holding him as he was holding her. He was almost on top of her now, big, warm, solid, leg to leg, hip to hip. Desire to desire.

Stop, shouted the voice of self-preservation, but desire hummed louder. Since the moment she'd seen Dylan standing by the pool and looking at her with those scorched-earth eyes of his, a battle had raged deep within her. He'd looked tall and strong, enduring, and for a dangerous moment, the desire to feel his arms close around her had overridden all else. To pretend for just a heartbeat, to dream. To return to the oblivion of the night they created a child.

But remembering was dangerous, because remembering made her forget. Remembering made her careless. Remembering made her wonder. What if she and Dylan had shared more time together before life exploded around them? What if he hadn't stormed out of the cabin? What if she hadn't run after him? What if there'd never been an ambush? What if the baby had lived? What if her father hadn't been called home because his daughter was in the hospital? What if his twin-engine hadn't crashed?

Pain sliced in from the past. She cried out, stiffening beneath Dylan as though she lay on needles, not a soft blanket.

Immediately, he pulled back. "Bethany?"

Her chest tightened. Who was this man, she wondered inanely. Who was this devastating man looking at her with gentleness in eyes that usually blazed with fire and passion. His hands were big and hard and capable of violence, she knew that, but the way he reverently skimmed his fingers along the line of her cheek reminded her of an artist putting finishing touches on a priceless glass figurine. He softly stroked the side of her face, easing the hair behind her ear.

She stiffened, knowing what he must see, not just in *her* eyes, but where her cheekbone gave way to hairline. Lance had wanted her to have the nasty scar removed, but somehow, that had seemed wrong to Beth. Not just weak, but dangerous. If she removed the reminder, she might forget the lesson.

"Don't," she whispered.

There was a shattered tenderness in Dylan's gaze, and it burned. "I'm not going to hurt you, sweetheart."

"So ugly…" she murmured.

"No," he said with absolute conviction. "You're the most beautiful woman I've ever known."

The words touched deep, caressing that dark, lonely place she'd tried to wall away. With his hand, he continued to stroke the side of her face, gently skimming along the faded line. With his body, all tense and leaning over hers, he kept the cold night at bay. And with his eyes, dark and brimming with a ferocity she couldn't begin to fight, he reached clear down into her soul.

With incredible finesse, the years between them dimmed, dissolved, the pain of betrayal fading into nothingness, hard-learned lessons dissolving into red-hot desire.

"Kiss me," she whispered. "Kiss me like you mean it." Like he had that night in the cabin, when he'd put his mouth to hers and reminded her of sensations she'd tried to forget.

He needed no more invitation than that. He lowered his face to hers, but she put a hand to the back of his head and sped up the process. Their mouths met somewhere in the middle.

Sensation whirred through her. Aside from that one desperate night, years had passed since she'd been touched like this, kissed, possessed.

"Bethany," he whispered, his mouth sliding from hers to skim her jawbone, nibble at her ear. "You're killing me…"

She arched beneath him, giving him better access to her neck. She loved the feel of his lips skimming the tender flesh there, his tongue teasing. Her nipples tightened and tingled, begged. The ache between her legs liquefied.

"Dylan…"

"Sh-h-h." His mouth returned to hers and sensation exploded anew. Need blurred everything. Coherent thought scattered. Mouths worshipped. Hands explored. Bodies slid. Legs tangled. She shifted beneath him, allowing him to settle between her thighs. She felt him straining there, felt the heat, the strength.

And she longed to feel it deeper. The need was acute, the desire overwhelming.

"Dylan," she whispered. "Touch me."

Something deep and dark and primal tore from his throat. He kept his mouth to hers though, communicating with his body not his voice. He deepened the kiss, making love to her with his mouth as thoroughly as he'd once loved her with his body. She felt him slide a hand to her waist, where he quickly worked his way under her shirt.

Deep inside she started to soar as his warm fingers and palm slid along her the flesh of her stomach. Her breasts tingled, ached. Longed.

But they were also denied. He stretched his hand over her stomach, spanning from below her bra to above her panty line. There he cupped, cradled.

It was shockingly intimate.

"Higher," she urged, and against her open mouth, she would have sworn he laughed. But he also obliged her. His hand slid to her chest, where he unfastened the front clasp of her bra. And then his fingertips were skimming around her nipples, softly, excruciatingly softly, little circles, feather soft touches.

The cry ripping from her throat barely sounded human.

She couldn't stand it, the measured, teasing torture. The anticipation. "Please…" she whispered.

And he did. His forefinger and thumb converged over

the tip of her nipple, rolling it into a tight bud and shooting tingles of desire to every corner of her body.

She didn't know who started to rock first. She might have lifted her hips, or he may have started grinding his. Maybe it happened simultaneously. She only knew that they moved together, hunger a fever in her blood.

"Bethany," he murmured, his fingers still playing with her nipple. He slid his other hand inside her pants and panties, easing his forefinger into the wetness between them. Then he groaned. "I never thought this would happen again," he murmured, then slipped inside.

Beth cried out. Her interior muscles clenched and convulsed around him. The desire to feel him fully penetrate her knocked the breath from her lungs…and the haze from her heart.

Dylan lay on top of her. She had her legs wrapped around his. His erection pressed into her; he had a finger stroking deep inside her. Her whole body was trembling and alive and on fire. Hungering. She wanted to let go of everything and step off the edge of the world once again, and just let herself fall.

And fall.

And fall.

But there was no such thing as an eternal free fall. Sooner or later, she had to crash back to earth.

Reality chose that moment to surface, reinforcements of preservation and memory spilling in from all directions. Beth abruptly pulled away, shocked. That was the danger of Dylan St. Croix, she knew. With him, she forgot everything she knew about caution and preservation. With him, she remembered only the glory of feeling and savoring.

"Bethany?"

She looked at him stretched out inches away, and felt her heart shatter. "I can't do this," she whispered.

Something flickered in his eyes. Something hot. "What's wrong?"

Everything, she thought desperately. Everything. She

was a prime suspect in a murder she hadn't committed, and she was carrying the child of a man she'd hoped to never see again. But here she was, as passion-drunk as her mother, about to surrender herself, her soul, to the man who was like her own personal albatross.

And her body didn't give a damn. It strummed and begged...

"This is wrong," she said, struggling to close the door deep inside, the door his kiss lulled open. Behind it burned the desire and intensity and recklessness he stirred within her, the out-of-control emotions that resulted in so much devastation. The miscarriage. Her father's death. "This isn't what I want."

The lines of his face, lines that had blurred with passion and desire only moments before, hardened. "You mean it's not what you want to want."

The disappointment in his voice, the scorn, the truth, scraped. She pushed up into a sitting position and wrapped her arms around her legs.

"Take me back to the cabin." She couldn't stay here with him, not alone like this on a blanket beneath the stars, where the embers of faded dreams echoed on the breeze. "Please."

Frustration tore through Dylan. She sat only a few feet away, but the wall between them jutted up to the night sky, thick and strong and as impenetrable as ever. He drank in the way the gauzy light of the moon played with the ends of hair his hands had tangled, her swollen lips and fathomless eyes, and cursed himself a fool of the worst kind. Clothes sex. *With Bethany.* He couldn't believe it. A few minutes longer and he would have done something he hadn't done since he was fifteen years old.

What the hell was he thinking?

He wasn't. That was the problem. He knew better than to touch her with his hands, much less his mouth. She'd always been his one weakness, able to make him forget truths he needed to remember. He didn't fit into her neat, orderly world, and she didn't belong in his. She couldn't abide the way Dylan muddied the waters of her life. And even though he knew with a few skillful touches he could turn her body liquid and wanting all over again, he also knew she'd never let him touch her heart.

With any other woman, that truth wouldn't matter. Sex was sex, and sex was great. Why tangle it with emotion? He could have her willing and beneath him and put out this dangerous fire between them, once and for all.

But this was Bethany, the only person who'd ever made him wish he was a different man. A *better* man. A man who could live in an ice palace without destroying the beauty.

"I was wrong," he ground out. "Maybe you will kill me, after all."

She watched him with those wary, exotic eyes of hers. "You mean like I killed Lance?" she asked quietly.

He stood and extended a hand. "I'm not scared of fire pokers."

She looked at his outstretched arm, his palm open, then straight into his eyes. "What are you scared of?"

His smile was tight. "A smart man learns to never reveal his weakness."

A shadow crossed her face. "So does a smart woman," she said, standing on her own. She stood there a moment, a lone woman with the cool breeze caressing her soft brown hair, the moon's light kissing the flawless skin of her face. Stars lit the night. The crater gaped behind her. Deep. Dark.

And for the first time, Dylan realized just what a steep fall awaited.

"Come on," he said, taking the fine-boned hand she'd denied him. Her skin was alarmingly cold, prompting him to curl his fingers around hers. He wasn't at all surprised she didn't return the gesture.

At the Bronco, Dylan helped her into the passenger seat,

but didn't say another word. He rounded the engine and slipped behind the steering wheel, closing out the pine-filled night gently, when he wanted to slam. They drove through the darkness and back to the cabin in silence. Went inside, in silence. Walked down the hall, in silence.

Slept. Alone. In silence.

Morning teased in through the sheer curtains. Beth stretched in the comfortable bed, not ready to leave the cocoon of cotton sheets and glorious down. The memory of the dream lingered. The same dream she'd awoken from the night before she married Lance. Of Dylan. Waiting for her at the altar. Tall. Strong. His ridiculously sensuous lips curled into a wicked little half smile. Those eyes of his burning hot and slow.

"Go away," she whispered. "Go away."

But, of course, Dylan didn't take orders or put on airs, didn't do anything to make life easier on those around him. Not the man, nor his dream counterpart. Otherwise, he would have left her alone the night before her wedding. He would have never forced her to confront herself that night in the cabin.

He wouldn't have kissed her *last* night.

But no. Not Dylan St. Croix. He came and went as he pleased. Took and gave. Lived. He called it honesty. She called it rebellion. He was so determined not to be like his dignified grandfather or playboy father, his ambitious cousin. He didn't want to move dutifully through a life preplanned from birth. If he wanted something, he went after it, whether it was politically correct or socially acceptable. Sometimes, Beth thought, he'd gone out of his way to make his St. Croix ancestors roll over in their elaborate graves.

Once, the wildness of it all, the spontaneity, had thrilled her like nothing else. For a short time the passion that drew them together blotted out the rest of the world. But in the end, it had also ripped them apart.

Because Beth wanted more. More than wildness and exhilaration, more than mind-numbing sex. More than a fire that burned everything in its path and made her forget about right and wrong. She couldn't go through life like her mother, so drunk on desire that she couldn't see straight. Think straight. That she hurt other people. That she didn't care about anyone or anything but being in Dylan's arms and his bed. Or the back of his truck. Or his grandfather's cushy study. Or the side of a lake. Or—

She wanted stability.

She wanted endurance.

She wanted love.

Dylan St. Croix couldn't give her any of that.

The truth cut deep, and suddenly Beth had to move. She couldn't lounge around in bed, reliving the past and fantasizing about a future that could never be. She had to do something, anything.

After pulling on a pair of light blue pants and a loose-fitting white shirt, she worked a brush through her hair, noticing that the woman staring back from the mirror looked tired, but an unmistakable glow shimmered in her eyes. And Beth smiled. The baby.

Dylan's baby.

Her chest tightened. She'd never fully be away from Dylan, she realized. Even if she never saw the man in the flesh again, she'd see him in their child. Maybe the easy smile, or the stunning green eyes. The shock of dark, dark hair.

Something deep inside stirred, and she abruptly turned from the mirror and headed down the hall. The aroma of coffee came first. Then the raspy timbre of his voice.

"I've got her, don't worry. She's not going anywhere."

Beth stopped abruptly.

Dylan laughed. "She can try, but sooner or later she'll realize that's impossible. There's nowhere she can go that I won't find her."

Her hand instinctively found her stomach, as her heart started to pound painfully against her ribs.

"I'll take my chances," he drawled. "Hell, Zito, who knows? I might even enjoy myself while I'm at it."

Disappointment stole her breath. Last night, his kiss had tempted her to believe he was on her side, but now here he was, talking about her to Detective Zito like she was a pawn to be moved at will.

Determination pushed aside the shock. Bethany Rae Kincaid St. Croix was nobody's pawn.

She slipped down the hall and into her room, closing the door and securing a chair beneath the knob. Slinging her purse over her shoulder, she eased open the window and crawled onto the wide porch. The scent of pine came to her immediately, drawing her attention to the early morning sun glinting through the pine forest. Without car keys she couldn't go far, but if Dylan thought she'd made a run for it, then he would look for her. She would slip back inside then, grab the keys and be off before he returned. Now, she had only to hide.

"Going somewhere, sweetheart?"

She spun to see Dylan strolling toward her, a cup of coffee in hand. "Damn you," she cried, then started to run.

Behind her, she heard the pottery mug shatter against the hard wood of the porch, heard Dylan swear and feet start to pound. Bare feet, she recalled, heading straight for the rockiest area she could find. Her sandals crunched down on gravel, pine needles and cones.

"Bethany!" Dylan shouted. "Stop it!"

She kept running.

"You can't outrun me," he warned.

But she didn't listen.

"You're pregnant, for God's sake!"

That got her. She put a hand to the small swell of her stomach, and stopped. Dylan was right. She could never outrun him. No good could come of trying.

''What the hell are you trying to prove?'' Dylan roared from behind her.

Lifting her chin, she turned to face him. He stood there barefoot and bare-chested, faded jeans hugging his hips and long legs, dark hair a little wild. And something inside her started to thrum. Those primeval eyes of his were dark, his mouth in a hard line. Whiskers covered his jaw, thicker than the night before, with just a trace of gray. He looked like he didn't know whether to throttle her or kiss her senseless.

''I heard you talking to Detective Zito,'' she said, and the words were breathy, winded.

He stepped closer. ''It's not against the law.''

''I was naive to believe you were on my side,'' she rushed on, before she did something foolish like lift a hand to touch the dark curly hair of his chest. ''You're in this with him, aren't you? Trying to get me to trust you and confess—''

''Whoa,'' he said, frowning. ''Back up. What are you talking about?''

''I heard you!'' The words tore out, desperate, broken. ''You told him where I am. You made it sound like a game! Like you're keeping me here until he's ready to file charges—''

''Bethany.'' In one svelte move he had her shoulders in his big hands. ''Listen to me, damn it! Yes, I told him where you are. Whether we like it or not, you're a suspect.'' His gaze bore down on her, hard, penetrating. His voice sounded like broken glass. ''If you vanish into thin air, that's going to raise more than a few eyebrows. And if it's all the same to you, I'd rather my child not spend his first night in jail before he's at least seventeen years old.''

She blinked up at him. ''Jail?''

''If Zito or Livingston thought you ran, they would put an APB out for you so fast it would make your pretty head spin. The D.A. would be chomping at the bit. The media.''

He pulled her closer. "I had no choice, don't you understand? *No choice!* For you. For the baby. I had to tell him."

The logic penetrated the haze of betrayal that sent her running into the cool morning. He almost made it sound like he was protecting her. No, she corrected. Not her. The baby. His baby. *Theirs.*

"There's nothing around here for miles—where did you think you were going?"

She glanced around, saw the endless sea of pine. "Away." He didn't need to know her plan.

"There is no 'away.' Not from the truth. No matter where you turn, it's always waiting." Regret shadowed his eyes. "Only cowards pretend otherwise."

"I'm not a coward," she said, squaring her shoulders. Her mother was a coward, too scared to take control of her life, too weak to resist temptation. Too wrapped up in her own wants, her own desires, to think about the people she let down.

Beth had done everything in her power to control and shape her own destiny. To make sure nothing ever swept her away.

"You can tell yourself you ran because you heard me on the phone all you want," Dylan murmured, sliding a hand from her shoulder up her neck, to the side of her face. "But we both know the truth is you ran because of what happened last night."

She stiffened. "Nothing happened."

"Nothing? Almost making love is nothing? You're going to pretend that wasn't you and me on that blanket last night?"

Making love. The words scraped over her. "No, Dylan. Almost having sex with you is something I don't ever, ever want to forget."

His eyes flashed. "Bethany—"

She grabbed his wrist and pulled his hand from her face. She didn't want him touching her.

"I thought I remembered what it was like between us," she said, giving him the brutal honesty he swore by. "Even though I tried to forget. I thought I remembered the intensity, the insanity. I thought I remembered the way you could play me like a song, the craziness of it all. But the night of the snowstorm I realized how wrong I was. I realized the images that hau—" She broke off the words abruptly, dangerously close to revealing too much.

"That what, Bethany?"

She sighed. "That the images were nothing more than pencil sketches." Incomplete. Faded.

"And the last time we were here?" he asked, as she'd known he would. Dylan never left loose ends dangling. While Lance had been a fan of the unsaid, Dylan demanded every blunt detail.

"That night was Technicolor," she admitted. "That night was 3-D." Hot, vivid, all consuming. Just like before. "There's no point in pretending something doesn't flare between us, but—"

"That something is passion."

"And that something is dangerous. It doesn't last. It's not what I want. And that's why I can't let myself forget. Last night is as close as I can come to going over the edge again."

The little muscle in the hollow of his cheek started to thump. "I didn't let you fall."

"No you didn't." Surprise lingered. "And for that I'm grateful." There between her legs, with a hand on her breast and a finger inside, he'd known full well how badly her body burned. Many men would have pressed their advantage, kissed a little deeper, teased her nipple a little more relentlessly, urging her mind to surrender to her body. One more touch and she would have gone up in smoke.

And they'd both known it.

But Dylan had practically ripped himself away from her, held himself back like a deadly force field separated them.

"I can't take the chance again," she told him, her throat unbearably tight. "My life is blowing up all around me— I could go to jail for a crime I didn't commit. I'm pregnant. I can't tiptoe through your land mines, as well."

He winced. "You're running."

"I call it surviving." Without waiting for his reply, she turned and walked back to the cabin.

The midday news paraded across the television, the cardboard anchor smiling from one tragedy to the next. Beth sat on the cushy sofa, her feet curled beneath her, one hand idly caressing her stomach. Dylan had vanished into his room half an hour before, taking the car keys with him. Shortly thereafter, the sound of running water had rattled the pipes, necessitating every scrap of her concentration to not imagine him standing naked beneath the shower spray.

Run, instinct had prompted. Leave. Now. She could, she knew. Technically, nothing stopped her. Except the truth.

The St. Croixs had nestled their cabin in the middle of nowhere. The nearest neighbor lived over ten miles away. And while a week before Beth would have preferred wandering the old-growth pine forests to being alone with Dylan, her pregnancy changed everything. She couldn't risk becoming lost or dehydrated, couldn't risk injury. She couldn't risk her child.

"We go now live to the Portland home of Sierra Landaiche, the new wife of world-renowned pianist Henrique Landaiche and mother of Bethany St. Croix."

Beth grabbed the remote control and ramped up the volume.

"You may recall Ms. St. Croix, ex-wife of Assistant District Attorney Lance St. Croix, is widely rumored to be a suspect in his murder. As of last night, she's also missing."

Adrenaline shot through Beth like poison. She surged to her feet, heart pounding.

"Crimes of passion," Yvonne Kelly began with a glint to her eyes. "Crimes of the heart. An abrupt divorce left a beautiful woman with nothing, and now a political star poised to soar lies dead instead. How can a fairy tale go so wrong? Just where does the shadow of innocence end, and that of guilt begin?" Turning to Sierra, the melodramatic reporter smiled. "Mrs. Landaiche, what can you tell us about your daughter's relationship with her ex-husband? Is it true she was desperate to get him back?"

An image of Beth's mother filled the screen, her magnificent blue eyes shimmering with tears. Her makeup was flawless, her clothes exquisite. She looked ready for an evening on the town.

"I'm so worried about her," Sierra lamented. "She's scared and pregnant and all alone."

The remote fell from Beth's numb fingers.

"Pregnant?" the reporter echoed.

Her mother dabbed at her eyes. "We just found out yesterday, after the funeral." She sniffed with practiced drama. "No one has seen Bethany Rae since."

"Do you think she's deliberately vanished?"

Sierra ignored the question and twirled down her own path. "Come home Bethany, my darling. *Please.* I know you're scared, but Henrique and I will stand by you. We'll be there for your baby if the worst comes to pass. We'll never let you down—"

The screen went black before the melodramatic appeal could continue. "Damn it," Dylan swore from behind her. "Doesn't that woman know when to keep her mouth shut?"

Beth stood there, sickened. Stunned. Her mother had always gone for the spotlight, but this plummeted to an all time low.

"How could she?" Beth whispered. "How could she use this to her own advantage like that?"

Dylan took her shoulders and turned her to face him.

"Zito knows where you are. You have nothing to worry about."

Her throat tightened. She drank in the sight of Dylan standing there, hair still damp from his shower, wearing only a pair of faded jeans. Moisture glistened on his chest, flirted with the curly hair there. He still hadn't shaved.

"Did you hear her?" she asked, ignoring the quickening deep inside. "She announced my pregnancy to the whole world!"

"A pregnancy is a hard thing to hide."

"But it's *my* pregnancy!" she shot back. "Not hers." Fury churned. Her mother had never been content to stay in the background. She'd craved the limelight, the attention for herself. Once, before Dylan, Beth had brought home a boy, and her mother had gone out of her way to monopolize the evening. The woman had worn a low-cut blouse and a high-cut skirt. The boy had drooled. Beth had been humiliated.

"She had no right to say a damn word," she said now. "I should be able to make the announcement when the time is right, not the day after Lance's funeral."

The dark green of Dylan's eyes bore down on her. "I can call the station, demand they not air the segment again—"

"Once," she rolled on, "just once, I wish she'd think about the consequences of her actions before she barrels ahead." The tears welled before she could stop them. "It's always about her, though. Her spectacle. Her dramas. Everyone else be damned."

Dylan lifted a finger to swipe the moisture from beneath her lashes. "You're nothing like her," he whispered. "Nothing."

It was his tone, more than the words themselves, that slipped through the anger. "What?"

"I know, Bethany," he said, and lifted his hand to cradle the side of her face. "I know why you've tried so hard to not rock the boat, to live that perfect fantasy life you used to talk about. I know why you chose Lance over me. I know why you stayed with a man you didn't love."

Chapter 10

Beth tried to pull away, turn away, but Dylan wouldn't let her go.

"You're not like her," he said again, this time stronger. "And you never have been."

The words punished, because she knew they weren't true.

"How can you say that?" she asked. "How can you say that after everything that's happened?"

The pain of remembrance darkened his eyes. "You weren't responsible."

"I killed our child!" she exploded, the words tearing from her heart, dark, damning. *True.*

She saw the small muscle in his cheek leap, the cleft in his chin darken. "An accident killed our child."

"No," she whispered. "You've never been one to lie, Dylan. Don't start now." Not when she knew the truth, had lived with it for years.

"I'm not lying."

"Yes, you are!" The room started to spin, just as it had

that long ago night when Dylan had found the stick of the pregnancy test. "I was hysterical," she remembered, the pain spearing through her all over again. "I wasn't thinking straight." She'd been too blinded, too emotional.

Against the side of her face, Dylan stroked his thumb. "You were scared," he said, his voice barely more than a rasp. And his eyes, dear God his eyes…

Sorrow scratched at her throat. "You told me to stay put," she whispered, "But I didn't listen. Couldn't. I ran after you."

Dylan winced, reminding her of one of those towering Douglas firs standing tall while someone swung away with a freshly sharpened axe. "My fault," he said hoarsely. "Not yours."

Outside, the land was vast, beautiful, but inside, the paneled walls closed in on her. The ghosts gathered closer. Emotion pulsed and burned. With every corner of her soul, she wanted to leap back in time and undo the damage she'd caused. Bring her baby and father back to life. It wasn't fair that she lived, when they'd lost their lives because of her recklessness.

She pulled free of Dylan's hold. "I wasn't thinking clearly," she said, backing away, but never looking from his eyes. "I was so lost in the fire, the passion, the excitement, I didn't stop to think. And because of that, people *died.*"

His gaze gentled. "And you've been punishing yourself ever since."

The accusation hit hard, his tone so achingly tender it made her chest hurt even more. She wanted to look from the unsettling glow in his eyes, the emotion she didn't come close to understanding, but could barely breathe, much less move.

"Bethany," he said in that druggingly low voice of his. "You can't blame yourself for the miscarriage. Or the plane crash."

The tears spilled over in earnest now, a sob tearing from

her throat. "He was coming home because of me," she managed through the tears. "Because of the miscarriage. Because his little girl was in the hospital."

The chill was almost unbearable, prompting her to wrap her arms around her waist, her child, this second chance she would protect with every ounce of strength she had. "The weather was bad. He never should have taken that stupid little plane up!"

And she should have learned from her mother. She should never have allowed herself to be swept away by the whirlwind that was Dylan St. Croix. She should have realized a passion that devastating would have an equally devastating price.

Every action, Lance had always warned, had to have an equal and opposite reaction. The shadow of innocence offered no protection.

Despite that, despite everything, she couldn't look away from Dylan standing by the sofa, all tall and strong, his jeans riding low on his hips, his hair still damp.

Part of her wanted to walk across the hard wood floor and lean against his strength, feel his arms close around her. Nine years ago she would have. Nine years ago he would have crushed her in his arms before she even had a chance to move. To think.

Now, they both kept their distance.

"Your father was a grown man," he said. "He made his own decisions."

"Because of me," Beth whispered.

"Because he loved you."

"That's just it, don't you see?" The place deep inside, the place she'd walled off with ice all those years, started to bleed. "Love hurts. Passion blinds."

"And that's why you married Lance." The words were matter-of-fact, stripped of all emotion.

Beth shook her head. "No."

"Because he never hurt you," Dylan rolled right on.

"He never blinded you." He paused, frowned. "I did both."

She bit back the pain of the truth. "He was good to me, a friend when I needed one." And now he was gone. She didn't mourn him as wife should mourn a husband, but as a friend would mourn a friend.

"I didn't kill him," she whispered.

Dylan's gaze met hers, hard, burning, but he said nothing. And suddenly Beth felt naked. Dylan was the one hardly dressed, but she was the one laying herself bare. She'd been showing the world a brave face, offering bravado when deep inside, she just wanted to be held. To have someone tell her they believed in her. To know she didn't stand alone.

Not just someone, either. *Dylan.*

He squeezed his eyes shut, the struggle clear. Then he opened them and embraced her without ever moving. Shattered her with two simple words.

"I know."

Beth just stared at him. "W-what?" Her heart hammered so hard she could hardly form the question.

"I know you didn't kill him, Bethany. I know."

The words nourished her like a life-giving spring. She didn't realize how badly she'd needed to hear them, until he draped them over her like a benediction. "You do?"

He moved then, finally, so swiftly and fiercely she had no time to prepare herself. He pulled her into his arms and held her tight, ran his hands along her back. "I know, Bethany, and so help me God, I'll give my own life before I let you go to prison for a crime you didn't commit."

The hoarse vow rushed through her and around her, strong, sure, doubt lifted like debris and carried away. Her knees went weak. She leaned into him, absorbed the strength she'd spent a lifetime trying to forget. The connection flared, her blood hummed.

And a knock reverberated through the cabin.

She stiffened, her mind flashing to the conversation she'd overheard earlier.

"It's about damn time," Dylan drawled. He put a quick kiss to her forehead and strode across the room, pulled open the door.

"Did you find everything?" he asked.

Through the crack, Beth saw a scrawny boy who looked to be in his teens, replete with red hair and freckles. "The book took me a while, but yeah, I've got everything."

Dylan fished into his pocket and withdrew a wad of bills, which he handed to the boy. "You're a champ, Paul. Thanks."

"No, prob, Mr. St. Croix. Nice place you got here."

Beth watched Dylan close the door and turn toward her, two paper bags in his arms.

"Supplies," he answered before she could ask.

Intrigued, she followed him into the kitchen, where he stocked the refrigerator with milk and cheese and butter, lettuce and olives, two thick ribeyes.

Then he turned to her with a book in his hand. "For you."

She took the book with a picture of a serene-looking woman in a rocking chair on the front cover. "You got me another pregnancy book?"

"The way I figure it," he said, the smile curving his lips somewhere between sheepish and terrified, "we have a lot to learn."

The extreme fatigue finally made sense. She'd written it off to stress from the string of failed artificial insemi- nations and the divorce. She'd thrown herself into her work at Girls Unlimited, finalizing an upcoming seminar on planned parenthood for unwed teenage girls.

The irony hadn't escaped her.

She now sat in the porch swing along the back of the cabin. Beyond, the pine forest rambled along the moun- tainside as far as the eye could see. Late afternoon sun glinted through the branches. A warm breeze played lazily, bringing with it the scent of Christmas. She missed the girls at the center, looked forward to returning to her extended family.

"There you are."

She glanced up to find Dylan lounging in the doorway, shoulder against the jamb, long legs crossed at the ankles.

"You okay?" he asked.

She stood and arched her shoulders. "Fine."

"You looked a million miles away."

True enough. "I just can't believe that after wanting a baby for so long, I completely missed the first few weeks."

Dylan grinned. "I know a few women who would trade just about anything to have missed the early stages of their pregnancies."

Beth actually laughed. "Me, too." But she'd never had morning sickness, not with the child she and Dylan had conceived in passion, nor the one conceived by accident.

Inwardly, she winced. She didn't want to think of the life growing inside her as anything other than precious. Already the shame and shock were fading, replaced by the most pure, profound sense of wonder she'd ever known.

"Dinner will be ready in half an hour," Dylan said, watching her peculiarly. "There's a warm bath waiting inside."

"A bath?"

"Last night you asked for a night without worries, without thinking about the past or the future." He smiled darkly. "I thought maybe we should try again."

Around her, the world blurred. All but Dylan. He just stood there, steady and unmoving. "A bath?" she asked again.

The dark smile turned teasing. "You know, water in the tub, bubbles, jasmine to help relax?"

She shook her head, the sense of wonder growing. "A bath," she said again.

Dylan laughed. "If I'd known this was all it took to render you speechless, I would have run the water long ago."

She was naked. In Dylan St. Croix's bathroom.

Beth stretched languidly in the enormous tub, loving the feel of warm water against her skin, the crackle of bubbles. Breathing deeply of jasmine, she glanced around the big room, her gaze lingering on the counter, where Dylan's toothbrush lay next to the razor he'd yet to use.

Warmth tingled through her, completely unrelated to the temperature of the water.

As with the rest of the cabin, the St. Croixs had spared no expense when designing the bath. A combination of white marble, mirrors and beveled glass lent the room a spacious, spalike feel. Dylan's athletic bag represented the only hint of the twenty-first century. A gray T-shirt sprawled half in, half out.

More warmth, more tingles. In more places.

There was something acutely intimate about being naked in a man's bathtub, and seeing his clothes strewn about. She couldn't help but wonder what else lay in that bag, whether he was still a boxer man, or if he'd defected to briefs. Or maybe those boxer-brief combos that hugged a man's body in all the right places.

"It's not too hot in there, is it?" came Dylan's voice from the other side of the door.

She stiffened, feeling insanely like a teenage girl caught cruising through her mother's Playgirl magazines. "Too hot?"

"The water. The doctor said it shouldn't be too hot."

She sank beneath the bubbles. "The water's fine." But oh, how her body burned.

"Good," Dylan said. "Dinner's in ten."

She swallowed, hard. "I'll be there." Relief swirled through her when she heard his footfalls heading from the door and out of the room. Or was that disappointment?

Ten minutes later she stepped from Dylan's room, wearing a light purple cotton shift she'd picked up at the mall. It was hard to believe barely twenty-four hours had passed since then. She felt like she'd lived more in the past few days than she'd lived in the past few years.

"What about 'get me the damn file' do you not understand?"

Beth went completely still. She stood just outside the kitchen, enticed by the rich aroma of steak, horrified by the hard edge to Dylan's voice.

"I don't care about the risks," he seethed. "I care about what's in those files. If you're not up to the job—" His voice broke off abruptly.

Beth peeked into the gourmet kitchen and found Dylan standing with his rigid back to her. His stance was that of a fighter ready to knock someone to hell and back.

"See to it that you do," he growled. "Call me when you know something." He slammed the mobile phone onto the granite counter, then swore viciously.

Beth didn't realize she'd gasped until he spun toward her. "Bethany." Fury blazed in his dark green eyes, quickly tempered by caution. "How long have you been standing there?"

"Not long," she said, struggling to breathe. The relaxation of the bath congealed into a palpable unease. "Everything okay?"

"Everything's fine."

Like hell. She knew Dylan well enough to recognize the muscle leaping in the hollow of his cheek meant he was working to keep his temper in check.

"This is hard for you, isn't it?" she asked, advancing across the hardwood floor of the kitchen.

"What is?"

"Being here," she said, knowing sooner or later they had to deal with the tension between them. "With me."

Dylan's eyes went a little wild at that, his body a little more tense.

"Away from all the activity," she clarified. "You want to be back in Portland, don't you?"

He yanked open a cabinet and pulled out two stoneware plates. "I want you safe."

She moved beside him and reached for two glasses. "We can go back."

"No," he said, pulling forks and knives from a drawer. "You need to be out of the chaos more than I need to be in the middle of it."

Reaching for the sparkling cider, she froze. The impact of his words rained down like acid. "We can't stay here forever. They could press charges. There'd be a trial."

Finally Dylan looked at her again. He set down the utensils and tilted her face toward his. The light glinting in his eyes could only be described as fierce.

"I'm not going to let that happen," he said point-blank. "No child of mine will be born behind bars."

The breath whooshed right out of her. "Dylan—"

"Go sit down, Bethany, before I have to send you back to the bathtub to relax all over again."

She stared at him a long moment, searching the severe lines and angles of his face for an explanation to the way her heart raced so frantically in her chest. Alarmed by what she saw, she pulled away and did as he asked.

Eating dinner seemed far wiser than cornering an angry male.

Beth stared out the wall of windows, toward the darkened land beyond. The sun slept now, the moon taking over as guardian of the skies. A thick blanket of clouds dimmed the light. Orion was nowhere in sight.

The blues drifted through the cabin. Lifting a hand to the window, she breathed deeply of the pine logs crackling in the fireplace. Reflected in the glass, she saw flames licking against the grate, smaller flames flickering from candles along the mantel and side tables.

She also saw Dylan moving toward her.

He'd been unusually quiet during dinner—steak and baked potato—answering her attempts at conversation with monosyllabic words or worse, masculine grunts. Tension radiated from him like heat from the sidewalk on a hot summer day. It seeped into her, as well, completely erasing the soothing effects of her bath.

But she didn't tell him that.

After dinner he'd practically ordered her into the sprawling great room, refusing to let her help with the dishes. She'd stood there staring into the darkness while he'd lit the fire, inserted the compact disc into the stereo. She'd stood there while behind her, he paced.

And now she stood there as he approached her.

Through the hazy reflection in the window, their gazes met. He stopped a few inches behind her, so close the heat from his body whirled around hers. So close his breath shimmied across the back of her neck. So close she couldn't begin to mistake the struggle in those primeval eyes of his.

"Dance with me, Bethany Rae."

The way he said her name caused her heart to thrum a little harder. A lot deeper.

Closing her eyes to the heat in his, she inventoried the thousands of reasons to say no. Absolutely not. To move away from him and walk to her room, shut the door, drag a chair beneath the knob. A thousand reasons to say no, and only one to say yes.

The need she didn't begin to understand.

Opening her eyes, she drank in the sight of him reflected there in the window, and felt something inside her shift. Loosen. Start to melt. His unshaven jaw was set, his eyes fiercer than usual. His stance was rigid, a strange combination of angry and unsure. Faded jeans hugged his long legs. His olive button-down shirt lay open at the throat, exposing the curly hair beneath.

The swift blade of longing stole her breath.

Last night you asked for a night without worries.

Just one night, she reasoned, the urge to let go of the tight rein she kept on herself strengthening with every heartbeat. His chest looked so broad and strong and...tempting. She remembered what it was like to rest her head there, to hear the steady strumming of his heart, to feel his warm breath feathering over her. His arms holding her.

Just for tonight. There could be no harm.

She turned to him and stepped into his open arms.

"You smell like jasmine," he murmured, pulling her close.

"You smell like sandalwood and smoke." Like before. Like always.

His hold on her tightened, and slowly they began to sway. He'd always preferred blues, whereas she'd favored a more upbeat tempo. But tonight the sultry melodies seemed...right.

The ambiance thickened, deepened. Tension arced and flowed, liquid lightning streaking through every nerve ending of her body. Instinct warned to pull away now, fast, but need and longing kept her in Dylan's arms. She loved the way his heart strummed a strong, steady beat, the way his chest expanded with each breath he drew. His hands skimmed her back. The front of his legs brushed hers. Another part of his anatomy pressed into her, as well. A very hard part she tried equally hard not to think about. But failed.

"I'm sorry."

The hoarse words surged through her, and she abruptly went very still. "What for?" she asked before she could stop herself. God help her, she didn't want to hear him apologize for the desire he couldn't hide. How did a woman respond—

He pulled back, cradling her face in his hands. "About what I said to you by the pool last week."

The sound of pain ripped from her heart before she could stop it. Suddenly she saw him standing by the chaise lounge all over again, tall and condemning. She remembered the surge of seeing him, the traitorous flash of joy. The sure knowledge that he'd pull her into his arms and make the nightmare go away.

Instead he'd accused her of murder.

"Don't be," she now said in a voice alarmingly thick. She needed to remember that moment, the rush of disappointment. The truth that this man could never give her what she needed.

Against her face, a single finger stroked. "I was out of line."

She laughed despite the tears scratching her throat. "Dylan St. Croix, out of line? Now there's a surprise."

Despite her teasing tone, his eyes went wild. "Damn it, I thought it was you!"

She'd still been holding him, but now her arms fell to her sides. Vaguely, she remembered hearing those same words that night.

He swallowed convulsively, the muscle in the hollow of his cheek thumping erratically. And his eyes, dear God, his eyes. She'd never seen the light blazing there. The emotion.

"I drove up to the house and saw the police cars and the ambulance," he ground out. "And I thought I was going to throw up. I thought I'd never have the chance to..." He broke off, wincing.

Her heart started to pound so hard it hurt. "To what?"

"It doesn't matter now."

"It does to me."

He squeezed his eyes shut, opened them a moment later. The ferocity remained. "No matter what else happened between us," he said, skimming his thumb along her lower lip, "I never wanted to see you hurt."

"So you accused me of murder, instead?"

"When I saw you sitting there," he bit out, "something inside me went a little crazy. I didn't want to believe what Zito said, but I had to know."

"Zito *had* to think that," she said, pulling out of his arms and backing away. She couldn't stand there like that, body to body, while they gouged out the gulf between them with the truth.

"It's his job," she pointed out, blinking back tears. "He doesn't know me. I hadn't slept with him a few weeks before."

Dylan went completely still. He stood there all rigid and towering, again reminding her of one of the timeless trees surrounding the cabin. And she'd just swung the killing blow.

Regret was swift and immediate. "That was out of line," she said, lifting her hands to his face. She knew better than to let pain talk, to let emotion run free. "I'm sorry."

His expression remained granite. "Don't be. I hurt you."

"We hurt each other," she corrected, and knew it was true. "But life goes on." It had to. "You promised me tonight," she reminded, and realized how badly she wanted to step back into his arms. Except this time, instead of feeling him holding her, she wanted to hold him. To wrap her arms around his waist and pull him to her, close her eyes and live in a pretend world where the past didn't have the power to rip her heart in two, and the future didn't hold the possibility of a prison sentence.

Just for tonight. That was all. Reality would come crashing down soon enough.

"If there's one thing I've learned about Dylan St. Croix," she said, loving the feel of his whiskers beneath the pads of her fingers, "it's that he's a man of his word. Let's not spoil what we have left with what we can't change."

Still, he didn't move, just stood there looking at her like he'd never seen her before. Like he had no idea what language she spoke. No idea what to do with her.

She slid her hands from his face to the back of his neck

and pressed her body to his. The surge was immediate, the rush, the sense of homecoming.

"Dance with me, Dylan. Please."

A hard sound broke from his throat, that of frustration and restraint and strength, but he lifted his hands to her waist and started to sway against her body. She felt him begin to relax, felt the tension drain from his tight shoulders and rigid back. Felt one hand slide around her waist and up her back, where he simply spread his fingers and held.

Felt her world, her resolve, shatter.

What was it about this man, she wondered in some hazy, barely functioning corner of her mind. What was it about this man that not only made her forget every hard lesson life had pounded into her, but made her *want* to forget? To simply enjoy the moment? When was the last time she'd danced in front of a fire? Danced at all. When was the last time she'd lived? *Really* lived?

The answer should have patched the cracks in the icy wall she'd erected around her heart, but instead, the thaw accelerated.

Across the room, the fire crackled, while the taper candles wavered valiantly. The singer's raspy voice filtered around her and through her, as drugging as the feel of Dylan's body moving with hers. They held each other tightly, fiercely, silently communicating what words could not.

"Look at me," he commanded softly, pulling back.

Three simple words, but they made her mouth go dry, her body liquid. She knew that intimate tone, had fought it in her dreams. Had surrendered to it the night they'd made a baby. Now, she lifted her eyes, wondering how she'd find the strength to tell him no. Tell herself.

"It was less than fifteen minutes," he said.

She blinked. "W-what?"

"The woman I brought here," he said, never looking away. "We were here less than fifteen minutes."

Her heart started to pound. Hard. A strange combination of elation and dread tangled. "I don't understand."

"No," he said with a slight smile, "I don't suppose you do. I'm not sure I do, either. Holly sure as hell didn't." He hesitated, sliding a hand from her shoulders to her neck, where he spread his fingers wide.

Beth braced herself. It was bad enough imagining Dylan here with another woman, here where she'd given him her virginity. But to hear him talking about it, about her, shattered.

"We came here for the weekend, but left before I unloaded the car. I never saw her again after I dropped her off."

Beth just stared at him, trying to understand what he was telling her. "She was that mad at you?"

"No, I was that disgusted with myself." His thumb cruised over her jaw and slid along her lower lip. "Seeing her here felt like a violation of something precious."

The breath stalled in her throat. "Why are you telling me this?"

"I needed you to know."

She quirked a smile, because deep down, she wanted to cry. Who was this man, she thought again. Who was this man who shattered her with gentleness every time she braced herself for passion?

"True confessions?" she asked with a wry humor she didn't come close to feeling.

His lips, those full, tempting lips of his, curved into a wicked little half smile. "Something like that."

But it was one confession she didn't want. Knowing hurt. Knowing ripped down one of those walls she'd thrown up between them, the wall of pain caused by thinking of Dylan making love to another woman, in the bed where Beth had given him her virginity. Where'd they'd loved and laughed, conceived a child.

But that wall was gone now, and without it, Beth felt like she stood in his arms, naked.

Through a foggy tunnel of time and space, she saw him lowering his head toward hers, felt the hand at the small of her back press her closer. Longing curled through her, hot, liquid, eager. She wanted to feel his mouth on hers again, wanted to drink of him, taste him, thank him for the precious, precious gift of his confession. And the child in her womb.

"You should go to bed now," he murmured, his lips cruising over her forehead.

She blinked, confused. She'd felt his body pressed against hers. His hard body. She knew how aroused he was, what he clearly wanted.

"Bed?" she whispered.

He nodded, turning her stiff shoulders toward the darkened hall. "Sleep," he said. "You've got a big day tomorrow."

Her body was hot and liquid and on fire, and he was sending her to bed, alone. But he was also grinning, the dark green of his eyes glinting with a promise she wanted to trust. "What's happening tomorrow?"

"A surprise."

She smiled despite herself, the ancient banter flowing from her as naturally as a spring bubbling from the earth.

"I hate surprises," she said, as she always did.

And he laughed. As he always did. "You'll like mine."

Chapter 11

The young elk looked up from the riverbed, startled. Nearby, a large female surveyed the dense pine forest.

Dylan stopped abruptly, taking Bethany's hand and pulling her to his side. He pointed toward the opening, where the small male once again drank from the edge of the crystal clear water.

"He's wonderful," she whispered, her voice barely carrying above the sound of rushing water. The Rogue River was running fast today, the warm temperatures melting off snow quicker than normal. Further down the mountain, Dylan felt sure the white-water rafting outfitters were in full swing.

He eased forward, bringing Bethany with him. Her hand felt small in his, soft, much like her body had felt in his arms the night before. The mountains always had that effect on her, helped her relax when nothing else could.

Sending her to bed last night, alone, had taken every ounce of strength he possessed. If she'd lingered one second longer, if she'd looked at him with those startling blue eyes of hers, if she'd touched him, he might have surrendered to need and carried her to the king-size bed instead.

But Bethany didn't need that from him. She didn't need blazing, in-your-face passion. She needed time. She needed space. She needed tenderness.

And even if it killed him, he was determined to give her what he'd been unable to nine years before.

Deep inside, he could no longer deny what his heart had been trying to tell him all along. No matter how damning the evidence, Bethany had not killed Lance. She was a compassionate, caring woman. Yes, she'd carved Dylan out of her life with brutal precision, but he'd broken her heart first by not sharing her immediate happiness over the child they created.

This time, he vowed, would be different.

The years separating them had given him a maturity and insight he'd not possessed as a rebellious twenty-one-year-old. He knew what was important now. What mattered. And even though the child Bethany carried had been conceived by accident, Dylan found himself excited about being a father.

"It's so beautiful," she whispered.

The smile in her voice warmed deeper than the sun glinting through the pines. He looked at the softness in her eyes, the glow to her cheeks, and knew he'd move heaven and earth before he let this woman go to prison.

She tugged on his hand and led him to the water's edge. They were far enough away from the elk now that they posed no threat.

Bethany stepped onto a boulder and tilted her face toward the blue sky, where a few fat white clouds drifted lazily across the horizon. "Almighty winds which blow on high," she said with a low laugh, "lift me now so I can fly."

Dylan just stared. She looked like a goddess standing there against the old-growth forest and the impossibly blue sky, her white shirt and khaki shorts the only hint she belonged in this world, and not mythology.

She tossed a smile over her shoulder. "Isis," she said. "When I was a kid, I watched the show every Saturday morning."

He laughed—he hadn't been that far off.

Bethany eased down on the boulder and pulled her knees to her chest, gazing upstream, where two more elk drank from a tributary leading into the river.

Dylan forced himself to remain where he was and not slip behind her on the rock, ease his arms around her and pull her against his chest. But for a moment there, he found himself wishing that make-believe world she talked of really did exist. That they could stay here and raise their child.

Their child. The thought stirred something deep inside. Something primal. Something unbearably soft.

He was going to be a father.

He picked up a flat rock and slung it into the water, watching it skip twice before sinking. He should already be a father. He should have an eight-year-old son or daughter. It was impossible not to wonder about what could have been, what would have been if he'd not stormed out of the cabin that night. If Bethany hadn't followed.

He looked at her now, at the faraway expression on her face, and felt his chest tighten. He'd once accused her of being a coward, but now he knew how remarkably brave she was. How strong. Being a suspect in Lance's murder was bad enough. But to be carrying Dylan's child, the child of a man she wanted to obliterate from her life, he couldn't begin to imagine what that did to her.

"Penny for your thoughts," he said before he could stop himself.

She glanced over her shoulder and slayed him with a smile. "A little over a week ago I was at the center, finalizing a seminar for planned parenthood. Now I find that by the end of this year, I'll have a baby of my own."

My own. Not his, not theirs. Hers.

She shook her head. "It's hard to believe how quickly life can change."

He picked up another rock, flung it into the river. "Some things," he acknowledged. "Others never do."

She frowned. "For six years Lance let me believe our inability to have a child was my fault. My problem. He lied to me, Dylan. In making himself feel like more of a man, he made me feel like less of a woman."

Anger blasted through him, ridiculously directed at a dead man. "I can't defend him, Bethany."

"But why you?" she asked, much as she had that afternoon in the convenience store. "Why would he think you'd go along with such a huge deception?"

Because he almost had. The truth ground through him as viciously now as it had then. "Because he knew me."

"He knew you? Don't be ridiculous. If he'd known you at all, he'd have known how much you hate lies."

Yes, Lance had known that. But he'd known more, as well. He'd known how to play his trump card. And he'd known how to send marbles scattering.

"Lance asked me, because he knew I never forgave myself for the miscarriage," he admitted in a voice suddenly tight and strangled with emotions he'd tried to destroy. "Giving you a child was a way to atone for the past and give you back the dream I destroyed."

For a moment, Bethany said nothing, just stared at him like he'd just admitted masterminding a plot to clear-cut old-growth forests. Then, slowly, she stood, shoving the flyaway hair from her face.

"Forgive yourself for the miscarriage? What are you talking about?"

The point of no return had long since been crossed and violated. Only the truth remained.

"The ambush."

Pain flashed across her face, darkening her eyes and

stealing the color from her cheeks. "That wasn't your fault," she whispered above the roar of the water.

Dylan couldn't stand it one second longer. Couldn't stand being apart from her, not when she stood there on that boulder, no longer looking like a goddess, but a woman who took penance too far.

He strode toward her, joined her on the rock, lifted a hand to her face. The sun blared down and a warm wind rustled the pines, but her skin was alarmingly cold.

"I walked out the door," he said. "I walked out that door when you needed me to stay."

He saw the moisture flood her eyes as she looked away from him, further upriver where the elk no longer lounged.

"It just all happened so...fast," he said, but the words sounded as lame as they felt. He'd been ill-prepared and overwhelmed. Scared. "I needed some time to think. To get used to the idea."

She looked back at him now. "And I just needed you."

He wasn't sure how he remained standing. "I didn't know about the ambush, Bethany. I swear to God I had no idea they were on to me."

"There's no point beating yourself up," she said with a punishing measure of acceptance. "It's over and done with."

"It will never be over and done with. Because of me, our child *died.*"

Tears spilled over, streaming down her cheeks like snow melt down the mountain. "I was the one who raced after you," she whispered, "even though you asked me not to. I was the one not thinking clearly, running on blind need and fear."

"Because of me." He'd been investigating a string of drug overdoses for the college newspaper, closing in on a meth lab selling a lethal concoction. Somehow they'd caught on to him, and had sought to eliminate him before he eliminated them.

They'd eliminated him, all right. They'd killed the best

part of him, leaving the rest of him to live with the aftermath. For as long as he lived he'd never forget the flash of headlights and the screech of tires, the shouting. The blood.

If the cops hadn't arrived when they had, Dylan would be dead or serving time for manslaughter.

"My mother always told me everything happens for a reason," he said, wiping the tears from beneath Bethany's eyes. "She said every life event prepares us for the next, but I've never figured out what the hell that night prepared us for."

An odd light glowed in Bethany's eyes. "This," she said, drawing his hand to her stomach. "Now." A soft smile touched her lips. "I'm carrying your child, Dylan. Again. We were too young before, too caught up in a fantasy we didn't realize couldn't come true. I let passion blind me. I didn't think straight. I didn't put the child first. I won't let that happen again."

The words of resolve hammered through him. "I wanted to tell him yes," he ground out, and the admission hurt as badly coming out as when he'd shoved the truth down deep. "I wanted to accept the devil's offer and erase the scar from your heart. But not through lies. Not through lies." He paused, swallowed hard. "I'm not going to let anything happen to you this time," he said, sliding the flyaway hair behind her ear. "So help me God, not to you, or our child."

Our child.

She closed her eyes, opened them a moment later. Sorrow no longer lurked in her gaze, but something harder. Darker.

"There's something you need to know."

Dylan's heart started to pound more violently than the water crashing against the boulders. His chest tightened. He'd been a private investigator long enough to know nothing good ever followed those six words. They usually represented the other foot falling.

"What?" Possibilities surged and shattered. She hated him. She never wanted to see him again. She would go to court to prevent him from being a father to their child. *"What?"*

"The fire poker was in my hands."

Dylan went very still. "W-what?"

"The f-fire poker," she repeated. "It was in my hands when I woke up next to Lance." The fear in her eyes deepened. "I was holding it."

Horror replaced shock, and finally he understood the terror he caught in Bethany's gaze when she thought he wasn't looking. Why she'd tried to run. "Jesus, Bethany," he muttered, taking her shoulders in his hands. The thought of her killing Lance in cold blood, of her going to prison, twisted him up inside.

"What the hell happened that day?"

"I d-don't know."

Years of training kicked into place. "Sweet God, you didn't tell this to Zito, did you?"

Her eyes met his, so blue and impossibly large, fringed by those dark, dark lashes, giving him the first unobstructed, unprotected view into a place he'd never thought to see again. Her heart. "I haven't told anyone, but you."

The soft words hit hard, but Dylan didn't have time to think about the implication.

"They'll find my prints," she whispered.

The fear in her voice made him sick. She'd been trying to be tough, to stare down a world that wanted to believe the worst about her. But he saw the fatigue in her gaze. The worry. The punishing possibility that she might be locked away for the rest of her life. That she would not be allowed to raise her child.

Their child.

Dylan wouldn't let that happen.

"The presence of your prints on the handle won't mean anything," he growled. A good defense lawyer would shred that piece of evidence in a heartbeat. "It's your house, your fireplace. It would be more odd if your prints weren't there.''

"But don't you see?'' she asked, and her voice broke on the question. ''Someone knocked me out. Someone took off my suit and dressed me in a negligee. Someone put that poker in my hands. Whoever this someone is, they went to a lot of trouble to make me look guilty.''

"All circumstantial evidence.''

"But will a jury see it that way? Like that vulture Yvonne Kelly is so fond of pointing out, my marriage was over. I'd lost almost everything.'' She hesitated. ''If anyone finds out about Lance's lies, that the child I'm carrying is yours—''

"Damn it, Bethany—''

She grabbed his forearms. ''Tell me you'll take the baby, Dylan. If the worst comes to pass, I need to know my child will be okay. I can't stand the thought of him or her being raised by my mother or worse—''

"Our child,'' he corrected, taking her hands in his. It was all he could do not to crush her in his arms. ''Our child. And no way in hell am I letting anyone take my son or daughter from me. From us.''

For a moment she just looked at him, her mouth slightly open, her eyes as pure and blue as the sky above. Except for the glisten of tears.

Then she shattered him with two simple words. ''Thank you.''

She might as well have swung an axe at him. Not in a million years, a million dreams, would he have believed they could be like this again, communicating and sharing, touching. He wanted to savor the moment, but even more, he wanted to put his mouth to hers and take away the fear trembling there. To chase the shadows from her eyes. To hold her tight, never let go.

"Come on,'' he said instead. He helped her off the big boulder, breaking the moment of acute intimacy. Even a strong man had his limits. ''There's a great spot up the

way, with the best view for miles. It's perfect for a picnic."

She blinked. "A picnic?"

"What else did you think was in my backpack?"

She glanced toward shore, where he'd left the big pack
resting against the base of a pine. "A picnic," she whispered.

His grin turned into a smile. She deserved more than a
picnic, but until he could get back to Portland and sort this
mess out—find out what the hell Lance had gotten involved with and why someone wanted him dead—ham
sandwiches and grapes were a hell of a lot safer than what
he really wanted to give her.

"It's beautiful."

Dylan turned from spreading a blanket across the expanse of dry, packed dirt to see Bethany standing on the
edge of the cliff. She had a hand to her stomach as she
stared over the dazzling vista. Sunlight glinted across her
long sable hair, lifted gently by a subtle breeze. A smile
curved her lips. Shadows no longer lurked in her eyes.

The sight fed somewhere deep inside.

"It's like I can see the whole world," she said, turning
to face him.

He smiled. "I come here when I need to think."

"Who can think with a view like this?" She turned
toward the edge, looking over the sweep of sky and mountain and pine. A couple hundred feet below, crushed between cliffs of basalt rock, the river raced with incredible
fury. The thundering water couldn't be heard up here, just
the caw of birds, the rustle of the wind.

"Careful," he said, starting toward her. The drop was
sheer and brutal. "My rock climbing skills are a little
rusty."

She laughed. "I didn't think any of Dylan St. Croix's
skills ever became rusty."

He ignored the flash of heat. "Yeah, well. It takes practice to achieve perfection."

A light sparked in her eyes. "So that's what you call it?"

Danger signs flashed everywhere. He'd brought her here to distract her, not torture himself, but his plan seemed to be working a little too well.

"Some things don't require practice," he growled, closing in on her.

Her smile widened. "Is that a fact—"

He realized his mistake too late. Her intent. Grinning, she stepped back from his advance...but no ground awaited her foot.

Dylan roared her name and lunged. Grabbing her shoulders, he thrust her to solid ground behind him. He tried to go with her, but momentum propelled him forward, and the world dropped away.

He'd always thought about learning to skydive, but trial by fire wasn't exactly what he'd had in mind.

Time slowed to a crawl as he plummeted over the side of the mountain. He heard the shout tear from his throat, felt the brutal impact of his body slamming against the hard rock wall. But none of it seemed real. Not even the sound of Bethany's scream caught between the cliffs.

Survival instincts kicked in. He grappled against the rock face for something to hold on to, but only felt jagged edges gouge his flesh. He kicked wildly, needing to keep his body close to the rock. There was a ledge about fifty feet down—

Pain splintered through him. He lay there, stunned, dazed, afraid to move. The ledge wasn't very wide. One misstep, and his skydiving would end abruptly on the rocks below.

"Dylan!"

He blinked against the severe midday sun and saw Bethany leaning over the edge. Or was that two Bethanys? Three.

Nausea surged.

"Oh, my God, Dylan!" the now four Bethanys cried.

He blinked rapidly, but the world wouldn't quit spinning.

"Bethany…" No voice came from his throat.

There were five Bethanys now, all staring at him. Close to fifty feet separated them, he figured, making it impossible to discern her expression.

But he sure as hell heard her words. They reverberated on the wind, blasted off the side of the mountain. *"I'm sorry."*

Then she was gone.

The sun inched across the sky, headed sluggishly for its bed on the Pacific horizon. Heat soaked into the land and radiated from the rock, drenched Dylan's body. The wind that had gentled before, now shrieked in concert with the river thundering below.

It was a hell of a way to die, Dylan thought grimly, perched like some sacrificial offering up on the side of a mountain.

He lay prone, the narrow ledge not granting him the luxury of moving. He'd managed to stand once, to grapple for jutting rock formations he could grab and use to pull his body up the mountain. But he hadn't been joking when he told Bethany his rock climbing skills were rusty.

And he'd never practiced when his vision blurred.

He lay there now, unmoving. The sun beat down without mercy. A few clouds, he thought idly, wouldn't be asking so much. Maybe a gentle cooling shower. Anything but the three crows circling. Cawing. Waiting.

"Bethany!" he shouted for the hundredth time.

But for the hundredth time, nothing answered but the echo of his own voice boomeranging between the basalt cliffs.

Damn it, he'd been a fool. He'd brought Bethany to this remote stretch of the mountain, thinking only of how much she would love the view. Never once had he thought about the opportunity he was handing her on a silver platter.

Without a watch, he had no way of knowing exactly how much time had crawled by since she'd disappeared, but the sky hinted at well over two hours. Plenty of time to reach the cabin and make it back.

Unless she'd gotten lost.

"Bethany!" he shouted again. "Bethany!"

Jesus. She could be lost, hurt, in trouble. And sunning himself here thirty feet below the top of the cliff and several hundred feet above the pounding river, he couldn't do a damn thing to help her.

Or she could be on her way to Canada.

If the worst comes to pass, I need to know my child will be okay. I can't bear the thought of him or her being raised by my mother.

He'd seen the resolve in her eyes, heard the kind of fear in her voice that made a person take chances, risks, they wouldn't normally consider. The car keys sat on the bathroom counter, back at the cabin. She would find them, use them. She could speed north and be in Canada long before Zito realized she was missing.

Even if he found some way off the mountain, he might never see his child.

A violent curse tore from his heart and ground against the wind. He couldn't let that happen. Couldn't lose a second child. Couldn't lose Bethany all over again.

The sight of the sprawling St. Croix cabin almost made her weep. Bethany stumbled out of the dense pine forest and ran for the porch. She'd never considered herself directionally challenged, but all those Douglas firs looked remarkably similar. She'd passed the same abandoned gold mine at least three times.

But now she was home.

She ran up the steps and threw open the door, a blast of cool air hitting her immediately. She didn't stop and gulp it in, just staggered to the kitchen and turned on the faucet. Water. She needed water. She splashed it against her face and let it run down her neck to her T-shirt. She cupped it in her hands and drank greedily.

But her heart didn't stop pounding, her breathing didn't even out, her thoughts didn't clear.

Dylan. Dear God, Dylan.

If she lived a hundred years, she'd never forget the horror of seeing him fall off the cliff. Because of her.

Guilt cut deep. She'd been so lost in the moment, the banter between them, she'd forgotten how close to the edge she stood. If Dylan hadn't lunged for her, she would have never survived the fall.

A keening sound tore from her throat, as her hands found her stomach. Her baby. *Their* baby. Already, love for the child she and Dylan had created filled every corner of her soul.

A hideous fear backed up in her throat. She couldn't lose this baby. The thought was too vile to even consider, not after waiting a lifetime to be a mother.

Dear God, she knew what she had to do, even if doing so bucked up against every survival instinct she possessed. She had no choice. Not anymore.

She wasn't coming back.

The reality wove through Dylan like a sharp needle, piercing deep. Let her be safe, he raged silently. On her way to Canada. He could live with that. He could live with anything so long as Bethany and the baby were safe.

Or at least, that's what he wanted to believe. Now wasn't the time to think of the child he would never see, never hold, the sloppy kisses he'd never receive, the skinned knees he'd never bandage. The grins, the laughs, the tears. Now wasn't the time to think about the son he would never teach to play baseball, the daughter he would never walk down the aisle.

If he did, he'd lose his mind.

But then, maybe that was happening anyway.

The sun slid westward, long shadows taking over for the glaring streaks of light. Everything was quieter now, the world gone still. Holding its breath. Waiting.

Dylan forced the swollen fingers of his hand to uncurl. Cuts and dried blood streaked across his dry skin, but he felt no pain. Even the throbbing of his head had stopped.

Acceptance, he figured. He'd tried like hell to find a way up the sheer face of the mountain, but had finally realized the impossibility of the task. Now he wondered how long he'd last without food or water, if he'd starve, or fall asleep and roll to the rocks waiting below. The crows would prefer the former, he thought, watching them circle closer.

He blinked, and the crows became a snake.

What the hell, he thought savagely, then realized the sun had taken a greater, faster toll than he'd thought. The hallucinations had already begun.

Dylan.

Bethany. Her voice was so sweet, as drugging as always. Somehow it seemed fitting, he thought as he watched the snake dangle closer, that she'd be the one to call him to his death.

Dylan!

He exhaled a ragged breath, wishing she'd quit yelling. A man didn't want to be yelled at when he took his final breath.

"Damn it, Dylan, can you hear me?"

Everything inside him went very still. The words were urgent, desperate. He blinked hard to clear his gaze, and suddenly the snake became a rope.

Shock jerked through him. He glanced toward the top of the cliff, straining to discern shadow from imagination.

And saw her.

Chapter 12

*B*ethany.

She looked impossibly real leaning over the side of the mountain, glossy brown hair cascading around her face. Shadows stole detail, but in his mind, he saw her startling blue eyes, the way they glazed over in passion.

It was a nice image to die by.

"Damn it, Dylan! Say something!"

"What do you want me to say?" he asked lazily. "Hello or goodbye?"

"Just tell me you're okay."

"I am now," he muttered. More than okay, actually. A strange sense of peace blanketed him.

"Can you grab the rope?"

"What?" He'd never heard of needing a rope to cross over.

"The rope. It's by your right hand. Can you grab it?"

He didn't want to look away from Angel Bethany leaning over the side of the cliff, but her voice was so damn insistent, he figured he better. He ripped his gaze away and saw the snake dangling by his hand. But it wasn't a snake. He'd forgotten. It was a rope.

"I've got it secured to a tree," came Angel Bethany's voice. "A knot like you taught me. Can you pull yourself up?"

He blinked at the thick rope, and suddenly the haze cleared.

"Dylan, please!"

Disbelief surged. Joy followed quickly behind. Angel Bethany wasn't here to help him cross over, but to help him up the mountain. She hadn't run, hadn't been ripped apart by a hungry bear.

"Bethany," he muttered, looking up at her. This time, he would have sworn he saw her smile.

"I'm here, Dylan. I'm sorry it took me so long, but...all those trees look alike."

He laughed. God help him, stranded there on the mountain ledge with the Rogue River thundering below, a rope his only means of survival, he laughed.

A second rope came plummeting down then, this one with a canteen attached.

"Drink first," Bethany said. "You've got to be thirsty."

He was thirsty, all right. Hungry. Starving. But mere bread and water would never satisfy the craving making him weak. He grabbed the canteen and pulled off the lid, poured the water over his parched face. He opened his mouth as he did so, let the liquid trickle inside. And almost wept. Not because of the water, but because of Bethany.

The desire to crush her in his arms, hold her, gave him all the strength he needed.

Very carefully, he eased into a sitting position, then stood. He remained very still for a second, careful to let balance settle around him before making any radical moves. One misstep, and the rocks would rush up to meet him.

"Careful," Bethany said, but didn't need to worry. He wasn't letting anything come between them now. Not again. He poured the remaining water on his hands, then wiped them against his torn khaki shorts. Then he opened and closed his fingers to ensure flexibility. Then he grabbed the rope and secured it around his waist. Then he climbed.

The wind roared at him and the rope wanted to sway, but he concentrated on pulling himself up, one hand at a time, walking his feet along the rock as he did so. All the while, he heard Bethany's voice encouraging him.

She grabbed him as soon as he heaved himself over the edge and pulled him back with her.

"Dylan...thank God," she murmured, holding him tighter than he ever remembered. "Are you okay?"

"I'm fine," he lied. He didn't want to frighten her with the truth that he vaulted somewhere between perfect and so consumed by need he could barely form words.

He pulled back and drank in the sight of her against a backdrop of pine, the tangle of her hair and flush to her complexion, the smudges of dirt on her left cheek and the tear to her white T-shirt. "It's you I'm worried about."

She gave him a wobbly smile. "No bears, no abandoned mine shafts, no porcupines. What more could a girl ask for?"

A whole hell of a lot. "You ran," he said, shifting a hand to her abdomen. "The baby?"

Her eyes met his. "Your son is fine."

The words were like a gut punch. "My son?"

She joined her hand to his. "Just a hunch."

A levelheaded man would end it there and give thanks for the solid ground beneath his feet, rather than step too close to the edge again. But Dylan had never been level-headed.

"Why?" he asked, and his voice pitched low. His passions had always driven him, as they did now. Straight into quicksand. "Why did you come back?"

She walked back into his arms and curled hers around his waist, but said nothing.

"You could have run," he pointed out. "You could have lost yourself in Canada before anyone knew you were missing."

He felt her stiffen against him, felt her pull back. But nothing prepared him for the expression on her face, the anguish in her eyes. "But then my child would never know his father, and…"

Her words broke off, broke him. "And what?"

She hesitated, her tongue moistening dry lips. "And I'd never know this," she whispered, then pushed up and put her mouth to his.

Shock stabbed through Dylan like a sky-to-earth lightning bolt, stark and beautiful. The current gyrated through him, searing from the inside out. He knew he should pull away before he charred her, as well, but couldn't have moved had his life depended on it. Which it did.

Slowly his arms lifted to surround her. He didn't know which was softer, the mouth nibbling at his, or the hair tangled in his hands. They both damned, making it impossible to summon the man Bethany had always needed him to be, the man his family wanted him to be. The stoic man who would untangle her arms and step back from temptation. The analytical man who realized trauma and near-death experiences often triggered primal affirmations of life. The rational man who knew instinctively that passion was not the answer. The considerate man who'd prompted him to bring her here, to the forest and the mountains she'd loved, to help distract her from the nasty media and police circus in Portland.

But none of those men could be found. They'd only been a figment, he knew. Illusions. A valiant attempt to fit into a world where he didn't belong. There was only Dylan now, Dylan as he'd always been, driven by passion and the need to possess this woman. Bethany. The only woman who'd ever slid into his heart.

For years he'd tried to deny her impact on him, how badly it had shredded him when Lance had ridden in on his white charger and given her the tenderness and space she'd needed. When Lance had helped heal wounds Dylan's in-your-face passion had caused. When he'd realized Lance could give her the life of stability Dylan could not.

"Damn it, Bethany," he growled, ripping his mouth from hers. "You don't know what you're doing."

She lifted her eyes to his. "Actually, I do."

"Then maybe you'd better tell me."

A slow smile glazed her eyes. "Dylan," she said, lifting her hands to his chest. Slowly, she began to unbutton. "I know good and well you're not out of practice with this, too."

The groan ripped from his throat before he could stop it. He wasn't used to being the one seduced. But he could no more have moved than he could have cut down the forest around them with a pocket knife. He watched in excruciating fascination as Bethany's fingers fumbled with the buttons of his chambray shirt. She slipped them through slender holes swiftly, then lifted her hands and eased the fabric back from his shoulders, down his arms.

"You're hurt," she whispered, lifting her mouth to kiss a cut along his rib cage.

He couldn't take it one second longer. He crushed her in his arms and put his mouth to hers, drank in every promise she had to give. The feel of her lips, soft and open, seared away every question, every doubt, every coherent thought he possessed. Only need remained.

He held her against him, running his hands along her back and lower, claiming every sinuous inch of her. Just like that night in the cabin. She felt like liquid fire in his arms, his body. He drank deeply of her, gave as deeply of himself.

Like so many other times during the past few days, nothing prepared Beth. Nothing could have, not memories, not even dreams that had her bolting awake at night, bathed in sweat and burning from the echo of Dylan's touch. For nine long years she'd lived with the memory of this man's mouth and hands. The memory of the mind-numbing passion he stoked in her, the feel of what it was like to be possessed by him. Consumed. And as often happened with memories over time, they'd faded, vibrant color washing out to a mere silhouette.

The night six weeks ago had changed that. Shattered her. Still, she'd told herself it was emotional vulnerability that had made that night so consuming. But now...now there was nothing faded about the man who held her in his arms, but didn't hold back. His mouth slanted against hers restlessly, hungrily, demanding and giving at the same time.

She'd never felt more alive in her life.

Lifting a hand to his face, she gave in to the temptation that had rocked her ever since they'd been in the mountains. The whiskers were soft not scratchy, unbearably masculine. She toyed with them, fingered them, loved them. Facial hair had never particularly appealed to her, but on Dylan, the dark, raspy shadow of his jaw stirred something deep.

The angle of his kiss changed then, his mouth sliding away from hers. She started to cry out, but then he closed his lips around her finger and gently suckled. This time she did cry out. Heat scored through her, arcing to every nerve ending. She would have sworn even her bones melted. "Dylan," she murmured.

He continued to make love to her finger, but pulled back enough to meet her eyes with his. She'd always thought of them as primeval, but even that descriptor felt tame now. The passion burning there stole the breath from her lungs.

"You're sure?" he asked, his voice dangerously hoarse.

"I'm sure," she answered, her voice dangerously strong.

On a groan, he lowered her to the blanket he'd spread for their picnic, countless hours before. Not much of the sun remained, only a few crimson streaks shooting up from the western horizon. The hazy shades of twilight settled around them, shadows from the wall of Douglas fir that held the rest of the world at bay. A breeze stirred gently, bringing with it the aroma of pine, but doing nothing to relieve the heat burning through her.

Dylan settled over her, supported by his arms. He kissed her deeply, possessively, his hands cruising along her body, not the back as before, but the front, where her tender breasts ached for his touch.

Impatience tightened through her. He was a deliciously thorough man, but she wasn't in the mood for deliberation. Not after running through the maze of pine and oak and hemlock, trying not to think about the very real possibility that she would not make it back to Dylan in time.

The survivor in her had insisted Dylan could take care of himself, that she had to think of the child, not the father. That she should seize the moment, the opportunity, and make a run for Canada while she still could. Before Zito had her arrested. Before she stood trial. Before a system designed to protect crushed instead.

Before Dylan's child was torn from her arms.

But she'd been unable to do that. Unable to turn her back on him after everything he'd done for her. Not just bringing her here to the mountains where she could breathe without choking on horror and scandal, but smaller things, like the clothes he'd brought her at the hotel, the pregnancy book he'd given her, the bath he'd drawn. The restraint he'd shown.

He showed no restraint now, though. He lay sprawled between her legs, his erection pressed against her thigh. She moaned softly, lifting her hands to his arms to push him back from her.

The look on his face said she might as well have ripped his heart from his chest.

Smiling, she rolled to her knees, then ripped something

else—the T-shirt from her body. Her bra came next, flung to the side and baring her chest for the world.

But there was only Dylan.

Her breasts were heavier now with pregnancy, her nipples larger, darker. And the ache. Dear Lord the sweet ache burned through her, the need to have this man's mouth close around her nipple and suckle.

Vulnerability bucked up against the haze of passion, but she refused to let it intrude. Instead, she cupped her breasts and offered them to the father of her child.

"You're the one who's made them ache," she whispered. "It's only fair that you give them relief, as well."

If Dylan hadn't already been on his knees, he would have fallen then and there. He'd never seen a more beautiful sight in his life. Earlier she'd mimicked the goddess Isis, but that's exactly how she looked kneeling there on the edge of the cliff, long hair blowing softly around her face, blue eyes glowing with a promise that could tear a man in two, her soft hands cupping her breasts and lifting them to him.

"Once," he rasped, "you told me *I* didn't play fair."

An unholy smile curved her lips. "Once, I was a fool."

And once Dylan had trampled the greatest gift imaginable. Not again. With damning clarity, he realized there was nothing he wouldn't do for this woman, to keep her safe, keep that glow in her eyes.

Keep her his.

In a move as swift as the river racing below, he lowered her to the blanket and put his mouth to her breast. He wanted to go slow, to trace lazy circles around the wide areola, to taste and tease and torture them both, but the way she writhed beneath him had him pulling the nipple into his mouth instead. She cried out and arched upward, wrapping her legs around his.

Desire crashed and surged. He savored the feel of her in his mouth, sucking gently but firmly, using his fingers to toy with her other nipple. Nipples that would one day soon nourish his child.

The thought rocked him to the core.

He was only vaguely aware of Bethany's hands at the waistband of his shorts, fumbling with the button and the zipper. But when she slid inside his boxers and closed her fingers around his shaft, vague awareness sharpened into excruciating reality. Her hand was soft, sure, squeezing and stroking and driving him half out of his mind.

Shifting his mouth to her other breast, he reached for the front of her shorts, only to have her hands join his there, as well. Together, they made quick work of her khakis and panties.

There between her legs, both of them naked and ready, he wanted to slide inside and step over the edge once again. Instead, he cupped her mound, his hand sliding lower to find her wet and ready.

"Dylan," she whispered, tilting her hips. "Please."

The broken word shredded him. He slid his fingers down further, then slipped inside, discovering her as small and tight as the night they'd made a child. But she was also warm and slick and when she cried out, he joined a second finger to the first. She rocked against him, prompting him to return his mouth to hers and absorb the mewl tearing from her throat.

Her hand found him again, and steered him toward her. This time he didn't hold back. Couldn't. Desire roared through him. Need. A sense of rightness he'd never before known.

Pushing against her opening, he heard something guttural break from his throat when her body didn't immediately take him in. He didn't want to push her, though. Didn't want to hurt her. Instead, he let her body adjust to his size, sprinkling gentle kisses along her cheekbone as he did so.

"Dylan," she whispered.

He lifted his head to look at her, the way shadows

played across her gaze. But these weren't shadows of sorrow like before, nor shadows of the past. These shadows stemmed from the evening around them, and in them, she looked even more beautiful.

"Don't hold back," she said, lifting her hips. "I want to feel you inside me," she purred, pressing a hand to his buttocks. "I want to feel you deep. I want to feel you come unglued."

Sweet mercy, he almost did right then and there. He stared down at the woman in his arms, no longer an ice princess, no longer in her ice palace.

"Maybe I want to take it slow," he muttered, grinning at the role reversal. "Maybe I want to savor every moment."

She bucked against him again. "And maybe you're not going to have a choice."

That was all it took. Her body accepted him, allowing him to plunge deep. She closed around him, hot and slick and possessive, little muscles holding him tight. He wanted to stay there forever, suspended in a hazy world where there was only him and Bethany, but need had him pulling back and sinking in again.

"Take me away," she whispered. "Take me back."

But he didn't want to take her anywhere. He wanted to give her everything, all of him, all he'd ever wanted to be.

They started moving together, him thrusting, her tilting her hips. Almost desperately he grabbed for her hand, threading their fingers together and stretching her arm above her head. She arched into him and cried out, and for the second time in one day, Dylan stepped over the edge.

But this time the free fall neither scraped nor burned, but shimmered and sizzled.

It was a long time before they landed.

Darkness blanketed the land, but not her heart. Beth lay naked in Dylan's arms, staring at star-dappled sky. Billions of pinpricks of light shone down, clear and unobstructed, dazzling and eternal. The breeze carried the scent of pine, and desire.

"Are you okay?" he asked, stroking a hand along her rib cage.

A delicious shiver ran through her. "Okay isn't exactly the word I'd use."

He swore softly. "Was I too rough? Christ, I'm sorry—"

"Sorry?" She lifted her head from his chest to see his face. "I'm not."

"I...got a little carried away."

Beth could only stare. The moonlight revealed the shadows in his gaze, the grim set of the mouth that had worshipped hers while evening gave way to night.

Slowly, tentatively, she lifted a hand and ran her fingertips along the stubble covering his jaw. She'd loved the way his whiskers had tickled her body as Dylan's mouth did deliciously wicked things to places long forgotten. And though the whiskers were soft, she felt sure they'd left their mark on her, as well.

The melting started all over again. For nine long years she'd shut herself off from the passion Dylan St. Croix stoked within her. She'd told herself that passion was bad, destructive. That it led to pain and heartache, that it didn't, couldn't, last. That it had been responsible for her miscarriage and the ensuing accident which killed her father. That if she let it rule her, she'd end up as self-centered and destructive as her mother.

That's why she'd left the cabin before dawn, that cold morning six weeks before. That's why she'd tried to forget.

But now, looking into Dylan's glittering green eyes, she could find no malice or danger in what they'd just shared. Only peace and happiness, a sense of contentment as brilliant as the night sky.

"You did get a little carried away," she said, sliding a finger from his jaw to his lower lip. "But I forgive you."

Her tone was purposefully playful, but his gaze remained serious. "Do you?"

She hated seeing him like this, her man of passion so still and expressionless. Sliding on top of him, she pressed a kiss to the side of the mouth she desperately wanted to see smile.

"I wanted it as much as you did," she reminded.

But he didn't give her the smile she wanted. "Not for making love to you, Bethany. For that night on the mountain. For mauling you, when I knew damn good and well you'd gone there to be alone."

And finally, at last, she understood. Their lovemaking had ripped down the walls between them, leaving only man and woman, truths as raw and unforgiving as the river thundering below.

She'd been so blinded by the enormity of Lance's murder and the discovery of her pregnancy, the soul-shattering revelation that Dylan had fathered her child, she'd never, not once, stopped to think about what Dylan must be going through.

His world had been blown apart every bit as brutally as hers.

Dylan had always been bigger than life to her, capable of dealing with anything. He was a man driven by passion, but principles, as well. Because of the hypocritical world in which he'd grown up, pretenses made him sick. Lies made him crazy. He'd turned crusading for the truth into his life's calling. But now, he'd not just gone against the moral compass that defined him, he'd shattered it.

"Dylan." She met his gaze with hers, gave him a smile born in her heart. "You've given me the greatest gift imaginable," she whispered, and meant. "What malice can I find in that? We were both there that night. We're both consenting adults. We both knew what we were doing. There's nothing to forgive."

He closed his eyes, but not before emotion flashed in green depths. "I don't deserve you."

The quiet words destroyed her. She looked at him lying beneath her, and wondered how she'd ever found the strength to walk away. If she could do it again. He'd been electrifying as a boy, but as a man...the hard-won combination of passion and strength and tenderness devastated.

And it was that man who deserved to know the secret she'd lived with for six long years.

"The night before I married Lance, I dreamed of you."

Beneath her, he tensed. His eyes came open, revealing a punishing combination of surprise and...dread.

"I dreamed of making love with you," she admitted. She'd thrashed restlessly in the bed of her childhood, heart hammering, blood heated, certain that he'd been there with her. "I dreamed it was you waiting for me at the altar."

Dylan swore softly, shifting her from his body and standing in one svelte movement. He jerked on his shorts and walked from her, walked from the confession that cost her so much, moving to stand at the edge of the cliff.

The rejection cut deep, but Beth wasn't about to let it silence her. She'd kept the words, the truth, bottled up for too long, never realizing what a coward she'd become.

"It was so real," she said, drawing her knees to her chest and wrapping her arms around them. "I woke up with my body on fire, as though you'd really been there in that room with me."

Through the hazy moonlight, she saw Dylan's shoulders stiffen, but he said nothing. He just stood staring out over the side of the mountain. She wondered what he saw in the darkness, if he saw anything at all.

Long moments passed. Long quiet moments punctuated by the ruffling of the wind and the urgent pounding of her heart. Long moments shattered by two words.

"I was."

Beth went very still, all but her heart. It strummed low and hard. Deep. "You were what?"

Dylan turned to her. "I was there, Bethany. I was with you."

Now it was her turn to step over the side of the mountain, and fall. "You mean figuratively, right?"

"Flesh and blood," Dylan corrected, but didn't move. He just stood there seemingly on the edge of the world, the star-filled night sky behind him, his expression as hard as a rock. "I knew you were marrying my cousin the next day, and I knew there was nothing I could do to stop you. But I wasn't ready to let you go. I wasn't ready to live my life without touching you one last time. Kissing you. Telling you goodbye."

Shock streamed through her, not hard and punishing, but languid and seductive. Her chest tightened. Her throat burned. Heat came next, the memory of his hands and mouth on her body, the lingering scent of jasmine. She'd jerked herself awake, horrified. What kind of a woman dreamed of making love with her former lover the night before she married another man?

Her mother's daughter, that's who.

She'd summoned the other memories as fast as she could, the screams and the blood, the baby she'd lost due to the blinding passion she felt for Dylan. And from those memories, she'd found the strength, the resolve, to walk down the aisle and pledge her life to a man who didn't send her world spinning.

"How?" she asked, standing.

For the first time, the hard lines of his face softened, and the side of his mouth quirked up into a smile. "Remember that window you showed me with the broken lock?"

She remembered, all right. It's how she'd sneaked him into her room after everyone else slept.

"Your grandfather never had it fixed."

No wonder, Beth thought wildly. No wonder the scent of sandalwood had mingled with that of her jasmine candle. "My God."

Dylan crossed to her and picked up his chambray shirt, then draped it around her shoulders.

Only then did she realize she'd begun to shake.

"You looked so beautiful," he said, lifting a hand to her face. "Peaceful. I stood there a long time letting that image override memories of the accident. Your screams…Jesus." He squeezed his eyes shut, opened them a moment later. "I can't tell you how many nights I jerked myself awake, convinced I'd find your blood on my hands all over again."

Horror staggered through her, bringing with it the need to comfort. She'd been so determined not to turn into her mother and casually hurt those around her, but somehow she'd never realized that in doing so, she'd hurt the only man she'd ever loved. There'd been a time she hadn't even thought that possible.

Now she knew how wrong she'd been. "It wasn't your fault," she whispered, running her finger along his bottom lip. "It was nobody's fault."

A hard sound broke from his throat. And his eyes… Dear God, his eyes. They were on fire. "It killed me seeing you with Lance, hearing you pledge your life to him, but I knew he was the better man."

"He was a different man, Dylan. There's no comparison."

"He made you happy."

"He made the scared little girl happy." The one who didn't want to follow in her mother's footsteps, not after seeing her break heart after heart. Including her father's. "He took care of her. But as that little girl turned into a woman…"

"What?" Dylan asked sharply. "As the little girl turned into a woman, what?"

"He…" It was difficult to put their marriage into words. They hadn't come together out of passion, but rather, common goals. "I don't know. We drifted. You were right, you know. Last week in the car, when you said Lance went his way, and I went mine."

Dylan's scowl darkened. "Then why didn't you divorce sooner?"

And come to me.

Beth heard the hoarse words as surely as though Dylan had spoken them aloud. "As crazy as it sounds, the vows we took meant something to me. I'd sworn before family and friends and God to make the marriage work for better or for worse and..."

"And you didn't want to be your mother."

The chill increased. "Maybe," she admitted, surprised by the insight. "But we were...content. Our marriage became more of a partnership than anything else. We got along. We were friends." She stepped closer to Dylan, needing his warmth, needing the man she'd just made love with to know the full truth.

"Last week you asked if I remembered the last time Lance and I made love."

Dylan stiffened, his eyes going cold. "Now's not the time—"

"We never *made love,*" she interrupted, pressing her body to Dylan's. They'd rarely even slept together. "We never shared what you and I always, always have."

"Don't lie—"

"He quit visiting my bed," she rolled right on, finding liberation in the truth, "after we realized we'd never make a baby the old-fashioned way. And I never invited him back."

Standing there in the moonlight, Dylan stared at her like she'd suddenly started talking in tongues. "It used to eat me alive thinking of Lance going home to your bed every night. Now you're telling me he didn't?"

"It wasn't like that between us." Never had been. In truth, she'd never quite understood why he'd asked her to marry him in the first place. "He had someone else," she told Dylan. "Someone whose bed he would visit."

Dylan lifted a hand to her face. "And you?"

She smiled at the way he was clearly bracing himself,

at the way he tried to keep the emotion from his eyes. Silly man. Dylan St. Croix could no more hide what he felt than she could yank the sun from the sky.

"Only one," she told him. "There's only been one man in my bed, my dreams. In my heart."

His gaze hardened, and she felt his body go rigid.

"You," she said as quickly as she could. "Only you."

He looked like she'd just slugged him in the gut, rather than given him a confession straight from her heart.

"Dylan, I—"

He crushed her in his arms before she could continue, pressing her against the warmth of his chest. The scent of sandalwood and desire killed her words, prompting her to hold him as tightly as he held her. He was murmuring something against her hair, but above the beating of their hearts, she couldn't make out the words.

"Kiss me," she whispered, lifting her face to his.

And he did. His mouth came down on hers with the same urgency she'd thrilled to nine years before. The same urgency she'd awoken from in dreams, heart pounding, body damp.

The cramp hit without warning. She cried out, her hands immediately finding her stomach.

Dylan tore his mouth from hers. "Bethany?"

She stood there, stunned, trying to catch her breath. But then another pain lanced through her midsection, this one so sharp she doubled over.

"Sweetheart, what's the matter?"

She was still naked except for his shirt, and through the moonlight, she saw the trickle of red down her leg.

"The baby," she whispered, looking up at Dylan. "The baby."

"Sweet Jesus, no," he growled, then scooped her into his arms and ran.

Chapter 13

You're not going to lose this baby!

The fierce vow echoed through Beth long after Dylan rushed her to an emergency clinic in nearby Medford. She lay on the exam table and prayed, while Dylan held her hand. And prayed. She remembered little of the trip down the twisting mountain roads, only the way Dylan had kept talking, kept touching.

Now, a cold fear twisted through her. She'd been careless. Reckless. Drunk on desire, she'd put her baby at risk. *Again.*

"The doctor should be back any minute. Can I get you anything?"

She looked at him and felt the ache in her chest deepen. His eyes were dark and wild, the lines of his face stark, the shadow on his jaw darkening. Even his closely cut hair looked disheveled. Scratches and dried blood streaked his chest and arms, bearing witness to the fact he'd picked her up and run into the pine forest without stopping to dress.

Now he held her hand tightly, giving her strength and warmth.

But the chill deep inside wouldn't go away.

"You should have someone look at those cuts," she whispered, her mouth too dry for anything louder. "The one on your shoulder looks pretty deep."

"I'm not leaving you."

His voice was hoarse, scraped raw, much like that long-ago night when a few careless decisions had shattered their lives. In excruciating detail, she remembered that dark night on the side of a mountain road, the paramedics frantically tending to her while violent cramps ripped through her body. And the blood. There'd been so much of it. Hers. Dylan's. She'd lain there cold and shivering, unable to look from the state trooper wrestling him to the ground.

"No," he roared. *"No!"*

"Hold still, son. Don't make this worse than it already is."

"You have to let me go to her! She's pregnant, for God's sakes. She's carrying my child."

"Maybe you should have thought of that before you dragged her into the middle of an ambush."

"Sweetheart? What's wrong?"

Beth blinked hard, bringing the stark lines of Dylan's face into focus. He held her hand in one of his, but somehow, he seemed to be retreating.

"C-cold," she murmured. "So cold."

He swore softly and glanced at the closed door, then slipped onto the narrow bed beside her. "I've got you," he said, and though he held her against the solid warmth of his body, the distance between them seemed to elongate. "I've got you."

"Mr. and Mrs. St. Croix?" came a voice from the doorway.

"Dr. Burns." Dylan was on his feet and across the room before the expressionless doctor took two steps. "How is she?"

The older man pushed his glasses higher on his face and glanced at his chart, then at Beth. "Your wife is fine, just a little overheated and dehydrated."

"And the baby?" Dylan and Beth asked simultaneously.

Dr. Burns smiled. "Everything's fine," he said. "The heart rate is strong and there are no signs of fetal distress."

Tears spilled over, relief and joy and thanks rushing through her as swift and beautiful as the river they'd hiked that morning. "Dylan—"

But he was already there, by her side and pulling her into his arms. He held her tightly, cradling and rocking, running a hand up her back and into her tangled hair, while the other stretched across her stomach.

"Thank God," he rasped over and over. "Thank God."

Beth absorbed the feel of his arms around her, telling herself she was only imagining the distance before. Her world wasn't shattering. Everything was okay. "Thank *you*, Dylan. Thank you for getting me here so fast."

"I'd like her to take it easy for a few days," Dr. Burns said, moving toward them. "No hiking or physical exertion."

Dylan pulled back and turned to the doctor. "I'll tie her to the bed, if I have to."

Once, the rough-hewn words would have coaxed a smile or a shaky laugh from Beth. Instead, the cold chill of certainty pierced deeper.

Clearly startled, the doctor hurriedly closed the chart and rattled off several warning signs, then advised Beth to see her doctor in Portland upon her return. "Other than that, Mr. St. Croix, just take your wife home, make her comfortable, treat her like a queen."

His wife. A queen.

The words tightened around Beth's throat, her heart, but she didn't correct the doctor.

Neither did Dylan. He merely agreed. "I will."

Dylan watched her sleep. She lay in *his* bed, in *his* bedroom, in *his* house, but he couldn't bring himself to slide *his* body next to hers. The need to stand guard tromped over every other need that tried to surface. Bethany didn't need to share a bed right now. She didn't need a lover. She didn't need to know the fire that burned in his gut. She needed rest and peace and the serenity she'd always sought.

In short, she needed what Dylan had never given her.

Take your wife home, make her comfortable, treat her like a queen.

The doctor's words had echoed through him the entire drive back to Portland. The entire *quiet* drive. Bethany had sat there in the passenger seat, staring at the darkened world whizzing by them, one hand on her stomach. Even with the soft strains of jazz drifting through the Bronco, he would have sworn he heard every breath she drew. Every beat of her heart.

But she'd said nothing.

And neither had he.

He didn't know what *to* say. Sitting there silently had been like wearing a straitjacket on his soul, but he didn't know how to put the terror and the relief and the lingering fear into words. At least, not the soft, gentle words she needed. Guilt would have twisted them. Intensity would have distorted. So instead he gave her silence. And time.

She hadn't fought him when he told her he was taking her to his house, like she had the night of the murder, when he'd walked back into her life. Less than two weeks had passed since then, but their entire lives had changed. In taking her away from Portland, they'd entered a whole new world, a world where the horror of Lance's murder didn't hang like a noose around Bethany's neck. A world where they could come to terms with the child they would share.

Bethany had always loved the mountains, and there amidst the old-growth pine forest, she'd come to life before his eyes. The thaw had awed him, seduced. To see her smiling again. To hear her laugh. To feel her touch.

It had been a long, long time.

For a few precarious days, he'd thought they were moving forward. Now he wondered if the momentum had carried them back instead.

"You can sleep in here," he'd told her upon their arrival at his secluded home just outside Portland.

The question flashed in her eyes. "And you?"

He wouldn't sleep at all. But she didn't need to know that. "I think we both need some time," he said instead.

Silently, she'd nodded, then walked into his room and shut the door.

Now, moonlight streamed through a wall of windows, spilling gently on the woman in his bed. She looked so damn right there. So…peaceful. He'd seen her like this hundreds of times before, in his dreams. Soft. Beautiful. Precious.

But in those dreams, she hadn't just almost suffered a miscarriage.

She shifted restlessly, her hair fanned across the pillow. He wanted to cross the room and touch her so damn bad, to put his mouth to her lips, his hand to her stomach.

But he didn't move, didn't trust himself to be around her without crushing her in his arms and never letting go. He could find none of the tenderness she deserved. Everything inside him felt jagged and broken, shattered. If he lived a hundred years, he knew he'd never forget the sight of her doubling over in pain, crying out.

What the hell had he been thinking? What the *hell* had he been thinking? Taking her into that remote area, out into the dense wooded area, being careless enough to fall off a cliff. Taking her right there on the edge, no holds barred, driving deep into her. While she carried a child. *His* child.

I let passion blind me. I didn't think straight. I didn't put the child fist. I won't let that happen again. I can't.

Nine years ago, his recklessness had almost destroyed

her, and now, despite his efforts to be the man she deserved, history wanted to repeat itself.

He wouldn't let it. Standing there in the darkness, he vowed to find a way to make everything okay. He wouldn't hurt her again. No matter what it cost him, he'd cut out his own heart before hurting her again, because that's what hurting her did to him.

And he wasn't going to let it happen. She deserved happiness and peace. She deserved to hold and love and nurture the child she'd always wanted.

"The f-fire poker. It was in my hands."

A violent curse tore silently through Dylan. In the morning, he would call Zito, find out the status of the investigation. Because God help him, somehow, some way, he'd find a way to give Bethany the future he'd once told her didn't exist.

Even if *he* ended up behind bars in the process.

He was gone when she awoke. Beth searched the spacious wood and glass house, but found no trace of the man who'd driven silently through the night. A disturbing emptiness accompanied her from room to room, every heartbeat deepening the chill.

Something was wrong.

She stepped onto the wide back porch and glanced toward the horizon, where Mount Hood rose against an azure sky. Normally, the song of the birds and the gentle warmth of the morning sun brought a smile to her face, but she couldn't find one now.

Never in a million years would she have dreamed fire and brimstone Dylan St. Croix would build a house so far from the hustle and bustle he thrived upon. Portland lay not too far to the west, but the city seemed a world away.

Why? Beth wondered. *Why?*

Dylan had been by her side nonstop since the moment he'd walked back into her life, almost two weeks before. He'd barely left her alone, not even when she wanted him to. But now, now that she craved the feel of his arms around her, he was nowhere to be found.

The ache in her chest deepened, sharpened, prompting her to draw a hand to her stomach. Her baby. *Their* baby. There'd been no more bleeding, no more cramping. She'd slept soundly, except the few times she'd awoken, hoping to feel the warmth of Dylan's body close to hers, but finding only cold sheets.

Now she found only cold certainty. She was back in Portland, back in the nightmare Dylan had taken her away from. There could be no more pretending, no more dreaming.

It was time to get on with the business of living.

"I have to admit I was surprised when your message said to call you at Dylan's house."

Beth squeezed a lime slice into a glass of ice water. "It's complicated."

Janine frowned. "With that man, it always is. What in the world was he thinking taking you away in the middle of a murder investigation? Doesn't he know how that looks?"

The uncertainty Beth had been fighting since waking alone scraped a little deeper. Janine seemed worried, upset. And when she'd finally called her back, she'd practically demanded Beth meet her as soon as possible.

"He told Detective Zito where we were."

"Well, he didn't tell anyone else. If this case ends up going to trial, that little disappearing act can be used against you."

Beth had never seen Janine so agitated. But, she added silently, most of their encounters had been over martinis at cocktail parties, not ice water to discuss murder.

"What's wrong? You said you've been trying to reach me?"

"Kent asked me to go through Lance's files."

Beth couldn't say why, but her heart started to pound, hard. "And?"

Janine hesitated. Her long blond hair was pulled severely off her face into some kind of twist, making it impossible not to see the fervor in the blue of her eyes. "How well do you know Dylan?" she asked.

Beth sat back in her chair, staring at her friend. "Dylan?"

"How well do you know him, *really* know him?"

The question pressed down on her chest, making it hard to breathe. "Why?"

Janine let out a ragged breath. "Jesus, Bethany, it might be nothing, but…when I was going through Lance's office, I found a file buried in his bottom drawer. A file labeled 'Dylan.'"

"A file?" Beth whispered. "What kind of file?"

Janine frowned. "About an investigation Lance was working on."

The restaurant started to spin. "An investigation?"

"Over the years Dylan has brought quite a few companies to their knees, forcing some to close their doors, in other cases sending management to jail. He's always been heralded for seeking out corruption. But from what Lance had in his files…" Janine took Beth's icy hands. "I'm sorry."

The chill Beth had been unable to shake spread deeper. Denial chased close behind, but couldn't catch up. Lance had never mentioned a word about investigating Dylan, but then, they'd made a point of never discussing Dylan.

I don't care about the risks, she suddenly remembered him barking into the phone while in the mountains. *I care about what's in those files. If you're not up to the job—*

"What?" she asked now. "What are you sorry for?"

Again, Janine hesitated.

"Tell me!"

"There's no easy way to say this, but there was enough

evidence in that file to make a strong case against Dylan for corporate sabotage.''

Beth curled her fingers around the edge of the table. ''Corporate sabotage?''

Janine frowned. ''It gets worse, Beth. There were… pictures.''

''What kind of pictures?''

''All I can guess is that Dylan discovered the investigation and was trying to put a stop to it by blackmailing the D.A.''

Somewhere along the line Beth had entered a hideous alternate universe, and she couldn't seem to find her way out. ''Blackmail?''

''The pictures were of the D.A. in a rather…how shall I say? Compromising position with what I'm assuming is a prostitute. There were notes, too. Notes demanding Kent step down or face exposure.''

Horror and disbelief crashed down from all directions, pummeling. Beth drew a hand to her stomach, tried hard not to be sick. ''There's got to be some mistake.''

Janine leaned across the table and lowered her voice. ''I wish to God there was. But until we know more, you have to be careful. I wouldn't go back there, if I were you.''

''What are you saying?'' Beth demanded.

Janine looked her dead in the eye. ''I know you're not capable of murder, Bethany. But Dylan St. Croix is.''

Janine was wrong. There was some kind of mistake. That was all. Beth had only to ask Dylan when he got home, and he'd explain. They'd probably both end up laughing about the misunderstanding.

But until then, she stood on his back porch, staring toward the west, where the sun slipped toward a massive cloud bank hovering over the horizon. Soon, twilight would take over.

Zorro chose that moment to make his presence known, weaving between her legs with a loud meow. Beth instinctively swooped the big black-and-white cat into her arms and held him to her chest. Dylan had brought him here the night Lance died, and he'd been making sure he was cared for ever since. That was hardly the act of the calculating, twisted individual Janine described. Dylan was a man of passion, not malice.

Passion. The word settled like a rock in Beth's stomach. Detectives Zito and Livingston had offered passion as a reason why she might have killed Lance. A crime of passion, Yvonne Kelly kept calling it. An explosion of emotion resulting in horrific consequences.

Beth and Lance had never shared passion. But Lance and Dylan....

"You and Lance were hardly the devoted cousins your grandfather wanted everyone to think you were."

"How could we be? The only thing we had in common was something two men should never share."

The memory chilled her. Born cousins, but raised as brothers, Lance and Dylan had shared a complicated relationship Beth had never understood. On the surface, they appeared civil. They played their roles to perfection. But beneath the pretenses, Dylan's passions clashed violently with Lance's addiction to image and power.

Beth couldn't begin to imagine how it must have galled Lance to approach Dylan about the artificial insemination. The humiliation. The shame. To keep his perfect, orderly world intact, Lance had possessed no choice but to turn to his cousin and ask him to provide a basic human function Lance could not. He'd had no choice but to let Dylan in on his dirty little secret.

To Lance, that would have been playing Russian roulette.

Maybe that's why he'd been investigating Dylan. To protect himself. To have a trump card in case Dylan decided to expose how far Lance had been willing to go to protect his secret.

Maybe Dylan found out about Lance's file. Maybe—

Zorro squirmed free, making Beth realize how tightly she'd been holding him. Frowning, she closed her eyes and hugged her arms around her waist, refusing to travel further down that dangerous, dangerous path. She wanted to just turn and walk away from the ugliness of it all, go back to the mountains, to before. But she wasn't a coward anymore, wasn't a scared little girl. She was a grown woman carrying the child of a man who'd promised to never hurt her.

Opening her eyes, Beth found that somewhere along the line, the sun had dropped below the thick bank of clouds, leaving nothing but darkness in its wake.

He found her on the back porch. Wearing a loose cotton shift, she stood with her back to him, hands curled around the railing he himself had installed. Darkness stole detail, but her rigid stance threw him back to that chilling night two weeks before, when he'd found her sitting in that chaise lounge, rocking vacantly.

She was retreating. He'd forced himself to stay gone all day, believing she needed time to come to terms with the chaos of the past twenty-four hours. But he'd been wrong. Not even the cool evening breeze eased the tension clogging the air.

A bad feeling settled low in his gut. He moved silently behind her and put his hands on her shoulders. The urge to ease her back was strong, but instinct warned him to go slow. "How are you feeling?"

She stiffened at his touch, his voice, but slowly, she turned toward him. "How did Lance know you'd keep his secret?"

The question caught Dylan with the force of a sucker punch. He didn't know what he'd been expecting her to say, but it certainly wasn't this.

"I gave him my word." He repositioned his hands, sliding one to her waist, the other to her nape. "Why?"

"You gave him your word," she repeated mechanically.

Her eyes were dull, glazed, determined. "But how did he know one day you wouldn't want to take everything back? That you wouldn't blow the whistle and expose his deception?"

"I don't go back on my word. Lance knew that." Suddenly he realized the shadows beneath her eyes had nothing to do with nightfall. "Why the questions?"

"You could have destroyed him," she whispered.

His gut tightened. The woman standing only inches away was not the woman he'd made love to twenty-four hours before. This woman was tense, on guard, caught in a vortex he didn't even begin to understand.

"What's going on?" he asked as levelly as he could.

Bethany glanced toward the three steps leading from the porch, where her cat lay bathing himself. The night was quiet, only a few crickets gearing up for the long hours ahead.

"Tell me about the Trigon Investigation," she said.

"Trigon?" Suddenly Dylan was ten years old again, grabbing at marbles scattering down a hill. With cold certainty, he realized that while he'd given Bethany space today, somebody had filled it with poison. "What about the Trigon Investigation?"

On a cloud of jasmine, the evening breeze pushed a strand of hair to her face. "Anything."

Dylan's fingers itched to slide forward, to skim across her cheekbone, but he kept his hand at the base of her neck. He didn't want to think he was trying to hold her in place, while she steadily slipped away.

"Trigon was a forest products company in financial trouble. To cover their losses, they not only clear-cut old-growth forests, but contaminated the drinking water of a small town in central Oregon through illegal dumping."

"And you brought them down?" she asked.

"I spearheaded the investigation."

"How did you know?"

An odd light glinted in her eyes. "What do you mean, how did I know?"

"What made you go after them?" she persisted.

Frustration boiled inside him. He didn't want to talk about ancient history. He didn't want to talk about Trigon. He wanted to talk about them, to tell her what he'd found out today from Zito. Yes, her fingerprints were on the fire poker, but the detectives could find nothing concrete linking her to the murder.

"A tip," he told her. "I found out through a tip."

"What kind of tip?"

"Jut a tip," he said as patiently as he could. "What's going on here, Bethany? Why all the questions?" And why did she look at him like she'd never seen him before, hadn't made love to him the day before, didn't carry his child?

As if on cue, she drew her hands protectively against the small swell of her stomach. "Can you think of any reason why Lance would have been investigating you?"

Dylan went very still. Deadly still. "Investigating me? What the hell are you talking about?"

Her gaze met his. "I'm talking about corporate sabotage, Dylan. I'm talking about an investigation Lance was conducting. I'm talking about blackmail and extortion. I'm talking about you."

Chapter 14

The transformation came over him immediately, shadows of concern tightening into hard lines of fury. The green of his eyes darkened. Even the whiskers that had looked enticing only minutes before became sinister.

The breath backed up in Beth's throat. Her heart pounded so hard she wondered if Dylan knew how hotly the blood poured through her body. He stood close enough she had to look up to see him, and yet, the inches between them felt more like a gorge, one that widened, deepened, by the second.

"Corporate sabotage?" he asked in a dangerously quiet voice that chilled her to the bone. "Blackmail?"

She shivered, not used to feeling any kind of chill around Dylan. "Yes."

"What the hell are you talking about?" he demanded.

The angry disbelief in his voice resonated through her, but she couldn't let intensity knock her off course. She had to know. She had to pull the weeds from their path before they choked out everything else.

"Trigon went out of business as a result of your investigation," she said as levelly as she could. "Their CEO committed suicide."

She hadn't thought it possible, but Dylan's expression darkened even more. "They were crooks, for crissakes."

Earlier, the distinctive scent of jasmine had brought a smile to her heart. Now, the sweet scent snaked through her as tightly as the vines curled around the porch railing, making it difficult to breathe, much less continue.

"What about the D.A.?" she persisted. "What about pictures of him and a prostitute? Demands that he resign or face exposure?"

"Christ almighty," Dylan bit out. Abruptly he released her and backed away. She'd never seen his eyes that cold, that remote, as though he looked at Judas and not the woman he'd made love to barely twenty-four hours before.

"I've been worried sick about you and the baby, but that's not what's eating at you, is it? It's me. It's us. You're wondering if you made a mistake up there on the mountain. You're wondering if you gave your body to a criminal."

The dangerous U-turn sent her heart slamming against her ribs. "I'm just asking a few questions," she insisted.

"And I'm answering them," he said flatly. "But you shouldn't even have to ask. You should know."

The chill inside her spread, reaching clear down to her soul. More than anything she wanted to cross the ravine between her and Dylan, put her body to his and curl her arms around his waist. Shivering, she reached instead for the blanket of numbness that had served her so well over the years.

"We've been apart a long time," she reminded softly.

His eyes caught fire. He started toward her, but stopped with violent abruptness, like a big, beautiful, charging Rottweiler at the end of his chain.

"Don't," he ground out, so still now that he barely looked alive. "Don't hide behind pretenses. Don't pretend you're pulling back because of my career choice, when we both know damn good and well it's because of what went down on that mountain.'' He paused, scorched her with his eyes. ''You're scared. Hell, I'm scared, too. But pretending this is about my career isn't going to help.''

Everything inside her that was female cried out to go to him, but she couldn't move. ''I'm not pretending.''

''Then that makes it even worse.''

The simple statement cut deep, because it was true.

''Who have you been talking to?'' he demanded. ''Who's pumped you full of lies?''

She shook her head, not wanting to drag Janine into this. ''It doesn't matter.''

He swore softly, the words a direct reflection of the stark disappointment in his eyes. Then he turned and walked away.

Panic stabbed into her throat. ''Where are you going?'' she asked, hurrying after him.

He kept right on going, striding around the side of the house to the driveway, where his Bronco sat parked. ''Away.''

''Dylan—''

He pulled open the door and pivoted toward her. The night was dark, making the glow in his eyes more pronounced. ''I don't trust myself with you right now. I don't trust myself not to put my mouth to yours and kiss some sense into you.''

Something deep inside started to crumble. ''Dylan—''

He didn't give her a chance to finish. He stepped into the Bronco, closed the door, and gunned the engine. Before her heart could even beat, he was gone.

Beth stood there numbly, arms wrapped around her waist. She'd hurt him. She hadn't meant to, had only wanted him to refute what Janine had told her, but by even asking the questions, she'd violated something between them.

Too late, Beth realized the truth. Trust. She'd violated

the trust. And to Dylan, a man who abhorred pretenses and swore by the truth, questioning his ethics was tantamount to stabbing a knife in his heart.

No matter where Dylan drove, no matter how fast, he couldn't get away from the sting of Bethany's questions. She'd just stood there firing one after another, relentless curveballs, an assassin on a mission.

A corporate saboteur? Blackmail?

It was an outright lie, but with cold certainty, Dylan could see his cousin creating such a file. Insurance, Lance would have called it, a way to make sure Dylan never let it slip how far Lance had been willing to go to maintain the image of the perfect, virile man who could one day be governor.

But blackmailing Kent English? Dylan couldn't figure how that fit in. He'd heard whispers that the embattled D.A., long at war with the press, might be leaving office, and now he had to wonder. Who stood to benefit from the D.A. stepping down in shame? Who would go to such dramatic measures to ruin English?

The answer settled in his gut like a jagged weight. He could think of only one person. But that man was dead.

Dylan had been a private investigator too long not to connect the dots. Someone *had* been blackmailing the D.A., someone who stood to gain from his demise. And now Lance, the heir apparent, was dead, killed in cold blood.

Dylan took an abrupt turn, his mind racing as fast as the car. If anyone knew what was really going on with Lance, it would be the woman his cousin had tried to pawn off on Dylan. Lance had been blinded by her stark beauty and forceful personality, but Dylan had recognized a man-killer when he saw one, and made damn sure their brief relationship never made it to the bedroom.

Lance might not have been so smart.

Janine never missed a chance to look down her nose at

Dylan. Hell, she might have even hatched the idea of investigating Dylan's role in the fall of Trigon Industries,
just to teach him a lesson. And if anyone knew about
Lance's dirty dealings, it would be her.

Less than fifteen minutes later, he entered the renovated
brownstone where she had her apartment and took the
stairs two at a time. He wasn't about to take the fall for
his cousin's misdeeds, or a murder he didn't commit. If
English found out Lance was behind the blackmail…

He knocked at Janine's door. Loudly.

From inside, the haunting sound of Celtic music drifted
through the cracks. He was raising his hand to knock again
when the door came open, and she greeted him with a glass
of wine in her hand. "Dylan," she said, and smiled. "I
figured it was only a matter of time before you showed
up."

He looked at her standing there in some slinky black
outfit, blond hair loose and flowing around her face. Fury
pounded through him, but he held the dangerous emotion
in check. Now was not the time to lose it.

He stepped inside her shockingly white apartment and
quietly closed the door. "We need to talk."

He found Bethany in his bedroom shortly after midnight, standing in a pool of moonlight and staring out the
window. The room was dark, save for the candles flickering from the dresser. She no longer wore the soft blue
shift from before, but a pair of fanciful pajamas, a tumble
of dogs and cats against a cream background.

Emotion tightened through him, the need to go to her,
hold her. The earlier anger had faded into a calm understanding. He could only imagine what it must have felt
like for her to listen to Janine's accusations, the shock.
The horror.

But she hadn't accused him. Hadn't turned on him.
She'd simply asked questions, giving him the opportunity
to tell her the truth.

Instead, he'd exploded.

The danger of passion, he knew. Yes, he believed there was honesty in passion, but he also knew it could take possession of rational thinking and lead a man to act like an idiot.

"Bethany."

Through the window, her gaze met his. There was a calm serenity in her eyes, an otherworldly quality that sent his heart hammering even harder. Quietly, he crossed the room and put his hands on her shoulders, just like he'd done four hours before, when he'd found her on the porch. Then, he'd been filled with questions and uncertainty.

Now, the need to apologize drove him.

"Are you okay?" he asked quietly.

She inhaled a raspy-sounding breath. "You're back."

"I never should have left." Never should have let emotion take over. "I'm sorry," he said. "I'm sorry for blowing up."

Beneath his hands, he felt her stiffen. "Don't apologize, Dylan."

"I shouldn't have walked out like that—"

"You're a man of principles," she said, meeting his gaze in the window. "I may not always agree with your methods, but I know there are some lines you won't cross."

God help him, he could hardly believe he'd heard her right. "You believe me when I say that file contained lies?"

"Yes." She didn't even hesitate.

But somehow, tension remained. "You're amazing," he murmured, easing her back against him. His body hardened at the contact, the need to reclaim her tangling with the need to take it slow. "If you'll let me, I'd like to give you something else pretty damn amazing."

She started to turn toward him, but he held her in place, sliding a hand along the soft cotton of her pajamas to press lightly against her stomach. He spread his fingers wide, extending from her mound to her breast.

"Dylan," she whispered, but he lifted his other hand to press two fingers to her mouth.

"I want to make love to you," he said in a strangled voice he barely recognized as his own. Heat poured through him in blinding waves as he slid his finger along her bottom lip. "I *need* to make love to you. To be inside you. To feel your arms and legs around me. To feel you beneath me and over me. Feel you come unglued."

Her reflection showed her eyes go wide and dark, as though he was torturing her rather than making love to her with words.

"But it's too soon for that," he said before she could speak. "As much as I want your body, I need your heart first."

A soft sound broke from her throat, and he literally felt her flesh heat, her limbs go languid. She tried to turn again, but he held her in place.

"I would do anything for you," he whispered against her silky hair. "Anything."

The pane of glass showed her eyes glaze over, her lips part. Showed his big hands sliding and roaming, claiming.

"I don't want you to do anything," she whispered. "I just want you to hold me."

The words rushed through him like a long sip of wine. When he'd left she'd been tense and upset, but this time the hours apart seemed to have brought them to a bridge, rather than the ravine of before. But he knew the divide still lurked in the shadows, knew he had to take it slow.

"You deserve more," he said, letting his index finger slip inside her mouth, while his other hand slid to cup breasts erotically heavy with pregnancy.

Through the window, her gaze met his. "I didn't mean to hurt you."

He tilted his hips against her, felt her inhale sharply when she felt the thickness jutting against her lower back.

"Hurting is part of loving," he told her. "But so is understanding."

He saw her close her eyes, felt her breathe, would have sworn he heard her heart thrumming low and deep. The wall of windows reflected them like a shadowy erotic photo, her sinuous body in front of his, his hands splayed wide, possessing the only way he would allow himself at the moment.

Need tore at the walls of restraint. He wanted to carry her to the bed, bury himself inside her, hear her cry his name and his name only. But less than twenty-four hours before, the intensity of their lovemaking had sent Bethany to the hospital. As much as he wanted her, needed her, even more, he needed to protect. It was too soon for passion. She needed tenderness first.

"I want to kiss you," he murmured. "All over. I want to taste you. Absorb you."

Her eyes opened abruptly. "Dylan—"

"Sh-h-h," he soothed, slipping his hand inside her pajama top to cup her breast. It was heavy in his hand. Perfect. "I want to show you how good it can be," he said, skimming a finger around her nipple.

Her head lolled back against his chest. "Do you enjoy torturing me?"

"Torture isn't what I had in mind."

She lifted her hands behind her to cup the back of his head, thrusting her breasts out even further. "Then what?"

He never got a chance to answer. A loud pounding reverberated through the house, the doorbell ringing over and over. Urgent. Demanding.

Bethany spun toward him, eyes wide and alarmed.

He took her face in his hands and pressed a hard kiss to her mouth. "Stay here," he commanded softly, then turned and headed out of the bedroom. He closed the door behind him.

Detective Paul Zito stood waiting on the doorstep. "Dylan," his friend said. "We need to talk."

Everything inside Dylan went very still. He knew that tone, knew that hard look in Zito's eyes. Neither had been present at the lunch they'd shared twelve hours before.

"It's after midnight," Dylan growled.

Zito frowned. "You don't need to tell me that, son. But you do need to tell me where you were three hours ago."

"Three hours ago?" Dylan's heart started to pound.

"Janine White has been attacked," Zito said in a mechanical voice Dylan barely recognized. "It was dark and her assailant wore a mask, but she remembers black jeans and an olive shirt. Surveillance cameras show—"

"Jesus." Dylan knew damn good and well what surveillance cameras showed.

Beth clenched the steering wheel tightly and concentrated on the blur of red taillights belonging to the car in front of her. The heater roared at full blast, but the chill in her blood deepened at an alarming rate.

Stay here, Dylan had instructed as Zito led him away. *Lock the doors and don't let anyone inside.*

But she couldn't do that. She couldn't tuck herself away in Dylan's house while the world was blowing up around her.

Janine.

Everything inside Beth tightened at the thought of her friend. Janine stood to gain nothing helping Beth, and yet, she had tried to help anyway. Now, she lay in a hospital room, badly beaten, and Dylan was downtown being questioned, because he'd been wearing an olive button-down and black jeans. Just like Janine's attacker.

One could have nothing to do with the other, Beth reasoned, but she'd never been a believer in coincidence. Questions gnawed, as relentless as they were punishing. She felt poised on the edge of something dark and horrifying, the rock beneath her feet crumbling.

Deep inside, she started to shake. It was hard to believe how hideously her life had spiraled out of control in just a matter of days. For a brief deceptive time in the mountains, she'd actually let herself believe that maybe, this time, things would turn out differently. Maybe the worst was behind them. Maybe the future held the kind of happiness she'd always dreamed about. They'd been close, she thought, fighting back tears. So horribly, beautifully close. If he hadn't stormed out of the house in a fit of passion—

The thought ratcheted up her pulse.

Passion.

Crimes of passion.

Emotion blurred her vision. No matter which direction she turned, which angle she played, which crime went down, everything kept circling back to passion. It was like a seductive narcotic, the wild giddiness of it enticing people to act in ways they wouldn't normally consider. Nine years ago, desperate, heart breaking, she'd chased after Dylan—

She saw the flash of brake lights too late. The car in front of her stopped abruptly, forcing her to swerve to avoid slamming into its rear. An elk, she wondered fleetingly, then stopped wondering at all. There was no guardrail on this dark stretch of road, just a steep drop-off bouncing down to a row of young pines and the creek they shielded, running horrifyingly fast with snow melt-off.

He saw her the second he stepped out of the elevator, and his heart flat out stopped. She sat in one of the rinky-dink chairs, face buried in her hands. Her shoulders were slumped, her whole body curled into itself. Her hair was loose and hanging toward the floor, dull and tangled, like she'd been running her hands through it the better part of the night.

Early morning sun squeezed through a small window, but not even the prospect of a new day chased the chill from Dylan's blood. Someone was playing him like a damn fool puppet, and because of that, he'd walked straight into a trap. Instinct warned the final act had yet to play itself out.

And Bethany was caught in the middle.

"What are you doing here?" He strode toward her, the question tearing out of him more roughly than he'd intended. He just hadn't been expecting to see her sitting there. Hadn't had the chance to prepare.

She looked up abruptly, exposing him to bruised eyes and skin parchment pale. He would have sworn he could count the blue veins streaking beneath the flesh of her cheeks and arms. She looked tired, exhausted.

"Dylan," she said, standing.

The urge to go to her was strong, to crush her in his arms and just hold her, but the way she hugged her arms around her waist warned him to keep his distance.

"I asked you to wait at the house."

She shook her head. "I—I couldn't." Her gaze searched his. "What happened? Are you free to go?"

"I can't leave town," he said flatly, "but they're not locking me away right now, if that's what you're asking." Sometimes, being a St. Croix wasn't all bad. Sometimes, it helped having a buddy on the force. Someone who knew him. Who believed in him. Who was willing to wait for forensics before nailing him to the wall.

"Let's get out of here," he said, reaching for her hand and reminding himself not to crush. Her flesh was cool and clammy, her fingers disturbingly nonresponsive.

"We can't go out there," she said when he headed toward the front door.

"Why the hell not?"

"Yvonne Kelly and company have been camped out all night."

"I'm not scared of reporters," he growled. In fact, he downright savored the prospect of giving them a bone to chew on.

But then Bethany lifted her eyes to his, and he saw the

fatigue swirling deep. The silent pleading. Maybe he was ready to take on an army of reporters, but she wasn't.

''The car's out back,'' she said, leading him to another hall.

He followed, wondering why it felt like she was walking away when he still held her hand. Because she was being so reserved, he knew. Because she was acting as though nothing was wrong, when they both knew the walls were closing in from all sides.

She'd brought her car, the one he'd had moved to his house while they'd been in the mountains. So he let her take the wheel, innately sensing that she needed to be in the driver's seat.

But still, she didn't speak. She kept her eyes on the road, her hands on the wheel. She might as well have taken a knife to Dylan's chest, and calmly, efficiently begun to carve.

Just looking at him hurt. Just looking at him reminded her of those precious days in the mountains, when the nightmare of Lance's murder had seemed a whole world away. The sight of those primeval eyes and the jaw always in need of a razor seduced her back to the night before, when he'd stood behind her at the window, so tall and strong and passionate, making love to her with nothing but words. They'd flowed through her and around her, shadows and desire creating the illusion of a bridge.

Funny how a few hours could change everything.

She'd avoided the pines, avoided the creek. But she couldn't avoid the truth. The past had roared back to life with punishing precision and slapped her hard. For close to an hour she'd sat in her car, surrounded by the cold dark night, trying to breathe. Trying to think. Trying to understand.

Fate had a hideous way of driving home lessons, again and again and again, harder and more brutal, until the message got through. Nine years before, her father and unborn child had paid the price of her stubborn resistance.

This time, she feared the price would be even higher.

The chill in her heart deepened. Dylan sat so close she could feel the warmth of his body, but from the moment they'd slid into the car, he'd gone quiet. Ominously quiet. Because Dylan St. Croix was never, never quiet. He was a man driven by his passions. He shied away from neither controversy nor confrontation. He roared and bullied and rocked the boat until everyone knew exactly where he stood. He never, never rolled over and played dead—if there was something he wanted, he found a way to have it. Even her.

Especially her.

Except now he was silent. And still.

Beth sucked in a deep breath, let it out slowly. Sooner or later, the dam had to break.

"It's okay," Dylan finally said. He took her right hand from the wheel and gave it a reassuring squeeze. "Everything's going to be okay. You'll see."

"Okay?" she asked in a hoarse voice she barely recognized as her own. She couldn't believe it. This man who'd long accused her of pretending, was now the one living in some fantasy land where their world wasn't blowing up around them. "Lance is dead, someone's blackmailing the D.A., and Janine has been assaulted. *How* can you say everything's going to be okay?"

"Because I won't accept anything else."

Deep inside, the tearing continued, faster, more stark than before. "This isn't about what you'll accept, Dylan. You might not have a choice." She glanced at him, found him watching her through curiously guarded eyes. "I know how the cops think," she reminded. "They'll think maybe you went there just to talk. Maybe Janey was upset. Maybe things got out of hand. Maybe you didn't mean to—"

"Is that what you think?" The question was hard, hot. "You think I roughed up Janine?"

"I didn't say that," she said as calmly as she could. "I'm just saying sometimes things spiral out of control." Terribly, horribly out of control. "Isn't that what you told me the day Lance died?"

"Lance didn't die. He was murdered in cold blood."

"I'm well aware of that." Would be for the rest of her life.

"This is the exit," Dylan said, and only then did Beth realize she'd been about to drive right by. She steered off the interstate and stopped at a red light, but the past and the present and future kept racing, twisting, tangling into one dangerous dead end.

"You should never have gone to Janey's," she said, trying not to let frayed emotions unravel any further. "You should have let the wheels of justice turn by them-selves—"

Dylan shifted, turning more fully to face her. "My cousin was murdered and someone is trying to set me up to take the fall, and you expect me to just wring my hands and see what happens next? How can you ask me to do that when I know damn good and well those wheels are being manipulated? I won't just lie down and let life roll over me or those I love."

And therein lay the problem. Therein had always, al-ways lain the problem. "No," she whispered. Of course not. "Dylan St. Croix prefers to charge headfirst into en-emy lines, with no regard for consequences."

From behind them, a loud horn blared obnoxiously, prompting Beth to jerk toward the road, where against the bright wash of early morning sun, the green light waited. She got them moving again, this time faster than before.

Dylan sat only inches away, but he might as well have been in another car. Another state. She felt the distance settling between them, stretching and thickening, the years between them stacking right back up.

"You could go to jail," she said through the tightness

in her throat. "You could leave your child without a father. All because you had to prove some stupid point."

Dylan just stared at her. "Christ," he swore softly. "Who did you think you were making love with in the mountains? I'm not Ward Cleaver and I never will be."

Beth turned onto his street, the bright sun glinting through the pines almost blinding her. "This isn't about making love—that has never been our problem. This is about the fact our world is blowing up around us, but I can't see past *you!*"

And because of that she'd put their child at risk.

Just like before.

But she didn't tell him about the accident, didn't want him to know. He'd go wild. Even more passion would blow up between them.

And that, she didn't want ever, ever again.

He shoved a hand through his closely cut hair, looking nothing like the sorcerer from the night before. He looked all man now, all angry, dangerous man. "Bethany, I swear to you, everything's going to be okay."

"No, it's not!" she exploded. "It *can't* be." She turned into his driveway, but barely saw the pines stretching skyward, the house looming beyond. She could see only two tombstones south of town, cold, silent reminders of the price of being blind to the world around her.

"No matter how badly it hurts," she said, fighting the emotion scratching at her throat, "I can't let this thing between us blind me into thinking otherwise. I've done that before, Dylan, and people got hurt. They *died.*"

"This thing," he clipped out, his voice acrid, "is love."

The hurt was swift and immediate, a jagged, tearing pain. She swallowed hard, but the emotion burning her throat didn't lessen. More than anything, she wanted to erect one of those ice walls, the kind she'd created in the days after the ambush nine years before, when she'd been quite sure her heart would simply bleed out. But she couldn't find those walls now, knew they'd all melted away.

For years she'd lived in a pretend world where the passion she felt for Dylan didn't still burn hot and bright. But now was not the time for playing make-believe. Everything inside her was too jagged and broken, just like all those years before. *This* was what she'd been trying to avoid. This horrible, out-of-control feeling, that if she let go even the slightest bit, her entire world would spin away from her.

"Everything's happened too fast," she said, needing him to understand, knowing he wouldn't, "...the murder, the pregnancy, the miscarriage scare, and now Janine. I need time to catch my breath."

Dylan's eyes went dead flat. "People 'together' don't retreat, Bethany."

"People 'together' don't issue ultimatums," she countered quietly.

"You're carrying my child."

Instinctively, protectively, she put a hand to her stomach. "I know whose child I'm carrying."

"Then turn off the car."

She wanted to. Dear God, she wanted to do as he instructed, to turn off the car and go inside. She wanted to go back to the mountains. Go back to before.

"You're the one always accusing me of pretending, Dylan. And you were right. But I can't do that anymore. I can't bury my head in the sand and ignore the truth. Lance is dead. *Dead!* Janine has been beaten and there's a hideous paper trail leading straight to you. But I don't care! All I want is to be in your arms and that's *wrong!*"

"And you're so determined to prove you're not like your mother that you're just going to walk away."

She stiffened. "This has nothing to do with my mother."

"The hell it doesn't," he bit out, his expression suddenly granite. "You think feeling is bad. You think it's a crime to want, to need."

"Dylan—"

"What happened to the woman in the mountains?" he asked pointedly. "The one who came alive in my arms, who came back with a rope when she could have run, who displayed more courage than armies of men? When did she become a coward?"

Panic flared deep within. The truth shattered. "She came home," Beth said quietly. "She came back to the real world, where nothing has changed. Call me a coward if you want to, but this is the hardest thing I've ever done in my life." She paused, swallowed, forced herself to continue. "Just because we have great sex doesn't change the fact that this…this out-of-control feeling is *not* something I can live with."

"Christ," he swore in a dead voice that terrified more than all the heat and bluster. "You're going to let the scared little girl win. You're going to retreat to her world of pristine white, just because things got muddy."

"Dylan—" Her voice broke on his name. "I'm sorry."

"So am I." With stunning abruptness he threw open the door and climbed out of the car, strode toward his house.

He didn't look back.

The swiftness of it all robbed her of breath. She tried to grasp what had happened, but was left with nothing but those jagged pieces she'd tried to hold together. They shattered now, raining down and slicing to the bone.

"Goodbye," she whispered to the gorgeous house of wood and glass. Through the silence, she would have sworn she heard her heart shatter just like that glass door so long ago. "Goodbye."

Putting the car in reverse and backing into the street was one of the hardest things she'd ever done, but she knew it was for the best. No matter how desperately she wished otherwise, there could be no future for her and Dylan.

When their paths crossed, everything else went up in flames.

She couldn't let that happen to her baby.

Their baby.

Chapter 15

Zorro lay on the back porch, perfectly centered in a swatch of early morning sun. The cat stretched languidly, reminding Dylan too damn much of the woman who'd backed out of his driveway, his life, not thirty minutes before. He'd stood under the cold spray of a shower most of that time, but eventually the cubicle of ceramic tile had turned into a prison cell, forcing Dylan to get the hell out as fast as he could. He'd barely taken time to dry, just pulled on a pair of old gym shorts and gone to the kitchen for a glass of orange juice, then headed outside.

Now he stood on the porch, hands curled around the railing. Beneath his fingers, he saw the small white flowers of the jasmine vines he'd planted upon moving into the house, then nurtured ever since. At the time, he hadn't let himself think about the fact Bethany loved jasmine, that she wore jasmine.

Now the tangled vines taunted.

He wanted to feel anger toward her. He wanted to feel contempt. After everything they'd been through, she still couldn't accept him for the man he was. She still thought passion was poison.

But he could find no anger. Only love. A love strong enough, pure enough, to let her go before he systematically destroyed her. He could live with a lot, withstand a lot, but he would never survive breaking Bethany. Not again.

That's why he had walked away. When their lives tangled like the vines around the porch rail, Bethany paid the price. She deserved so much more than that. She deserved the serenity she'd always wanted, the fairy tale he told her didn't exist. Because of the child, they'd never fully be apart, but nor could they be fully together.

No matter what it cost him, he would never, ever hurt her again. He had to figure out who was playing them like a puppet, and what the hell had gone down with Janine White. He couldn't shake the bad, bad feeling that Lance's murder and the subsequent ordeal for Bethany were somehow linked to the alleged file found in Lance's desk.

The ringing phone interrupted his thoughts. He went inside, picked up the kitchen phone, but found only silence. "Who is this?" he demanded.

Nothing.

"I don't play games," he said, but then the line went dead, and a dial tone droned into his ear.

Swearing softly, he returned to the porch and picked up his orange juice, drank deeply.

I don't love you, Dylan. I never did.

Nine years ago, he'd accepted Bethany's denial and simply walked away. Now a stark realization hit him hard. Normally he was a crusader of the truth. He pushed and prodded until he got it. But then, he'd merely accepted her broken words as gospel. Now he knew why, what a hypocrite he was. In preaching the truth, he'd been lying to himself all along.

The irony burned. Once, he'd sworn he would kill for her. He just hadn't realized the person he would kill was himself.

''Brooding becomes you, Dylan.''

The amused words jolted through him, prompting him to spin toward the side of the house. She stood there with her hair loose and silky around her face, a glint in her pale blue eyes, and a gun in her hand.

Bethany slowed the car in front of the beautiful house that had never been a home. Yellow police tape no longer stretched across the perimeter. The tulips had faded. The petunias and impatiens were wilted from thirst.

A chill ran through her as she realized she couldn't live here anymore, didn't even want to go inside. No way could she return to that sterile white life, not after Dylan showed her so many evocative colors—the clear blue of mountain lakes and companionship, the green of old-growth pine forests and laughter, the vivid red of flowers and desire.

The truth hit her hard. All her life she'd worked hard to not rock the boat, not hurt anyone or anything. She didn't want to destroy like her mother had, but with startling clarity, she realized she *had* destroyed. Herself. And Dylan. She'd staunchly denied her feelings for him, believing the passion between them would ruin everything in its path. It took finding the courage to walk away to show her how wrong she'd been. Sitting there in her idling car, staring at the gorgeous sterile house, she realized it was the denial of passion that hurt, the loss of it that made her chest so tight she could hardly breathe.

Rattled from the accident the night before, the woman she'd become had deferred to the girl she'd once been, letting her make a terrible mistake. Walking away, pretending, wasn't the solution. Fighting for what she wanted was.

Dylan St. Croix was the only man she'd ever loved. The only man she could imagine sharing her life, her child, with. She deserved his anger, but no way could she just walk away. She was a strong woman. She needed— wanted—a strong man.

No way was she going to let Dylan St. Croix write "The End."

"Hello, darling."

Dylan went very still. "Yvonne." He took in the malevolent light in her crystalline blue eyes, the gun in her hand, and with cold certainty realized Yvonne's preoccupation with Lance's murder had nothing to do with getting a story. "What the hell are you doing?"

She laughed. "Every good reporter knows you can't just sit around and wait for stories to happen. Sometimes you have to nudge."

Christ. "Put down the gun," he instructed, starting toward her. But his legs would barely move. They felt leaden.

Again, she laughed. "What's the matter Dilly, darling? Not feeling so good?"

The world swayed. Suddenly there were two Yvonnes, two guns. "What the hell?"

She motioned toward the empty glass on the porch rail. "I would have thought a smart man like you would know better than to leave a drink unattended."

He fought the fog thickening through him, the web spreading over his muscles and his organs. "Y-you d-drugged me?"

"A girl can never have enough insurance. A big strong boy like you wouldn't think twice about charging me..." she waved the gun "...wrestling away my little friend here." She flashed her infamous on-air shark smile. "Now you can't."

Disbelief whirred through him. He reached for the rail, held on, sucked in a breath. Yvonne Kelly had a reputation for going for the jugular, he'd just never realized she'd go for the kill.

"It's really quite tragic," she said blithely. "Lance always said you didn't know how to leave well enough alone."

He blinked, holding his eyes open when they wanted to slide closed. "Wh-hat are you t-talk-king about?"

The two Yvonnes stepped closer. "Prince Lance's death, of course. If the cops can't bring themselves to arrest Little Miss Perfect, if her fingerprints on the murder weapon aren't enough evidence, then maybe a suicide will make them stop and think."

"S-u-u-cide?" The word roared through him. "You m-mean murder."

A black-and-white blur ambled over to Yvonne, weaving between her legs. She muttered something and shooed it away.

"Bethany has fooled everyone into thinking she's pure as the driven snow, but you don't have that same affliction, now do you? You like things dirty. Everyone knows you play rough." Another laugh, this one laced with malice. "No one will question whether the nifty little file I planted on your misdeeds is fact or fiction. No one will know I've elevated creative writing to a whole new art. No one will care. You'll be dead, the paper trail will be stark, the poor, poor D.A. relieved, and the investigation into Lance's death will stop cold."

The effort to stand grew more difficult. Dylan concentrated on his leg muscles, refusing to let them buckle. Maybe the lethargy sapped his strength, but his mind clicked rapidly, the nasty pieces falling into place with brutal precision. "You k-killed him," he realized sickly.

Yvonne's face was one blur now, but he would have sworn he saw a flash of pain.

"I loved him," she said thickly. "I loved him with all my heart."

"Th-then why?"

She swiped the tangled blond hair blowing into her face. "He didn't understand. He didn't understand how deeply I loved him, how far I'd go to prove it. For over a year he shared my bed. I gave him everything he wanted—everything, no matter how kinky, how dirty. All I wanted in return was a commitment. That shouldn't be asking too much, should it?'' Her voice broke, and for a moment there was only an ungodly silence. ''He thought he could just dump me like trash and move on. He thought he could walk away.''

The drug clouded Dylan's vision, but the picture in his mind crystallized with startling detail. ''S-so you killed him-m instead?''

''No!'' Yvonne shouted. ''No! I loved him! I understood him, thought like him, told him I'd make sure no one ever discovered his dirty little secret.''

''W-what secret?''

A malevolent smile twisted Yvonne's lips. ''We could have had it all, Lance and me. I wanted the same things he did, namely Kent English out of office and Lance on his way to the top.''

''English?'' Dylan asked, realizing he had to keep her talking. It was like some cruel joke standing there staring at Yvonne and her gun, knowing what she had in store for him, but also knowing that if he followed instinct and let go of the porch rail to charge her, she'd gut-shoot him before he took two steps.

''He didn't deserve to be D.A. He was as amoral as the scum he sent to prison, and I had the pictures to prove it.''

The pictures. Of the D.A. and a prostitute. The evidence of blackmail Yvonne had used to try and incriminate him.

''But he didn't understand, told me I was crazy. Told me he was going to turn me in.'' Pain flashed in her blue eyes. ''I had no choice but to point out he was no more innocent than me. That I knew about his shenanigans at the infertility clinic. I knew about the bribe. And I was prepared to let all of Portland know, too, starting with Miss Goody Two-Shoes. Not so good for a man who'd built his reputation on family values.''

Dylan just stared. ''H-how did you f-find out?''

''I'm an investigative reporter!'' she snapped. ''I know the importance of covering my bases.''

"But you didn't expose him," Dylan pointed out sickly. "You k-killed him."

The wind whipped harder, sending wisps against Yvonne's cheekbone. "He called me a coward, told me I didn't have the guts to go through with it. I didn't have a choice, don't you see? I didn't have a choice but to go to Bethany's, tell her everything, convince her to press charges." She stepped closer. "Lance followed, tried to force me to leave."

"But you w-wouldn't," Dylan stalled. With shocking clarity, the scenario flashed through his mind.

"You wanted him to leave. He wouldn't. Maybe he grabbed you. You only picked up the fire poker to protect yourself. You never meant to hurt—"

He'd been right all along. He'd pegged the scene *exactly,* he'd just had the players wrong.

Crimes of passion, Yvonne herself had said during one of her news reports. Crimes of the heart. A fairy tale gone bad.

She'd all but confessed on-air.

Except no one had been listening.

"I loved him," Yvonne said again. "I never wanted to hurt him. But he kept insisting that I was wrong, that he was sorry, that he'd expose me if I exposed him. He wanted me to leave…but I wouldn't. He…" Her voice broke, and her eyes filled. "When I called him a coward, he lunged at me. There was only a second to react. He was coming toward me, his face contorted. I didn't stop to think. I reached for the first thing I could find."

"The f-fire p-poker."

"It happened so fast," Yvonne whispered. "He never knew…I never knew."

Dylan lifted a hand and wiped the sweat that had started sliding into his eyes. He'd long known Lance's misdeeds and manipulations would catch up with him one day, but he'd always expected it to pertain to his job, his political aspirations, not the fact he wasn't man enough to admit his sterility, that he made up for his own perceived inadequacies by bedding the wrong woman. "You hit Bethany?"

"I had to! I wasn't guilty of anything but loving him. *She* never did. If he was willing to cast her by the wayside, why shouldn't I?"

"You hur-rt her." The thought filled him with a cold rage. He clung to that emotion, gathered it close, deep, used it for strength.

"Bruises heal," Yvonne spat. "A broken heart never does."

"W-what now?"

Her laugh sounded more like a cackle. "You should have left her alone, Dylan. You should have stayed away. Now I have no choice. I can't let you and Zito look any further."

He kept his eyes on the gun. "M-men don't s-suicide with p-pills."

"I know that!" she snapped. "And don't worry, you won't either. Whoever finds you will find a gun in your hands." She waggled it at him. "Lance's gun at that. Sweet, isn't it?"

"Never b-believe. No note."

"No need," she countered. "But if it makes you feel better, I'll type something up before I leave." She took another step. "Now we wait, darling. We wait until you pass out. Unless you'd rather get this all over with now."

"Not so fast," came a steely voice from the side of the house.

Yvonne swung around, just as Dylan saw Bethany round the corner. He didn't stop to think. He lunged. Through the haze he heard a female scream, but couldn't discern its owner. He landed hard against Yvonne's back, sending them crashing to the ground. As they fell, he reached desperately for the gun, but the impact sent it clattering across the wood planks of the porch.

Bethany picked it up, held it firm. "Not another move."

Dylan straddled Yvonne, pulling her hands behind her back and manacling them with one of his. "Now who's laughing?" he growled with deliberate precision.

She struggled beneath him, twisting back to look at him. "W-what?"

Fury pounded through him. His body still felt woozy and leaden, but he was a strong man. "It takes more than a few damn pills to incapacitate me, Y-Yvonne."

He saw the instant awareness hit. "You tricked me!"

He glanced at Bethany, standing strong in the morning sun, the gun in her hands. Zorro rubbed against her legs. "Call the police."

"I already have. Zito should be here any minute."

"You weren't supposed to come back," Yvonne said in a broken voice. "You were supposed to run like a scared little rabbit!"

Bethany stepped closer. "How did you know about before?" she asked. "How did you know about the night on the mountain?"

Yvonne glared at her. "Your life is hardly a secret."

Dylan looked at Bethany. "What about the night on the mountain?"

Bethany lifted a hand to her face, easing the hair back to reveal a nasty bruise at her temple. A bruise that had been hidden from him that morning. "Yvonne thought she could play God. Yvonne thought if she could make history repeat itself, have you taken to the police station and force my car off the road, then I'd walk away from you, just like I did before." Moisture glinted in her eyes. "And it almost worked. But she didn't count on the fact that I'm not a coward anymore." She looked down at Yvonne. "I came back because I love him," she said. "And when I saw your car in the driveway, I recognized the license tag from last night...the car that stopped abruptly and forced me off the road."

Dylan saw black. If he hadn't already been straddling Yvonne..."You had an *accident?*"

"Yvonne played the wrong card," Bethany said, her eyes meeting his. "Are you okay?"

He looked at her standing there, determination in her eyes, strength in her stance. She'd come back. For some incredible reason, she'd come back, after he'd walked away. And she'd said she loved him.

The need to destroy the distance between them and crush her in his arms drove deep, but he wasn't letting Yvonne move until Zito arrived. "I'm fine."

A smile curved Bethany's lips. "You're also one hell of an actor."

He laughed. "You have no idea," he growled. "No idea." But he intended to clue her in as soon as they were alone. He, purveyor of truth and prosecutor of pretenses, had been acting for nine long years, pretending he didn't love her with every corner of his heart and his soul. But now he knew the truth.

Soon, she would, too.

"You were wrong in the car," she said, and her voice was strong. "That's why I came back. I don't want a world of white." She hesitated, smiled. "I'm still not too fond of the mud, but the color…I want the color, Dylan, the red, the blue, the green, and everything in between. I want *you.*"

Beneath him, Yvonne started to sob.

"I never meant to hurt you," he told Bethany.

"You didn't. I did that all by myself." She looked so beautiful standing in the soft light of early morning. Emotion swirled in those slumberous blue eyes, an emotion so pure and real it would have sent Dylan to his knees, if he hadn't already been there.

"I love you," she said, and slayed him with a smile. "I love you with every corner of my heart. That's why I came back. No way am I going to let you write the end."

"I don't want to write the end," he told her. "I'm much more fond of beginnings."

Her eyes sparkled. "Then tell me how it starts."

That was easy. At the time, there'd been no way to know what chain of events lay in store, but he'd been no more capable of turning his back on her than he was of living without a heart. The need to feel her in his arms, to show her just how much he loved her practically overwhelmed him, but for now, he settled with the power of memory and the promise of what lay ahead.

"It began one dark snowy night," he told her. "With a kiss in the dark."

Epilogue

An urgent cry intruded upon the silence of the night. He awoke abruptly, heart hammering, adrenaline surging. Disoriented, he sat upright and blinked against the grainy dryness of his eyes, brought the fireplace into focus. The cabin was dark, shadows blurring detail. Nothing moved save for the frenzy of snowflakes outside the window.

A dream, he realized. A memory from that night nearly a year ago, when innocent intentions had combusted into heat, launching him and Bethany on a life-altering journey. The memories were stronger here in the cabin, shimmering from every direction like dewy wildflowers kissed by the sun.

So much had happened since that snowy night, Lance's death and the subsequent investigation, the ultimate discovery of Yvonne Kelly's twisted life. She'd been in love with Lance, desperate to keep him. So desperate, she'd been blackmailing the D.A. to force him to step down, clearing the path for Lance's ascension. So desperate she'd tried to blackmail Lance himself about his diabolical scheme at the fertility clinic.

So desperate, passion had turned to murder.

In some ways, Bethany had been right. Passion could be dangerous. Passion could lead people to act in ways they'd never consider when not under the influence. But passion wasn't the culprit, just the impetus. In the right hands, with the right people, passion was a gift, a celebration.

He and Bethany had been celebrating for ten months, looked forward to celebrating for a lifetime.

Yvonne was locked away now, where she could never touch them again. And Janine had recovered fully from the attack Yvonne had paid for, hoping to rattle Bethany's faith in Dylan. After Kent English had stepped down, Janine had been the natural replacement. She was remorseful over her role in Yvonne's scheme, realizing she'd let the fact Dylan had turned down her romantic overtures shadow her professional judgment.

And then there was Bethany. She—

He heard it then, another cry, this one louder than before. And he realized it was no dream. He was off the sofa and running barefoot down the darkened hall, toward the closed door at the end. They'd only meant to stay a few days, but a particularly exuberant snowstorm had necessitated other plans.

For a moment he was catapulted back in time, to the night he'd reached the door at a dead run, thrown his body against the wood. But he didn't need to do that tonight. He needed only to put his hand to the knob, and turn.

The sight greeting him almost sent him to his knees.

Moonlight teased in through the windows, casting his girls in a heart-stopping play of shadow and light. They sat in the rocking chair he himself had made, seemingly oblivious to his presence.

"There, there," Bethany cooed. She had her leopard print nightgown open, allowing Ella to suckle hungrily. "You've no need to cry, sweet girl. Mommy's here now."

"So's Daddy," he said from the doorway.

Bethany looked up and smiled. "Dylan. We didn't mean to wake you."

Dylan was across the room in a heartbeat, kneeling beside them. "Waking to the two of you is better than dreaming."

"Really?" she asked, quirking a brow. "Better than dreaming? I can think of a few dreams you've awoken from that certainly seemed...*better*."

He caught her meaning, knew the dreams to which she referred, the erotic images that he'd groggily rolled over and played out in real life. "Well, maybe not *all* dreams."

"That's what I thought," Bethany said. A knowing light sparked in her slumberous blue eyes, the only trait mother shared with the daughter. It still blew Dylan away how a baby girl dressed in pink could look so much like a grown man.

He felt his throat thicken, realized he was about to make a damn fool of himself. "I'd offer to help," he said lamely.

Bethany laughed. "Oh, there's plenty you can do to help me," she promised. "Starting just as soon as I get Miss Priss here satisfied."

"She is her father's little girl," Dylan pointed out, grinning. "She might not be satisfied that easily."

Bethany's smile widened. "I might have learned a trick or two."

He heard the promise, felt his body tighten. Nine years before tragedy had driven them apart, but the love had survived. Strengthened even. Now that they'd found their way back together, Dylan knew deep in his heart that nothing would ever drive them apart again. There would be no endings, only a lifetime of beginnings, hope and promise, love.

Passion.

Leaning forward, he put a hand to his daughter's cheek, a kiss to his wife's. "I can hardly wait."

* * * * *

Don't miss
Jenna Mills's next heart-pounding read,

THE PERFECT TARGET

With deadly enemies seeking her at every turn,
Miranda Carrington has no choice but to trust
her dark and dangerous companion, Sandro.
But is Sandro a loyal friend or deceptive foe?
And will her heart ultimately pay the price?
Time is running out for both of them...

On sale March 2003
from Silhouette Intimate Moments

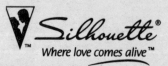